Immortality, LLC

Volume 6 of the continuing adventures
of Glen Wilson...

Ken Coffman

Other books by Ken Coffman

Fiction

Steel Waters (Glen Wilson #1)
Alligator Alley, by Ken Coffman and Mark Bothum *(Glen Wilson #2)*
Twisted Shadow, by Ken Coffman and Mark Bothum *(Glen Wilson #3)*
Glen Wilson's Bad Medicine (Glen Wilson #4)
Toxic Shock Syndrome (Glen Wilson #5)
Hartz String Theory
Endangered Species
Fairhaven
The Reluctant Queen, by Ken Coffman and Kristen Lolatte *(Fiona #1)*
The Moon Maiden, by Ken Coffman and Kristen Lolatte *(Fiona #2)*
The Sandcastles of Irrakistan
Fiancetto

Nonfiction

Real World FPGA Design with Verilog
Buffoon: One Man's Playful Interaction with the Harbingers of Global Warming Doom

Short Story Collection

Mesh, by Ken Coffman and Adina Pelle

© 2020 Ken Coffman

This book is a work of fiction. Names, characters, places and incidents are the products of the author's fevered imagination or are used fictitiously. Any resemblance to actual events, locales or persons (living or dead) is entirely coincidental.

Print ISBN 978-1-949267-60-0
eBook ISBN 978-1-949267-61-7

Glen Wilson illustration on the back cover by Pav Kovacic

STAIRWAY PRESS

www.StairwayPress.com
1000 West Apache Trail, Suite 126
Apache Junction, AZ 85120

Glen's Story So Far...

IT'S HARD TO coherently summarize Glen's wild adventures, but out of courtesy for readers encountering Glen for the first time with this novel, I will try.

This overview will be unsatisfactory, so I urge readers to absorb the books from the beginning.

On his own, Glen, though indefatigable, is silly and hopeless. Somehow, he assembles a team of supporters who, when working together, achieve remarkable results.

In *Steel Waters*, Glen has a brief career as a drug mule running cocaine from South America to the United States. Along the way, he encounters his old Army sergeant Robert 'Steve' Stephens and briefly meets magician Walter Crowley (Dr. Zalooq).

In *Alligator Alley*, at a computer trade show, Glen's wallet is stolen by a drug lord and he travels across Florida to get it back. Along the way, he meets Benjamin Franklin Jackson, Elke Rittenhauer and her soon-to-be lover, police officer Margaret Murphy.

In *Twisted Shadow*, Glen assembles a team and runs for U.S. Congress in Alaska. He wins the election, but is ruined and imprisoned by the humorless powers-that-be.

In *Bad Medicine*, Glen returns to Seattle and takes a contract from the distraught mayor to solve their homeless problem.

In *Toxic Shock Syndrome*, Glen goes on the road with David 'Raz' Smith and his progressive metal rock band.

In *Immortality, LLC*, most of the Glen Wilson team gathers to create a highly successful, high-tech company offering an odd form of immortality to rich patrons.

The Luckiest Guy in the World

OUTSIDE THE REINFORCED window, there was a muffled click and clatter. Glen's eyes flew open. On his back, he looked at the ceiling for a minute, thinking. His thoughts were random and unfocused—he felt very strange. All memories more than a few months old were vague and unfocused.

Who am I?

He was two people at once—half of his memories were of a harsh, hungry life in a hot, crowded urban environment while the other half was a collage of images, people and places like nine foreign movies spliced into a disturbing, surrealistic dream sequence.

A Portugese word came to mind.

Favela.

What was it in English?

Shantytown.

Like a dream, his brain was filled with random images.

Cocaína. Stacks of brown-paper wrapped cocaine bricks and blocks of clear, cello-wrapped cash. Pistols. Machetes. Women. Highs and lows. *Bailes funk* discos and raves. He'd been shot and stabbed. A flow of desperate emotion surged. He'd stolen from the *Comando Vermelho milícia* and was marked for death.

Why did he think he could get away with it?

There was no escape.

Unconsciously, his fingers reached to explore the scars on his thigh and chest.

Fingers.

His hand was mutilated. Hacked up. The wounds had not quite healed and were wrapped lightly with gauze.

What did they do to me?

He was not fully connected with objective reality. The world was confusing and weird—all bright lights, poking needles and stifling, claustrophobic captivity. He was trapped in a glass cage like a zoo animal.

Clank, whirl, click. The sounds of the meal cart. Time was disconnected from meaning—the prison was isolated from the outdoors—but there were clues, like gelatin-with-mixed-fruit or a plastic cup of pudding in the meal he thought of as dinner. He reflected on the schedule with all the foggy concentration he could muster. Rosa was his best hope. But, that's not to say there *was* any hope. Meals and doctor visits were accompanied by nurses, technicians and guards who always appeared in threes and fours, never alone.

The guard rattled stainless steel chains. Glen put his hands into slots in the wall and cuffs were closed, tightened and locked. He pulled his hands inside, then, with a buzz, the cell door slid open. It was Rosa with the biggest guard, Roman. The outside guard was invisible, but Glen smelled the licorice pellets the man habitually chewed.

For an unknown reason, he knew the Portuguese name for licorice, *alcaçuz*—and the brand the guard chewed. *Halter Liquorice* bonbons. It troubled him. His mind roiled with unwanted and useless information.

The outside guard was a mean one who carelessly clamped the cuffs on Glen's flesh, sometimes pinching hard enough to draw blood. Glen leaned back and looked over his shoulder. The staff was trained to not interact or even make eye-contact, but sometimes Rosa would see him. Really *see* him. And, there was kindness in her eyes—kindness mixed with a sad desperation he knew well.

He flashed back to sweaty, teen-aged, brown-skinned sex machines moving their asses to heavy Roland TR-808 booty beats—deafening bass and drum machine rhythms with one aim, to make the body move. And move, they did, like slinky, well-lubricated hydraulic robots seeking sensual escape if even only for one glorious night.

Rosa had needs and the world weighed heavily on her. Someday, perhaps, that would be something he could use.

He put everything he had into a carefree, confident grin. Women liked protectors, providers—heroes; he emoted every strong and positive emotion he could muster. Compassion. Kindness. Love. Learn to fake these things and dealing with the world was easy.

How did he know? He just did, that's all.

Rosa, my friend. I will help you with your problems. I will shield you from evil and despair. I will grant you solace and absolution. Gently, he rattled the steel chains. Did she pick up his message? How can I save you if I'm locked up like a laboratory rat?

Her gaze lingered on him for a long few seconds. It could have been his imagination, but her eyes seemed touched by his warmth.

What did she want?

He flicked his eyes to her chest covered with layers of crisp, clinical hospital-blue cotton. Under the uniform, she was a woman—all woman. She had desires. She wanted to be dominated, conquered and owned. Protected. Cherished. Loved.

Yes, he nodded.

He sent the message with his eyes.

I promise to give you everything you need.

Wearing latex gloves, Rosa pulled the sheets off the bed and stuffed them in a large canvas bag. She pulled his dirty underwear from a drawer built into the wall. It was an intimacy—with her fingertips, she lightly stroked the soiled clothing more than professionally necessary and yes, there it was, her lips bore a subtle hint, a micro-expression of smile. Once the laundry was attended to, she worked off the gloves, discarded them, then arranged his dinner on the plastic table epoxied to the concrete floor.

Quietly, he sang a phrase from a song he'd heard her hum. It was a Brazilian melody and he was surprised he knew the words—as far as he knew, he'd never been to Brazil. Wait, no, he was born and raised in the slums of Rio. The paradox remained unresolved.

Eu abro o meu Neruda e apago o so.

The guard did not like this.

"The client will remain silent," he said with a harsh edge of warning on his voice.

Client.

It seemed like an odd word. He certainly did not feel like a client or guest—he felt like an inmate. However, when he misbehaved, they did not beat him. Invisible air outlets emitted a calming vapor and he'd find himself drifting in mindless tranquility for a few days. Because all he had was his wits, he hated that fog and what it did to his head. In the cage, his body, though young and strong, was powerless. Security was air-tight and there was no hope, but, he would escape or die trying, he knew that.

He *was* young and strong, it was true, though he did not know how that could be—young and strong and filled with energy. Inside, part of him was old and broken, but on the outside, he was fit and toned. In the stainless steel cabinet or, when the light was right, reflected in the glass, he could see himself. Brown skin. Brown hair. White teeth.

They'd worked on those teeth, he knew that. One day, his mouth was filled with rotten teeth like putrid tombstones. On the next day, he had perfect but gappy, off-white teeth that felt like they were made of aerospace plastic. For weeks, his mouth was a foreign, alien place and his gums ached. He lived on soft, pureed fruits and vegetables, but slowly, his mouth healed and he got used to the feel of the new choppers. His cheeks and eyebrows were surgically reformed and slowly the sutures were removed, the wounds healed and the scars faded. His face didn't look like anything he half-remembered.

They did his hand last and it ached. Relentlessly, it ached.

That was one thing he would never forgive. One day his hand was whole and perfect, then later he woke with bandages and when the bandages were removed, his hand was mutilated and two of his fingers were truncated stubs. This seemed right, but at the same time, seemed very wrong.

What did they do?

And, why?

Rosa dragged out the bag of laundry. He turned and stretched and again leaned back as far as he could. She did not turn around again, but, humming, carried the Brazilian tune into its following phrase. Once the door was closed and tested, the outside guard released the cuffs. Glen turned and rubbed his sore wrists.

Had she left extra steamed carrots because she knew he liked them?

They monitored him continuously, so he ate the carrots with delight written on his face. How did she know he liked carrots? Was she watching? He winked at the one-way glass and raised sporked carrots in salute to the cameras, one-by-one. Once he was done eating, the utensils melted into a puddle of liquid and then evaporated.

How did they do that?

He did not know. It didn't do any good to try to hide the spork or knife, they just left cold, wet spots in his pockets.

After the utensils and bowl, cup and plate disappeared, he watched a video on a wall-sized screen. They always picked movies that seemed familiar—ones he vaguely remembered liking a hundred years ago when he'd first seen them. Then they showed pictures and film clips which he enjoyed. There was a central actor he liked, a hatchet-faced older man who was both alien and intimately familiar—a man who vaguely resembled Glen's resculpted face.

Was he my father, grandfather, a trusted mentor or what?

There were other faces too, a hundred and three of them

shown over and over. He grew to know their names, voices and mannerisms. Why? He didn't know. There was one in particular, a strikingly beautiful young blonde lady named Gerusha Wilson. Over time, his reaction to her photographs and video clips grew more intense. He wanted to own her. He wanted to hold her face in his hands and kiss her until the world ended. He wanted to penetrate and plunder her.

At the same time, he knew he'd kill her without a thought if she stood between him and something he wanted. He'd kill anyone. Rosa. The guards. In an instant. He knew this was wrong and that he should not feel this way, but, he did. In the final tally, their lives meant nothing compared to his goals. But, what were these lofty goals? He had no idea. It didn't matter. He walked the Earth for an important reason and he'd kill God or the devil himself if they stood in his way. Ignoring the throb in his mutilated fingers, he clenched and unclenched his strong hands. It was wrong to be willing to kill so readily, but how can you help what you feel—or don't feel?

Despite perfectly designed systems, humans were imperfect. Eventually one would make an error and he'd strike like a cold-blooded viper.

His fists clenched, then unclenched.

Where was he? Though isolated, there were clues. Once the air conditioning and pink noise sound-masking system failed for a half hour—the still air grew unbearably warm and humid, so it was clearly a tropical climate. In that brief stillness, he could hear gibbering animals. Monkeys? And, the whomp-whomp of a helicopter. There was a small chip in the reflective glass and if he moved his chair just right, he could see a little of what happened in the hallway. Staff moving to and fro, servicing the other rooms. How many chambers like his were there? He counted eight in his hallway, but how many hallways?

One day, he glimpsed another inmate being escorted from a room—a stocky woman immaculately dressed in a wool business suit—with lacquered hair in elaborate swirls wearing a colorful paisley scarf wrapped around her neck. She looked like a younger version of Margaret Thatcher. He didn't know why he knew anything about anyone named Margaret Thatcher, but he did.

She was famous, right?

Everyone knew her. The woman was given a fond farewell; hugged and kissed on the cheek. He couldn't understand it. Inmate? Guest? Was this a sanitarium? Drug or alcohol treatment facility? A health retreat? One of those mysterious CIA facilities where rendered people were disappeared, sometimes forever? Some kind of new-age or religious cult programming or deprogramming facility?

The next day, from the opposite side of the hall, a youthful L. Ron Hubbard emerged, but he was not treated with as much friendly regard as Maggie Thatcher. Who was L. Ron Hubbard? Glen didn't know. Besides, it couldn't be L. Ron Hubbard, because that man was old and certainly dead. Perhaps this was some weird Scientology facility—that would explain a few things, but the explanation didn't feel quite right.

These thoughts were confusing; he didn't know the boundaries of what he knew, or how he knew anything at all. It was as if he was completely stark, raving mad—halfway through conversion into someone new. His body resisted, but why? He wasn't really a prisoner—he had a vague recollection of signing a contract in a tall, modern office building and getting cash money, a lot of it, to distribute to his friends and family. What choice did he have? The *milícia* had marked him for death. Their reckless pre-teen assassins watched for him and wanted the reward—a move up in the organization.

His kids.

He had children, but they would not have a father. Even in his old life, they didn't have a father because he spent his time hustling on filthy streets to earn the temporary solace of hot fluid eased into his veins from a dirty needle.

What streets?

The hillside of Rio de Janeiro. A leaky tile roof. Raw

concrete walls covered with graffiti like *Viva Elektro*. Random Spanish and Portuguese words mixed with English in his head. Street vendors and the oily smell of fried onions and *Malaguetinha* peppers on a heaping plate of *prato feito*. Kids playing *futebol* in a plaza. A fire on a ghetto hillside. Brown water and mounds of filthy trash in a ditch.

The air vents hissed—mist dissipated in the room and he drifted into sleep.

Later that evening or the next, the doctor came for the daily visit. It was the same routine each time; Glen's hands were cuffed and chained to the table. The doctor was escorted by two orderlies. Everything was carefully designed. No matter how much he stretched, he could not reach the doctor. The orderlies stood by the door—they too were out of reach. There was nothing to throw. He was helpless.

"How are you feeling, today, Glen?"

"Fine, I guess."

"Do you know who you are?"

It always seemed like an odd question, but his identity waxed and waned like something just out of reach.

Glen shrugged.

"I'm Glen Wilson."

"Where were you born?"

"Medford, Oregon."

"What year?"

"1953."

"What was your mother's name?"

"Nancy."

"Your father?"

"Ramon."

With a jerk of his head, the doctor looked up from his tablet.

"Sorry, who?" he said.

"Ra—, ah, Ray. My father's name was Ray."

"Why did you mention another name?"

"Everyone gets confused sometimes. I know who my father is. Ray. Ray Wilson."

"Fine. Do you know where you are?"

He knew what he was supposed to say.

"I'm recovering my health in a hospital."

"That's right. You were in a horrible automobile accident and you had a serious head injury, but you're coming along very nicely."

Fucking liar.

Glen knew the doctor was lying. There were surgical scars on his head, but there had been no accident.

They kidnapped him and held him prisoner.

Why?

He did not know.

Because they were psychopaths. Sadists. Assholes. No, that wasn't right. He rubbed the inside of his elbows. The needle marks had faded and were nearly invisible, but he could still feel them—along with the craving for a hit.

Heroína.

He wanted to drift in temporary, artificial peace.

He knew he'd agreed to be here—he remembered endless pages of contracts, but still, he was filled with a hard-to-control, violent rage. One day, he'd kill this doctor and the guards and burn the compound to the ground. Glen pushed the unruly thoughts down and stifled them. It wouldn't pay to let on—it wouldn't serve the mission.

It would be counter-productive.

He smiled.

"I must be the luckiest guy in the world to have such wonderful doctors and your fabulous medical care."

One Month Earlier

Glen Wilson—Primeiro

The Second Luckiest Guy in the World

OUTSIDE THE HEAVY curtains blocking the morning light, there was a muffled click and clatter. Glen's eyes flew open. He lay on his back for a minute, thinking. His thoughts were random and unfocused—he felt very strange.

It was a game he'd played far too often.

Where am I?

As his mind cleared, he absorbed the clues. The smell of French hair conditioner on the pillow beside him. The feel of the cool silk sheets. The dark-stained hardwoods of the bed frame and paneling of the room.

Click.

Clatter.

There was no hope of sleep now. Stark naked, he threw aside the covers and stomped to the window. He tugged the drapes aside and pushed open cut-glass French doors. Outside on the roof, a man worked on replacing a slate shingle.

"I thought we agreed," Glen said. "No work on the house before ten A-M while the master is trying to sleep."

The man grinned—his gold tooth gleamed in sunlight streaming through a gap in woolly clouds. He spoke with a calm tone, as if reasoning with an unruly toddler.

"What time do you think it is?"

Glen growled like a bear.

"I'm surrounded by sad impudence and nauseating incompetence."

From behind, Gerusha spoke. Glen turned. Light streamed from the steamy bathroom. She tossed her blonde hair while working dangly earrings into her earlobes, then spoke with a mock-scolding tone.

"I thought you were going to work today for a change. You have a date with the procedure, remember?"

She was fully dressed and gorgeous from peep-toe, sling-back high heels to the feathered blonde locks framing her face. Panty hose, a bright orange dress. Around her perfect neck, black and tan Tahitian fresh water pearls gleaming like charcoal lightning. Glen felt a stirring in his loins. He ran to her and wrapped her in his arms.

"We should get naked and climb endless mountains of passionate rapture."

"That's what you said last night, but instead, it was more like molehills of boredom. I watched the ceiling for five minutes while you worked up a spurt, then you rolled over and fell asleep. To top off my wonderful evening, you snored like a wildebeest. Besides, don't you have something important on your schedule today?"

"Crap, you're right. We'll have to save your world class, cataclysmic orgasm for later."

"Until then I'll somehow struggle through my sad and depressing life."

Through the silky dress, he massaged her perky breast.

"Keep the girls safe for me."

"Glen?"

"Yes, dear?"

"You're a filthy, disgusting pig."

Glen shrugged and grinned.

"My very best qualities."

"Put some pants on."

Glen sighed.

"Yes, dear," he said.

She kissed his whiskery cheek.

"I'll see you in forty-eight hours."

With both Rose and Marcus in the kitchen, there wasn't much room for anyone or anything else. While Marcus was tall and broad, Rose was squat and broad. They were dressed twin-like in tents of denim bib-overalls splashed with paint—though Rose was more colorful with dabs and streaks of many colors while Marcus bore the few basic neutral colors of the interior walls he painted.

"You're standing between me and my coffee," Glen said.

Rose tapped a paint-splattered finger on his chest.

"I told Marcus there would be no sexual penetration until we're married and I'm sticking to that vow, but I consented to allowing him to pleasure me orally and it didn't seem right to be selfish and not return the favor. Are we doing the permitted or are we hell-bound sinners?"

The unwelcome images of these two huge people having sex filled Glen's mind. He covered her mouth with his palm, then thought about where that mouth had been. He wiped his hand on his trousers, then elbowed past her to wash his hands at the sink.

"Both," Glen said, "I've told you, I don't want to hear anything about your sexcapades."

"Glen, this is important."

Glen sighed. "Do what you want, but keep it to yourself. That's according to Revelations or Psalms or Genesis or some damned something." There was only one subject that would derail her from talking about sex. "Don't you have a painting overdue for Raz's new record? How is that coming?"

Marcus talked around a mouthful of glazed donut. Rose tenderly brushed sugar crystals from his beard.

"That's something I want to talk to you about, Glen,"

Marcus said. "Ten thousand dollars for one of Rose's original paintings seems light. Raz is a famous and rich rockstar. What do you think he would say if we politely asked for twenty-thousand?"

Rose's latest painting was called Obama's Care—an illustration of a surgery theatre filled with maniacal politicians wearing blood-splattered three-piece suits while they hacked up infant children with scalpels. It was gross, controversial and disturbing, all things Raz liked the most.

Raz would probably pay a hundred-grand without blinking. It was ironic because Glen paid all the household expenses and Daniel's Art Supply store bills while Rose's money accumulated in a bank account she didn't need and paid no attention to.

"That's between you and him. What's something worth? What one damned fool will pay and another damned fool will take. Nowhere does Glen Wilson factor into that equation. Leave me out of it." Glen poured cream in his coffee. "Are there any of those donuts left?"

Solemnly, Rose and Marcus shook their heads.

"But you could buy more while you're out," Rose said. She raised her glass of Tang. "I have an announcement." She gestured at a scrap of paper taped to the refrigerator door. "The proper Tang does not quite match Pantone Sunrise Orange 1375. Not enough grenadine, so we're switching to Pantone Starfish Orange 178." She pointed her finger at Glen. "And, I'm not pointing fingers, but someone does not stir the Tang properly, so there are crystals at the bottom of the pitcher. That's disgusting and unacceptable." She switched to baby talk. "We no like. Okay?" She reached out and cupped Glen's jaw and nodded his head for him, then spoke in her normal tone. "We understand and promise to do better in the future? Right? We're all good?"

It was hopeless to argue with her.

"Yes, it's understood, totally," Glen said. "We'll track down the criminal and execute her."

Rose beamed and patted Marcus's shoulder.

"I told you. He totally gets it."

Beyond groping Gerusha, there was one additional pleasure in Glen's morning. The swoopy 1950 Jaguar XK-120 that came with the house had been fully rebuilt and its replicated olive-green paint (Pantone 15-0522 as proclaimed by Rose) gleamed in the overhead lights of the refurbished garage.

It started instantly and the engine's rumble coupled pleasantly to Glen's loins through the leather clad seats. The AM radio tubes were slow to warm up and the sound drifted in and out from the ancient, crackly speakers, but Glen refused any updates to the classic car. It was stupid to drive a drop-top convertible in Seattle's misty weather, but Glen could not resist taking it out once or twice a week instead of the more practical Lexus sedan leased for him by the company.

Through Seattle's side streets and stop-and-go traffic, Glen drove to the Immortality, LLC headquarters on Fremont Canal east of the Chittenden Locks. In the parking garage across the street from the three-story chrome and glass Immortality building, he had a reserved double-spot—he parked square in the middle of the two spaces. Anyone who scratched the Jaguar would face a painful death or worse.

Today was a big day for Glen. Finally, the secrets of the company would begin to be revealed. Although he worked there for over a year, his concept of the service they delivered was shaky. What could be worth a billion dollars to the richest people in the world? True immortality was impossible, of course, but all of his inquiries were deflected or ignored. Did they offer expensive, non-FDA-approved hormone injections? Blood transfusions from youthful athletes? Exotic cosmetic surgery? He didn't know. His job was to schmooze the oil sheiks and movie stars and then, when the sale was made, pass the customers on to the technical team.

In modern business, there was a concept of *eating your own dog food.* This meant using the services the company offered to more thoroughly understand the product and its usage. Glen was tired of pretending to know what was going on; today he would begin the process of eating the Immortality, LLC dog food.

While walking through the entry area, he nodded at Lori-Ellen, the pretty receptionist. At the same time, he ignored the lobby-rat sales-droids lurking about. Make eye contact with any of them and the next thing you know, a half hour you'll never get back elapses and you'll stagger on, punch-drunk with brochures clutched in your hands with buzzwords echoing in your ears.

It's better not to engage.

He could badge in at the private, employee entrance, but it was his habit to rub the head of his bronze bust. Because he moved it himself, it was prominently displayed and illuminated by a showcase lamp at the side of the lobby. He loved it. Glen Wilson, Co-Founder in gleaming metal.

He strolled into the main conference room precisely on time, only fifteen minutes late. Walter Crowley looked up from playing Angry Birds on his iPad. Walter was tall and skeletally thin. His long, bushy white hair was perfectly groomed plumage that made him look like an albino rooster.

"Good of you to join me," he said.

"Let's order in pastries," Glen said. "I didn't get breakfast." He held up the palm of his hand. "Don't ask, long story. You gotta get up really early to beat big-eaters to breakfast. One donut, would that be too much to ask when we buy them by the dozen? And then they want to talk about their sex habits. Do you want to watch elephants mate? I don't. Who cares, right?"

"Glen, please, I have a busy morning. Let's get right to it."

"Fine. Go."

Walter opened an app on his tablet.

"First of all, what is the thing you fear the most?"

"Falling—falling from a high place, I guess. I hate heights."

Walter grunted.

"A lot of people say that. We'll see."

"What do you mean by that?"

"Shut up. I'm working."

There was a tap at the door. A college intern wheeled in a cart holding coffee, orange juice and fourteen types of fresh pastries. This kept Glen busy for a while.

Glen popped a final morsel of a cherry tart into his mouth.

"That should hold me until lunch," he said.

"The way you eat, you should weigh three-hundred pounds," Walter commented.

"Lucky in the metabolism department, I guess."

"Whatever," Walter replied. "I've warned you and I'll warn you again, things will be intense today."

"Yeah, yeah, I know. You don't know intense—intense is my middle name. I'll show you intense. Ever had a Nazi point a Luger at your head? Ever had a finger hacked off by a machete or pruning shears? Ever had a battle of wits with a psychopathic teeny-bopper who wants to stab you in the guts with a Bowie knife? Ever been the only straight man in the studio audience of an Ellen DeGeneres TV show taping?"

"Glen, do you ever shut up? I've given you fair warning. This procedure is necessarily traumatic. Let me give you one more chance to change your mind and back out. My best advice is to forget this whole thing. It doesn't work like you think and it should only be used by the determined and desperate. So, smarten up and pull out? I promise, you'll have a much more pleasant day."

"Glen Wilson does not back out. Glen Wilson does not run away. Glen Wilson does not shy away from danger."

Walter held up his hand.

"Okay, I get it. Stop talking about yourself in third-person perspective."

Glen's tongue felt thick; he had trouble forming the words.

"Glen Wilson forges forward, relentlessly and always."

"Enough, already. We're doing this. The reason we don't explain the procedure is because we found the results are better if the client goes in cold."

"I feel funny."

"You could have gone easier on the orange juice."

Glen tried to stand, but his knees were spongy.

"What have you done?"

"See you on the other side," Walter said.

The medical team did not mess around—they roughly picked Glen up and dropped him on a gleaming steel gurney.

Watching, Walter grinned.

"Don't mind me, there's no reason to be gentle with him. He's a prick."

They threw a crisp green sheet over Glen and wheeled him toward the back of the building. Walter followed along and joined Bennie in the media room. Bennie was still young, but the years weighed on him. He was still in his early twenties, but there were gray strands in his nappy black hair and his ebony skin was imprinted with worry-wrinkles. He'd been working nearly nonstop for several years and it had taken its toll.

Bennie was the key technologist for the Immortality technology. He conceived the ideas, prototyped the algorithms and worked through all the complications. He had 125 bright engineers working for him and implementing his will, but they all needed to know what to do, and Bennie told them.

With surgical shears, they cut off Glen's clothes. Naked, the lax, gray, waxy skin of his scrawny body looked pathetic.

"He doesn't look like much, does he?" Walter commented.

"Some men transcend their physical body," Bennie responded. "I hate doing this to him."

"He insisted."

"I know."

"Besides, this will be an interesting one, won't it?"

"Yes," Bennie said. "Interesting."

They strapped Glen in the custom-built magnetic-resonance-positron chamber and hooked up hundreds of subcutaneous steel probes until he looked like a Clive Barker nightmare too scary to write about. Low-power, laser-generated images were projected into Glen's pried-open eyeballs. Headphones poured sound into his ears. A bizarre cocktail of drugs and hormones were fired into his veins. High frequency generators whined. Magnetic coils screamed from high-current stress. The air crackled with high-voltage fields.

Bennie tugged Walter's arm.

"Control room," he said.

"Right," Walter replied. "It's not safe in here."

The terrified client generally screamed for up to ten hours while the data was collected. Glen was no exception.

Glen was inexplicably hungry. He reached for a pecan scone.

"I thought we were in a big hurry?"

"It's done, Glen. We dosed you with anti-inflamatories and pain killers, but I'll bet you feel something. It was quite an ordeal you went through. Physically and mentally."

Glen flexed the muscles in his arms. He felt fine.

"Bullshit."

He stood up, but felt dizzy, so he sat back down in a hurry.

"You probably still think it's Monday."

"It is, isn't it?"

Walter grinned. "No. Wednesday. We're done."

"Bullshit."

Walter shrugged. "You'll catch up quick enough."

"Okay, now that it's supposedly done, you can quit being so obscure. What did you do? What is the procedure this company sells for a billion dollars a shot?"

"Can I call Bennie? He's better with the technical explanations."

Glen winced.

"I don't want a technical explanation. Just give me the

predigested, English version."

Walter steepled his fingertips.

"Fine. Here goes. First of all, the thing you fear most is *not* falling."

Glen shrugged.

"Then what is it?"

"Being alive, strapped down and gnawed to death by rats. It's odd, there must be some prehistoric root to that fear because it pops up so often. It's as if it's hardwired to the primitive brain. For forty-three percent of the people tested, that's the real number one."

"Don't be so damned obscure. Just tell me these things straight. Forty-three percent of what?"

"So far, for forty-three percent of our clients, being gnawed by rats is the absolute worst thing that could happen to them."

"I swear, Walter, if you don't get to the point..."

Walter held up a palm to stop him.

"I'm getting there, Glen. Try to emulate a little patience, please." He took a deep breath and then a sip of water. "You've heard the hoary cliché about how a man's life flashes before his eyes when he faces death?"

Glen shrugged.

"Sure."

"It turns out there is a physical basis. When faced with mortal danger, all your memories are weighed and measured and the important ones are flashed into storage deep in the root of the brain. All your thoughts and feelings and memories—all the things that make you *you* are grabbed and stored and locked away. One of Bennie's key insights was to imagine a way of using Positrons and magnetic imaging to tap into that flow and *hack* the data."

"You're fucking with me."

"You asked me to tell you and I'm telling you."

"But there's no way to decode data with such complexity."

"We don't decode it, we capture it. We copy it and port it

to another vessel. We don't have to understand it to copy it."

Glen stood on shaky legs, then paced around the conference room table.

"I think I'm catching on. You port the captured data to a new vessel. A younger vessel."

"That's the fundamental strategy."

"Okay, take me one more layer in."

Walter sipped more water.

"The data is too complex to fully port, but Bennie had a brainstorm. He creates a transfer function. So, given a situation, 99.3% of the time the vessel will respond or act like the donor."

"I don't get it."

"What is a key part of your personality? What is your essence? It's how you behave, right? Beyond some metaphysical spirituality, you could say that anything that always *acts* like you, *is* you. Bennie ports the transfer function to the new vessel. We augment it with deep immersion into life-events, people and places—all the memories we can mine, and there you have it. Immortality, LLC."

"It doesn't seem worth a billion dollars. It's not real immortality as most people would describe it."

Walter's grin was wolfish.

"Rich people are not like normal people. In fact, they seem to love themselves to an inordinate degree. When given a chance to bond with someone amazingly just like themselves, they are happy to pay us handsomely to pass along the life-in-progress and thus, work their will in the future. Like all good American marketers, we add glimmer and glitz and downplay the negative aspects. And, as it turns out, it doesn't have to be perfect to be worth a billion dollars to some people, so, from Bennie's wonderful technology we created a very profitable business."

"Wait, pass along? How do we keep this process from getting out of hand? Do we allow two, three, four versions to coexist?"

"No, we don't, we have a policy. I think that's enough to

process for one day." Walter grabbed a macaroon from the pastry tray. "We'll chat more later."

"So, you grabbed the essence of what makes me, me. When do I get to meet this fresh, new Glen Wilson? He's probably a great guy. Suave, sophisticated, well-read, intelligent, sweet-natured and otherwise all-around wonderful."

"Right," Walter said with his lips twisted as if he'd bitten into something bitter. "Six months, that's how long it takes to bring the vessel online."

"Have you gone through the procedure yourself? Is there another Walter running around? Which Walter are you? Number one or number two?"

Walter turned away from the door. His face held a passive expression, though a bit of humor leaked into his eyes.

"It's not my kind of thing," he said. "I don't want the competition."

"What about the Feds, the Federal Food and Drug Administration and all the other fuckwit government alphabet agencies? They're not going to let us do anything interesting."

"The actual work is not done in the United States. We have a lab. Its location is a closely guarded secret. The locals are paid handsomely to look the other way and leave us be."

"Give me a hint."

Walter sighed.

"It's probably in an isolated region in Brazil, though Uruguay disputes location of the border in that region. We pay off both sides, so we don't care."

"Wait," Glen said. "What about these vessels? Are they people who already exist? How the fuck does that work?"

But, it was too late.

Walter was gone.

Glen held out his hands and wiggled them. He felt a little strange—as if partially disconnected from his body, but he assumed that was the work of the painkillers. Some of them didn't alleviate the pain so much as make it seem like the pain was happening to someone else.

Odd, that.

To avoid having to engage with anyone, he walked a circuitous route around the building to Gerusha's office. He stood in the doorway and watched her work. She shuffled papers while keeping up a steady dialog with a team on a video-conference call. She held her index fingers to her lips to tell him to stay quiet. He walked around her desk and nuzzled her neck. She pressed a button to mute the phone and disconnect the camera.

"How did it go? You don't seem any worse for the wear."

"It was interesting. We're not exactly in the business I thought we were in."

"Hang on," she said. She demuted the phone. "The photon microscope came with an eighteen-month warranty. Why are we paying four-hundred grand for an under-warranty repair?"

To Glen, she whispered, "We'll talk more later."

He scowled, but took the hint. It was lunchtime anyway and this version of Glen Wilson was ravenously hungry. His spacious office was on the top floor at the south side of the building overlooking the canal. He enjoyed watching the ships, sailboats and pleasure craft motoring up the and down the channel in a useless back-and-forth churn. He called Padrino's and ordered a double Nizza. They liked his generous tips and could generally get him his meal in an hour. Soon he was happily munching his favorite pizza with Ahi tuna, hard-cooked eggs, gorgonzola cheese with Italian dressing.

While eating, he daydreamed about having another version of himself to talk to. Someone who could read his mind—because they shared the same mind. Would it be boring because every word was predictable? Or, would it be infinitely stimulating to communicate thoroughly and intimately? Glen knew his intellect, though unconventional, was prodigious.

It would surely be a great benefit to the planet to have two of me on it.

While leaning back in his leather chair, he drifted into sleep. A plastic forkful of lettuce slipped from his hands onto the gleaming Brazilian cherry hardwood floor.

He was trapped in a tight, dark space and his bones and muscles ached with merciless intensity. He wanted to move, to stretch, to flex, but he couldn't. The cold walls of his cage would not budge. He heard the skittering of little claws and the squeak and chatter of their ugly voices as the wave of gray teeth grew closer. No matter how he moved, he could not avoid the gnawing teeth—they started with his toes, ripping into the warm meat and tearing out gobbets of flesh. Blood flowed like geysers.

Barely holding back a scream, he woke and jumped from his chair desperately brushing invisible rats from his arms and legs. In flashes, he could see the rodents, but he could also see the bright lights and stainless steel of the clinic mixed with the hardwood splendor of his office.

What had they done to him?

He knew. They had laid bare his deepest fears, then immersed him in them and tapped the flood of protective responses. It was a horrible procedure, torture—the worst thing you could do to a person.

"You okay, Boss?"

Glen turned. Bennie stood in the doorway. As the shakes subsided, Glen studied Bennie and thought about how he'd changed so much in so very few years. He thought of Bennie as a child, but that was no longer accurate; Bennie was a young man. Tall and thin as a twig, he was hunched over as if to disguise his towering height. His skin was black, black as an eggplant, and there was a shred of paper stabbed into the mat of his dense, lumpy hair.

Bennie continued, "Did Walter tell you about the echoes of nightmares you'll have for a while?"

Glen gestured for Bennie to sit down.

"No," he said. "But I got a free sample, so I think I get it."

Bennie frowned.

"That's plain mean. After the trauma you've been through, flashbacks are perfectly normal and they'll subside in time. It's better that you know about them so you can keep things in a proper perspective."

"The things you did, they're inhuman."

Bennie shrugged.

"I tried to talk you out of it. I told you I'd never do it myself."

Bennie was right, he did try to dissuade Glen, but Glen was not the kind of man who responded to rational dissuasion.

"You should have tried harder," Glen said.

"Maybe. You're going to want to know everything at once, but I don't have time. Let's do it this way—I'll answer one question, then I'll go back to work, how about that? You'll get a fresh question tomorrow."

"That's bullshit, how about you sit your ass in that chair until I tell you that you can go?"

"Was that your first question, Glen?"

Glen flopped into his chair, turned to the boats drifting in the channel and leaned back to think.

"Tell me about the vessels," he said.

"That's not a question."

"Bennie, don't bust my balls. Tell me about the vessels."

Bennie sighed.

"That's a big subject. There are a lot of hopeless people in the world."

"Right. So?"

"We buy them. We try to pay a million, but we'll pay five or ten million if we like closeness of the match-up. We try to find people with similar physique and we pay off their families. For some of these people, it's the only positive thing they've done in their life."

"Do we kill them?"

"Finally, a question. No, we don't kill them, not exactly. In fact, you could say the opposite occurs. But they cease to exist as they were. We turn them into the host—or as close as we can."

Bennie got up.

"Wait, what did you mean when you said *opposite*?"

"Question-time is over, Glen."

"Sit back down. We're not done talking."

Bennie smiled.

"I think your three-o'clock appointment is here."

The offices in this section of the building shared an administrative assistant. Monique. She was perfect—it was as if she'd popped off the cover of a French fashion magazine. Perfect face, perfect hair, perfect figure, perfect stylish dresses and jewelry. Glen didn't trust her—he didn't trust anyone who appeared too perfect. When Bennie opened the door to leave, Monique was there. She poked her head in and scanned the room.

"Did I hear you screaming a few minutes ago, Glen?" she said.

"No," he said.

"Let me know when you're ready. Your three-o'clock appointment is here."

Glen watched Bennie amble away; he had a loose-limbed gait like a giraffe.

"Okay, Monique. Give me two minutes, then send him in."

"Her, Glen. It's a her. I'll send *her* in."

Glen shrugged.

"Whatever," he said.

In his bottom desk drawer, he kept a bottle of sixty-four-year-old Macallan single malt whisky, but he kept it disguised in a screw-top Jim Beam Bourbon bottle. Just a shot, that's all he needed. He poured a finger into a plain water glass and savored the aromatic fumes before tossing it back.

The door opened and Monique ushered in his guest. She stretched her words as if Glen would be slow on the pickup.

"Mr. Wilson, this is Sarah Sumner, Special Agent with the Internal Revenue Service."

"Thank you, Monique," Glen said.

He waved her away—she slipped out and closed the door. Glen gestured toward the Jim Beam bottle.

"Care for a snort?" he said.

She shook her head. "A little early in the day," she said. "You don't strike me as a Jim Beam kind of person."

Glen put the bottle away in its drawer.

"Looks can be deceiving," he said. "Are we going to dance around or are you going to get to the point so we can communicate effectively?"

While Glen studied her, she studied him. Her black eyes darted around weighing and cataloging. Her hair was dyed artificially black. She was squat like a fireplug and appeared to have the same sense of humor. None. From under her wool blazer, lacy white cuffs appeared; they flapped when she waved her hands. It would be wrong, dead wrong to underestimate or needlessly aggravate her.

"Thank you for seeing me," she said.

"Refresh my memory."

"Ah, okay. This is a courtesy visit—a friendly, informal chat."

A fishing expedition to see if I'm stupid enough to reveal anything self-incriminating.

"Excellent. I've had many a cheerful interaction with government employees over the years."

"Yes, I'm sure you have. You're an interesting person, Mr. Wilson."

"Please. Call me Glen."

"Very well. Glen it is. Over the years, your personal tax returns seem to be—intermittent."

Glen shrugged.

"My financial affairs are complex. When I have income, don't worry, it works its way through the corporate umbrellas and you parasites get paid."

"Parasites, Glen?"

"I'm sorry, did I say parasites? I meant to say 'honorable public servants.' My benevolent Uncle Sam gets his share from me. Always and without question."

"You're not the first person to hide behind a tangled morass of corporate entanglements."

"And clever Jewish attorneys. Don't forget them."

Sarah sighed.

"Right, clever lawyers of Semitic heritage. I'll remind you, Glen, that fraud does not have a statute of limitations. We can go back ten, twenty, thirty years if we want to."

"My life is an open book. Do you mind? This kind of talk makes me thirsty."

He pulled the bottle from his desk drawer and poured a generous inch.

"I'll join you this time," she said.

Glen looked up, surprised. He pushed the glass over with his index finger, then pulled out another for himself.

This woman is wiser than she appears.

She sipped, then poked her nose into the glass to sniff the liquor. Slowly a smile stretched across her face.

"This is not Jim Beam, not by a Scottish mile."

Glen reached across the broad expanse of desk to click his glass against hers.

"Well said."

They sipped in silence. This was a clever strategy—some people cannot abide silence. Like a golfer concentrating so intently on *not* hitting the ball into a pond, then, of course, plopping the ball right in the dead center of the hazard, sometimes a nervous interviewee will direct a conversation exactly where they don't want it to go. For all of Glen's faults, this was not one. He would let her speak first.

"Delicious," she said.

"By chance, do you know anyone looking for a job? For the

right candidate, the salary and quarterly bonus pay-outs are very generous. We're looking for smart people who think creatively, rain-makers. For the right person, it's a job that pays well and won't even seem like work at all."

Knowing the game, she smiled.

"It could be I know someone, but it's hard to say unless I know more about the position."

Game on.

"I could tell you a little more about what we do here..."

As if I know myself...

"That sounds perfect."

"To keep things efficient, bring me up to speed on what you know and I'll fill in the blanks for you."

This was a test. She was carefully and thoroughly trained to not reveal anything. The purpose of this type of interview was to gather information that could be built on to prosecute tax evaders and money launderers. According to her training, she would answer all his questions with additional questions and reveal nothing. If she disclosed anything, it meant she was serious about fishing for a job in the private sector or she was more clever by far—highly skilled at gathering incriminating information.

She pushed her glass across the desk and held her thumb and index finger a half-inch apart.

Glen grinned.

This was going to be fun.

Walter Crowley

Walter had met with executives from Proctor and Gamble in the morning; his afternoon meeting was with an intense and humorless team from Jacobszen, International.

It was a tough choice: to go public and hang around for the required two years before absconding with the IPO money. Or, sell out to a mega-corporation and try to negotiate a quicker exit strategy. Staying around and building the business to 100 Billion in yearly sales, which seemed inevitable, would take too long—their plan was to take the quick money and move on to something more interesting.

The lead negotiator was a hawk-faced, Holland-born expat named Dirk Schellinkhout who currently lived in Singapore, so he fully understood the nooks and crannies of doing business in the margins of society. He could spend ten billion and borrow another ten billion, so his potential offer was viable, though marginally.

"The best way for me to value your technology is to go through the process myself," Dirk said.

"If only I had a billion dollars for everyone who said that…" Walter replied. "That option is off the table."

"I'm not buying an alley cat in a sack."

Dirk's assistant leaned over and whispered in his ear. Dirk corrected himself.

"A pig in a poke."

"Right, of course," Walter said. "I understand. So, we're stuck and that's it." The Jacobszen team began gathering their papers and closing their air-book computers. "However, there's someone I'd like you to meet before you go."

Walter tapped an icon on his communicator.

"Please send him in," he said.

"Who?" Dirk said.

Walter smiled.

"You tell me," he said.

The young man that entered the room was about twenty-five years old. He was slender and had a dark-brown swath of thick hair on his head. He wore an earring and had a mouthful of straight, perfect, pearl-like teeth. He flopped in a chair and slouched like a teenager.

"Hallo, hoe gaat het, neef?"

Hello, how are you, cousin?

"I will not entertain silly games or parlor tricks," Dirk said. "Good day, sir."

The young man switched to English.

"Do you remember Hendrika, cousin? What we did to her? How many people have you told about that? I know how many I told. None. No one."

"This is nonsense," Dirk said.

"I have an even better one. Alfons. Need I say more?"

Dirk's face went pale, as if all his blood had drained into his shoes.

"I don't know anyone named Alfons, I never did and I never will."

"Right, I understand. Remember the German streetwalker we pitched into the Prinsengracht? That's a safer subject, isn't it? She was wrapped head-to-toe in a mink coat. Her high heels, they were tiger-striped, right? You asked her to kiss *der schwanz*, and she told you to *pissen* off? So, into the canal she went and we ran off laughing like jackals. You were fourteen. I hope you can hold your beer now more than you could back then."

Dirk studied the young man's face.

"Who are you?"

The young man laughed.

"I'm not going to tell you. Guess, Cousin. Go ahead. Ask me anything you like."

"Fine. Who was your first wife?"

"That's too easy, Cousin, but I'll play. Many people think it was Gusta, but we know better, don't we? It was a long weekend in Petersburg, and Ulyana would only sleep with us if we pretended to be married. Was the priest we woke in the middle of the night legitimate or not? Who knows? She was willing to try anything as long as there was cocaine involved. And, her brother the policeman? It's lucky we had lots of cash for bribes that weekend, isn't it, Cousin? Now, hit me with something hard—something only you and I would know. As your older brother, I showed you a whole new world, remember?"

"Oom? Uncle Neeltie? This is impossible. You're an old man."

"Yes, impossible, but here I am, all young again."

Dirk studied his face.

"You don't look the same at all."

"Do you think that's a disadvantage? You can pick—you want to look much like you did, just tell them. I still have the same—desires and preferences, shall we say no more? I might not look exactly the same, but my energy and appetites, they are the same."

"Can you stay? Can you talk?"

"I have a plane to catch." The young man laughed. "But, it's a private jet, it will wait. I live in Sao Paulo now and I'm having the time of my life."

"Clear the room, please," Dirk said. "Everyone out."

"Everyone but me," Walter said.

Dirk looked at him coolly.

"Fine," he said. "If we're going to be in business together, there's no need for much secrecy, am I right?"

"That's the way I see it," Walter said.

"This thing you've done—it's not a miracle, it's somewhere beyond a miracle."

"I know," Walter said in a flat, neutral tone.

Three Stories

Special Agent Sarah Sumner loosened the scarf around her neck and pulled off her sensible shoes which she pushed to the side of her chair. Glen's veins were warmed by the alcohol. He wasn't drunk, but felt like all was very well with the world.

"Do you mind if I tell you three stories, Glen?"

"No, please go ahead."

"The first one is about a former coworker. I don't want to use his real name, so let's call him Tim. Tim was assigned to investigate a narco money-laundering operation centered in Houston. He was a good investigator and worked hard to gather evidence against a Swiss transnational person-of-interest named Fritz Platten. When the case was very nearly ready to be filed with the Attorney General's office, Tim's wife died in a car accident. I don't know for sure, but people say Tim and his wife were not getting along and he was on the frontier edges of a nasty and expensive divorce. Then the chain of evidence fell apart and the Platten case was abandoned. Six months later, Tim retired to Costa Rica and lives in a lovely villa in comfortable obscurity raising a second crop of sons and daughters with a Tica wife named Lidia. Lidia is half his age, a former escort girl and quite lovely, as I understand it."

"Interesting," Glen said.

"The second story is about a young Mormon man from Boise. In an appalling deficit of creativity, let's call him Tim, too. This Tim was only twenty-five, but already with three kids, a Chrysler minivan and another bun in his wife's oven. Tim was a Boy Scout, not literally, but figuratively. Energetic and a straight arrow all the way. Like a terrier pup, once he got his teeth into something, he would not let go. He was investigating tax evasion by a big, well-known construction contractor, one who built one of the Hells Canyon bridges over the Snake River as a random example. Not big-time, but doing well. Part of this contractor's success was intimate relations with several trade unions and there were rumors about mob ties to Big Tuna Chicago-Accardo and other heavies back east. One day, Tim got in his government-issued Ford econobox sedan to drive to work and he and the car were never seen again. At the time, the big construction project in Boise was the Eighth and Main Tower where a lot of concrete was being poured. I have my suspicions about what happened to Tim, but the cadaver dogs smelled nothing and Tim's body was never found."

"Do you have any thoughts about the car?"

Sarah shrugged.

"Chop shop? Melted down at a recycling facility? Stripped and shipped to a Juarez wrecking yard? It doesn't matter. The car was never found and never will be. That's my opinion and you're free to disagree."

"I'm with you," Glen said.

"The third story isn't really a story. I worked for a few months side-by-side with a legendary DEA old-timer I think you know. Steve Stephens. Sometimes, over a drink like we're having right now, your name came up in conversation, so I know a fair bit about you. From your mutilated hand and the hawkish look in your eyes, I now tend to believe a few more of the wilder tales I used to discount, but you know how stories are—they inevitably accrete drama over the years and the retelling."

"I've known Steve for nearly half a century. He's known as an embellisher."

"Maybe, but maybe not. So, Glen, what do you think I take from these stories?"

Glen rubbed his chin and pondered.

"That's a great question. I think it's safe to assume you are a worldly person fully aware that sometimes the truism is wrong—crime does sometimes pay. And, you want to do a good job, but, perhaps, not too good of a job."

"That's well-put, Glen." There were a few scant drops left in her glass. She drained them. "Let me describe a scenario and see what you think. I don't have any grandiose ambitions, I just want to land a GS-15 rating and move up a couple of steps. I max out my federal retirement contributions every year and I want to retire at fifty-five and live comfortably in a big, paid-for house with a pool and a handsome pool boy in Scottsdale, Arizona. Here's the scenario: we pick a small, non-criminal accounting error, say an IRC section 461H non-compliance with international revenue procedure and the end result is a Notification letter and an amount due of something nominal, say a hundred and three thousand dollars. We close the books up to last year and you don't marshal your team of expensive downtown tax attorneys."

Glen leaned back in his chair.

"GS-15? That's good. I'll bet your superiors think of you as an excellent agent who really *produces*. Am I right?"

Sarah grinned.

"You're not wrong."

Glen tilted his chair back toward his desk and reached out his mutilated hand.

"Let's do this thing," he said. "A hundred and three grand—not a penny more." She shook his hand with a firm grip. "Where to tomorrow?"

She smiled.

"A local company, Omnitron."

"I like your style."

"I like to reach out and touch the money tree to see if anything will drop gently into my hands. There are others who think a chainsaw is more productive."

"And you have one in your back pocket if you need it."

She shrugged.

"That's correct."

"At the same time, private companies are funny kinds of trees that can move if the forest gets too—inhospitable."

"True that." She studied Glen's face. "I'm not the kind of Fed you need to worry about." Glen waited her out to see if she'd continue. She made a decision to say more. "As an example, I know of an FDA man named Charles Benson. Don't call him Chuck and don't call him Charlie. He's got an auto-immune disease—his body hurts from head to toe, so don't touch him, not even to shake his hand. You'll find him very, uh, humorless. Relentless and humorless."

"That's a bad combination in a government bureaucrat."

Sarah nodded.

"According to talk around the water cooler, he's *interested* in what you are doing here."

"Thank you, Sarah, I appreciate the heads-up." He studied her face. "If you hear of anyone looking for a private-sector job that handsomely rewards creative-moxey and initiative, don't hesitate to give me a jingle."

Sarah worked her feet into her shoes.

"I'll keep an eye open and see if I can find someone for you," she said.

There was only one place where Glen could smoke a Cubanos cigar and be left alone—the roof of the building. The weather was often cold and damp, but he had a shelter built like a greenhouse with leather-clad furniture and radiant heating from hot water coils in oak flooring. It hadn't been properly broken in because he hadn't talked Gerusha into having sex there yet, but that was inevitable. One day, he'd wear down her defenses or she'd want something bad enough to give in.

He grinned.

It was as sure as the dusky smoke in his lungs.

It seemed odd to be involved with a business he knew so little about—one that had made him rich again, but he was used to living on the far fringe of control. He'd go nuts if things were too settled and predictable. After the session with Sarah Sumner, he felt overheated. He pressed a cold bottle of water to his forehead. Life had dealt him many twists and turns and it was odd to think that most of his adventures were in the past, not the future.

Old. Old-old-old. I'm an old man or on the razor-edged fringe.

Wouldn't it be nice to live a fresh new life? To keep all his memories and experiences, but carry them in a strong, lithe, powerful body? The name of the company along with the stainless steel mobius-infinity logo hanging at the front of the building explained everything, though most people thought the symbol was pure advertising agency, empty, dot-com, vapor-cloud, hyperbolic imagery with no substance. He was in good shape for his age, but didn't have the stamina of his youth. He could ride a bicycle, but not up a steep hill. He could walk a mile, but not run. He could have sex with Gerusha, but not five times a night and he couldn't make her walk like a bowlegged cowpoke for a week thereafter.

Immortality. The fountain of youth. It was something kings, emperors and khans craved for millennia. Now technology delivered this gift to anyone who could come up with a billion dollars worth of gold or DigiCoins. He mulled over how this must work. Something Walter said stuck in his mind.

No, we don't kill them, not exactly, in fact, you could say the opposite occurs.

That was an odd thing to say. What's the opposite of killing someone? Letting them live? That didn't feel right. Maybe he wasn't parsing Walter's words properly. What's the opposite of *we don't kill the donor*?

He tapped Robusto ash into a crystal bowl and studied the smoke curling in the still air of his plush gazebo.

We don't kill them, not exactly.

Was there added emphasis on the *we*, or did he imagine it?

Maybe Bennie would tell him. He dialed the front desk.

"Lori-Ellen? This is Glen. Please connect me with Bennie's cell."

Because so many people bothered him, Bennie's watch-phone got a new IP address every week.

"I have him, Glen."

"Thank you. Bennie? Come up to my gazebo."

"Glen, I can't, I'm with a candidate. A promising one. Tsinghua University. He knows about cell protrusion—projecting bacterial comet tails and cytokinesis."

"Tell me about...."

But, Bennie was already gone.

"Shit," Glen muttered.

He pressed the listing for Emma's watch-phone, but she did not answer.

"Damn it, am I a C-level executive or not?" he muttered. "People have to talk to me, don't they?"

He tried Gerusha.

"What's up, Glen?" she said.

"Come up to the gazebo. I have something important to talk

to you about."

"Bullshit. You've been smoking those horrible cigars and you want to have sex with me."

"I'll turn on the exhaust fan. You won't smell a thing."

"Right. And, according to your admin, you've been drinking. There's no way I'm coming up there. Forget it."

"Baby, please, I haven't seen you in two days. I need you."

"Glen, we're married, so I'll have sex with you, but not now. Tonight in the big bed, I promise."

"Baby—baby?"

It was too late, she'd disconnected the call.

"Goddamn it," he said.

His cigar was out. He rekindled it with a butane lighter, and then leaned over to rest his head on the glass wall of his enclosure to watch a forty-foot schooner putt-putt by on the canal. At the wheel was a huge, swarthy man, at least three-hundred pounds. A young woman dressed in Spanx blackout tights, CamiTank and Patagonia parka coiled a rope. When Mr. Big Sailor called, his girl-of-the-month would come running, or else.

If I wasn't blissfully married, that's the way I'd run things.

He imagined what Gerusha would look like in those tights and the image pleased him. He made a mental note to order up a dozen. She didn't need the reshaping, but the skin-tight fit, oh boy. Walter's unwanted voice echoed in his ears.

No, we don't kill them, not exactly, in fact, you could say the opposite occurs.

There was a bell that rang through the building whenever a sale was consummated—it meant the contract was signed and the bank transfer had been confirmed.

Ding, like a ship-Captain's bell.

It was the sound of money and Glen never grew tired of hearing it. It came surprisingly often. One lucrative day, the bell rang twice as husband and wife owners of a luxury cruise line signed up.

It didn't seem like there could possibly be that many people who could afford to spend a billion dollars, but maybe there were a lot who could borrow that much. He didn't know. He didn't care. The company did not accept IOUs or empty promises. The potential buyer couldn't even get an introductory meeting until their net worth passed an audit. Want to get rich? Easy. Figure out what people want and give it to them.

Glen wasted the afternoon daydreaming. Then, to avoid talking to anyone, walked down the fire escape and across the street to drive his Jag home. He had black moods and learned not to take them too seriously; life often seemed more worth living in the morning after a good sleep. Besides, he had sex with Gerusha to look forward to.

Young Gerusha was silky and slippery and—this was a continual surprise to Glen—generally willing. It was as if she felt some obsolete traditional obligation to her husband, but Glen would not complain or guide her to understanding the errors of her ways. He loved her firm flesh and her slim body where everything was as it should be—untouched by the relentless evils of middle age. The inevitable evil was there—lurking in a gentle roll of fat or a protruding vein—but did not yet reign. This was in contrast to Glen where wattles and wrinkles and flab were hidden away under imported, custom-fitted silk suits.

The early evening was dark and damp. Overhead, the ceiling of clouds was thick and relentless. The roads were wet and even the traffic lights were sad and dripping tears. His home was dark. Down the long hallway, Marcus and Rose were doing whatever it was they did to the sound of 60's music—stomping like hippos and laughing like hyenas. He didn't want to know.

It was pleasant enough; The Monkees and The Rascals drifted into the kitchen as he foraged in the refrigerator for dinner. He ended up with a feast for kings; a glass of Arrogant Bastard Ale and an organic Hempler's hotdog dipped in a bottle of dijon mustard. There were hotdog buns, but they were all dusty with green mold. They were probably a good source of penicillin, but he didn't have a staph infection. Besides, most staph was resistant to penicillin these days. Doubly disgusted, he threw the moldy buns away.

When Gerusha got home about eight o'clock, she brought a take-out container of tofu Pad Thai. He evaded her defenses and landed his chopsticks in the box several times to grab a few bites. She liked to watch TV when she came home. To separate herself from the stress of the job, she liked brainless sitcoms and melodramatic shows with doe-eyed nurses and muscle-bound doctors. She didn't much mind him groping her, so he unfastened her bra and pretended to watch the TV with her.

At ten o'clock, she yawned and was ready for bed. He waited patiently while she washed off her makeup and brushed her hair. She spoke quietly while standing at the foot of the bed.

"You still up?"

He sat up.

"Why, what's wrong?"

"Nothing. I promised to be your lover, but I didn't want to wake you if you're already asleep."

Right, like there was any chance.

"Oh, yeah, I forgot. Come to me, princess—we'll ride a magic carpet of love over an endless desert."

"Right. Try not to take too long, I'm still sore from the last time."

Rats, an endless wave of filthy, disgusting rats with yellow teeth and an insatiable appetite for living flesh. Their teeth were embedded in his raw flesh and he could feel every quiver and munch.

He woke with a spasm of twitching muscle. He sat up on the bed and rubbed cramp from his calves.

What did they do to me?

The lingering images were vivid and real.

Gerusha was only partially awake.

"Are you okay, babe?" she said.

"Yeah. Go back to sleep."

It was another hour before he fell into another restless sleep. When he woke, she was gone.

They will answer my questions today, or else, he vowed.

After a long shower, he dressed for work—taking time to get a diagonal-striped silk Hugo Boss necktie knotted just right. He did this sometimes, obsessing over a detail no one else would notice. Who else would spend a half-hour knotting a tie? Was this the way the world ends? Zeroing in on infinite detail that can never be perfected, then never getting anything done?

He was in one of his moods. It wasn't like he hated his job or really had anything that could honestly be described as a job, but he was stalling. He didn't want to go. He considered taking the day off.

Would anyone notice?

It boiled down to boredom. He had had everything a man could want. He stopped checking his checking account balance when it reached ten-figures. It was more money than he could imagine spending on anything. A new car? The Jaguar would go for more than $300,000 on eBay and he'd essentially paid nothing for it. A better house? Who wanted to maintain more than 15,000 square feet? A better watch? The battered old Casio suited him fine. He'd had it so long that the retro-digital style was back in fashion. For the house, there were already two or three people working on estate maintenance and repair, full-time. He had a beautiful young wife who tolerated his mood swings and catered to him, mostly. He had endless creature comforts, but his life was unexciting. Sure, it was fun to have a battle of wits with a clever IRS special agent, but he was used to being out in the world and living on the edge—letting the world challenge his wits in life or death struggles.

He poured a cup of coffee in the kitchen and wandered to the library. When he opened the door, he was assaulted by a thick wall of blue smoke. Inside, Marcus sat in the main chair with a leather-bound book and a crystal glass of something amber.

"Aren't you supposed to be painting something?" Glen said.

"I'm on my lunch break."

"You're smoking my Robustos…"

"Do you mean Rose's father's?"

"And, what are you drinking? It better not be the Harvey's Oloroso. That stuff is irreplaceable."

"There are at least 700 bottles in the cellar. We can relax and enjoy a couple. It's sweet. I'm developing quite a taste for it."

"What are you reading?"

"The History of Circumcision by a Doctor Remondino. 1891. It's fascinating. Did you know some people consider circumcision to be a form of penis worship?"

"No." Glen gestured. "You're an asshole. Read it over there—not in my chair. Will you help me rob a bank?"

Marcus tilted his head like a dog. "Excuse me?"

"Ah, forget it. I don't know why I said that. Just move. And stay out of my Cuban cigars."

"Yes, sir," Marcus said. "They're not that good anyway—I don't think the humidifier is working quite right."

"You wouldn't know a good cigar if it crawled up your pant leg and bit off your foreskin."

"You say odd things sometimes."

"Shoo."

Marcus moved over to an upholstered lounge chair. Glen had just settled in the vacated poet-style leather chair when his cell phone tinkled. His ringtone was Oldfield, Tubular Bells.

"Crap," he grumbled.

He was going to ignore it, but glanced at the screen. It was Bennie. He had to answer.

"Bennie, what's up?"

"Where are you? I want you to meet someone. Can you be in the Hangout conference room in five?"

"Bennie, I've been trying to get your attention for a month and now you want me to drop everything for you? I should appear at your command at the drop of a hat to take the abusive neglect you dish out, eat it all up and ask for more?"

"Yes," Bennie said.

Glen looked at the phone's screen. Bennie had disconnected. Glen spoke to the dead phone.

"Why, yes, Bennie, obviously this is important, so I'll be happy to come in and do you this favor. No problem."

He stood up. Marcus looked up from his book.

"It shouldn't be a big bank," Glen said, "a small, regional bank, not one of the big multi-national branches where the security is carefully designed."

Marcus returned his attention to his book.

"Weirdo," he muttered.

The instant Glen was gone, Marcus moved back to the Poet's chair.

Soul Men

On the third floor of Immortality headquarters, Glen tapped on the door of the Hangout conference room. Bennie came out. He seemed overheated and jittery.

"Thank you for coming, Glen."

"What am I doing here?"

"I can't take any more of this guy."

"That's not an answer, Bennie. What do you want me to do?"

"This is one of our early prototypes. Talk to him. Let me know what you think. His jet has a flight window—he's leaving in forty-five minutes, so be quick about it."

"Quick about what?"

"I'm nervous about what we're doing, get it? You are a more worldly person than me, you *read* people better. Scope out this guy and tell me what you think."

Bennie turned and began walking away as if he was in a hurry to be somewhere.

"Bennie? I don't know what you're asking me to do."

From ten feet away, Bennie spoke over his shoulder.

"Before you let him go, ask him about a girl named Sybylla."

Glen's hands clenched. He loved Bennie, but wanted to strangle him. He took a deep breath and squared his shoulders before entering the room. This was one of the smaller rooms—an informal meeting space without a central table—it held two couches and a scattering of casual chairs and end tables. The window overlooked the courtyard. Outside, well-groomed evergreen trees dripped with misty rain. Inside, the man was about thirty, slender and clean-shaven with brown skin and gleaming, perfectly-straight white teeth. Glen held out his hand to shake—the young man mauled Glen's hand with a crushing grip.

"Glen Wilson," Glen said.

"Neeltie, that's a surname, but you can call me Neel—it's an easy name for Americans to remember."

"I'm pleased to meet you."

"No you're not. You're just saying that because you think it's polite. But, it's not polite to say things you don't mean. Instead, it's rude and dishonest and phony, but that's the *gelul* American way, I understand."

For an instant, Glen was taken-aback. Then he remembered, the Dutch are direct and value getting to the point. It's rude, but the Dutch don't consider it so. They once ruled over a great percentage of the world and in their minds, they still do. Eye-contact. Glen looked directly into the man's face and engaged his eyes.

"How old are you?" Glen said.

The man considered. "My body is thirty-three, but I'm over 80." He thought about it for a few seconds. "82. It's a miracle."

"The Immortality service? You're satisfied? We delivered everything we promised?"

"Yes."

Glen leaned back in his chair and studied the ceiling for a minute.

This is a good chance to learn more about the mysterious process.

"The nightmares, they were bad at first, then they faded?"

"Yes, exactly."

This is going to be the world's shortest interview.

"I'm curious about what you remember."

"Ah, okay, fine. I was old, dying, in fact. I wouldn't have lasted another year, but it was a great life. I had many good years to look back on. What more can a person expect beyond great memories after a long, eventful life? I began hearing rumors about your company, but I was suspicious about your technology. What good things have Americans created? Coca Cola? MTV. Bad movies and filth on HBO? But, I have to give credit. Your *niglet* is remarkable. Bennie, Benjamin, right? A smart black, really smart. There are many wonders in the world."

"You arrived at our clinic here?"

"Yes, I came here to Seattle. The bad weather here is like Lelystad, my homeland. That's good, it builds character—you can't laze around in the sun all day like a *kaffir*."

"Why did you come back?"

"You pay me, I come. One-hundred-thousand dollars for twenty-four hours. To convince my nephew. It's okay, for that, I leave the sunlight for five minutes, no problem."

"And you were one of the first?"

"I didn't know until later. Slippery, you Americans. I was the very first that survived. Mad, the others went. They died screaming."

"What did you pay for the experimental procedure?"

"Ah, I didn't pay. Free. Gratis. That's good because I had no money. And, what did I have to lose with so much to gain? I agreed. It took only a minute. I agreed, though maybe your Walter did not tell me everything? I understand. I forgive. Why not?" He raised his hands like a preacher. "Life is good."

"Where did your new body come from?"

"They didn't say. I don't care. It's a good, strong body." He laughed and made a back-and-forth piston motion with his fist. "Much stamina. Fuck like stallion—come like geyser. They told me to stay away from Barcelona. I saw a postcard of La Rambla. Forced to guess, I'd say I was a pickpocket there. Brown trash no one will miss, I'm sure. I get a flashback from subways and crowded streets. Echoes. Old memories. I don't love tourists. It's okay, I don't need to go to Spain. I get everything I need from Brazil. The donor-person sometimes struggles to emerge, but I push back. Slowly, he dies and I live. Okay. Enough? No extra time, is that how you say it? Overtime." He stood. "Time waits for no one."

"One more thing. Tell me about Sybylla."

"What's to say? Beautiful girl—daughter to my second wife. Was I even really the father? Our marriage was bad by then—I had other lovers and so did she. Who knows? Was it wrong? Even if I was the father, in a new body, is it incest? Legally? Morally? I wanted her and I seduced her. Twenty-two years old. She was willing; no stranger to *lullen*, that's for certain. Where's the harm? I wasn't her only lover, though I was her last."

He stood with his hand on the doorknob.

"Wait," Glen said. "You were her last lover?"

"She was nothing, a pretty nothing."

"Did something happen to her?"

"She had an empty head. She was all handbags, lipstick, expensive shoes and cigarettes. The world didn't blink when she died."

"Did you kill her?"

Neel laughed.

"No, it wasn't me. Her boyfriend was unhappy." He lifted his shirt to expose a three-inch gash in his side. "See, he got me too, but her? He cut her until she was dead. Then he cut his own throat. It was okay—better this way, maybe. I was done with her."

Glen visualized the scene.

"He didn't cut his own throat. You didn't kill her, but you

watched *him* kill her, then you killed him."

"The police said it's hard to cut your own throat—ear-to-ear—but apparently it's possible, technically. Who knew? Young lovers can be so passionate. I must go now."

He left the room. Glen sighed and spent a sad hour craving a drink while looking out at the dreary rain battering the window before Bennie poked in his head.

"Glen, I've been looking everywhere for you."

"Heaven forbid you look in the last place you saw me."

Bennie pulled the door closed and sat down—leaning forward to study Glen's face.

"What did you think?"

"He's a certifiable psychopath."

Bennie made a rude *splat* noise with his mouth.

"That's it? A third-grader could figure that out. I expected more from you."

"Don't play games, Bennie, I'm not in the mood."

"I'm worried, Glen."

"I will beat you to death with a chair if you don't get to the point. What are you worried about?"

"It will sound funny if I say it."

Glen leaned back and rubbed his forehead.

"I've officially lost patience. Be gone, young annoyance."

"I—I..."

"Are you still here? Go away."

"When we make the *transfer* from donor to client, I don't think everything makes the transition. The clients are not wholly *human.*"

"Bennie, no one who earns enough money to spend a billion dollars is fully human. Haven't you noticed this? Generally, they are a rare breed with ruthless ambition and cold-blooded, hard-headed, raw, insatiable appetites. They are more like sharks than men. Now it's *you* disappointing *me.* Take a hike, mate."

"There's more to it, Glen. You haven't seen as many clients as me. There is something wrong with them. All of them.

Something's missing. I'm scared."

"What do you think is missing?"

"You'll laugh at me. In spite of a practiced shtick you manipulate people with to make them misunderestimate you, you have insight. You know what I'm talking about. Please don't make me say it."

"I enjoy my solitude. I'm all alone."

"Dog-gone you, Glen. You are one-hundred-percent aggravating."

Glen pointed his finger at the door.

"You can find your way out, I'm sure."

"I see what is happening. You don't want to say it either, do you? Don't play stupid—you know what I'm talking about."

"Go," Glen said.

"I'm going already."

With passive-aggressive spite, Bennie left the door open; Glen had to get up to push it closed. He really wanted to be alone with his dark thoughts. Outside, the gray day descended into evening.

After giving up on being alone, Glen walked to his office. It was seven o'clock in the evening, but many of the researchers were still working—about half the day-staff members were present. He stopped to watch three Indians, a Korean, a Pakistani and a Latino argue over a protein fault tree analysis. For no good reason—he didn't understand anything of what they talked about—he stayed long enough to identify the Latino's accent. Lima, Peru. He pulled up an application on his laptop and found that Walter was still in the building—in the third-floor break room. Glen walked quickly to get to Walter before he disappeared.

"Walter, don't run off," Glen said.

"Places to be," Walter replied.

Glen grabbed Walter's arm to hold him in place.

"The clients take over the body of the donor, I get that."

"Is that your question? Are you asking me to verify that is company policy?"

"No, my question is this—what happens to the old version of the client?"

"Oh, that's easy. We discard them. Now, I really have to get going. I'm meeting Angela for dinner and I'm already late."

"We kill them, don't we?"

Walter laughed.

"No, that's silly, of course we don't kill them. What you must think of us."

"Then what? What does it mean to be *discarded*?"

"Glen, once we start digging into this, it will be a multi-hour conversation I simply do not have time to entertain. I'm not trying to be evasive; I'm just trying to get you to focus so I can bring you up to speed efficiently."

"Wait."

"Truly, Glen, I've answered two questions already. I need to go. Get your next question ready. Focus like a proton beam and we'll talk more tomorrow."

"You're a festering pain in my rectum."

"Likewise, Glen. Very much likewise. See you tomorrow."

Glen drove home and found Gerusha in the kitchen eating a take-out chef salad from plastic box.

"Did you bring me one?"

"No," she said.

He pulled a fork from the flatware drawer.

"Fine, then you can share."

"Eat a hot dog."

He stabbed a slice of boiled egg in her salad.

"Washington is a community property state, I get half."

Rose, wearing a huge, flapping kimono waddled into the kitchen. She poured a glass of Tang and examined the color in the bright kitchen lighting.

"Hmmm, close enough, I guess," she said. She took a trial

sip. "Good." She looked at Glen from head to toe. "You're an ugly man, and I can imagine how nauseating your scrawny body would be, but I want to paint you. Nude."

Glen and Gerusha looked at each other.

Where did that come from?

"It's not going to happen," Glen said.

"Why not, Glen?" Gerusha said. "You're always up for an adventure, right?"

"I'm sure she'll get around to you next."

Gerusha emitted a snort of laughter.

"Right."

"If it will make you more comfortable," Rose said, "I will disrobe too. I'm not ashamed of the body God gave me."

Unbidden, Glen had an uncharitable thought.

God and ten thousand cheeseburgers...

Rose continued, "It's not the bare flesh that is sexy, it's the mystery hiding under the clothing."

With that, Rose strolled back toward her bedroom.

"Every now and then, she says something that halfway, sort-of makes sense," Glen said.

"Bring me a Haagen Dazs bar when you come up to watch TV."

"Wait," Glen said. "Have you noticed how weird Immortality is?"

"When I worked at Starbucks, the engineers from Adobe would come in. If you want to see weird, try those guys. Oh, boy. Their tattoos had tattoos."

"This company is into seriously twisted shit. Do you know what we're doing? We're recording people and duplicating them in different bodies so they can pretend to live forever."

"Glen, do we have to talk about work? I'm tired. All day, I was trying to get SpectroDynamics to honor a software configuration initialization per a clause clearly denoted in the purchase order so the team can get busy with something called RNA trans-sequence convolution. Engineers. Doctors. Lawyers.

Mediators. Regulatory Agencies like alphabet soup. Do you want to talk about that? I don't. I just want to watch Oklahoma City Housewives until I can fall asleep. Okay?"

"We scare the shit out of people to record their memories."

"No sex if you keep talking about work."

Glen opened his mouth, then shut it.

"Yes, dear," he said.

Sales Pitch

In the morning, Glen walked in the front lobby and rubbed his bust. This always made him feel good. He stopped to talk to the receptionist, Lori-Ellen.

"Where's Walter? He turned his locator off."

"He's in the theater."

"I didn't know we had a theater. Where is it?"

She pointed an ivory-painted fingernail over her shoulder.

"First floor. Follow the marble tiles. Don't bother him while he's pitching."

Ha, pitching. This I want to see.

"Thanks," Glen said.

He'd never spent much time on the first floor, so he was not sure what-all was there. He followed marble inlays in the bamboo flooring—after a few turns, he stood before a huge, arched doorway. The massive doors looked like they'd been rescued from an ancient church and refinished. The guard nearly filled the doorway, he was a monster.

Glen gestured.

Let me in.

The man shook his head.

"You're not on the list." Glen's blood pressure spiked. He waved his badge. The man grinned. "I'm kidding, Mr. Wilson. I know who you are. Slip in quiet and no one will notice you. To keep the theater dark, please don't open the inside door until I close this one."

The guard pulled open the door. Inside, through a short

hallway, there was another large door. Glen walked in and stood by the second door. When the outside door was closed, Glen was in complete darkness. For no reason, he stood for a full minute before pulling the door open. Inside, the small stage was brightly lit, but the room was dark. Glen slipped into a rear row seat to watch the show. Walter was on stage wearing a headset while images moved on the screens behind him.

"Show a caveman a light bulb and he'll think it's magic, but we know how they work and take them for granted. Flick a switch and the light goes on. Flick again and it goes off. Is it a technological miracle or just an everyday convenience? The answer depends on context."

Glen wriggled his butt in the seat. It was wide and plush—very comfortable. He wished for popcorn. As his eyes adjusted to the light, he studied the other people in the audience. The theater capacity was about 100, but there were only ten people scattered around in the cavernous room. Old. They were all ancient, mostly men, but there were two thin women wearing expensive wigs—fake hair coiffed in elaborate swirls. They looked like iguanas in dresses.

A beautiful actress was frozen on the video screen. She was well-known from her role on a Netflix series. She wore a sheath-dress that seemed painted on her infamous curves. Her image morphed into three dimensions, then four as she started moving. She walked off the screen and onto the stage to join Walter. There was a smattering of applause.

"Is she magic or is she real? You should be the judge."

On impossibly high heels, she walked down the stairs from the stage to shake hands—she held out her cheek for a kiss from each of the members of the audience. When it was his turn, Glen reached out as if to touch her chest. She batted his hand away.

"Don't be naughty," she said.

"You seem real enough."

Glen's comment raised a titter of laughter, though Walter scowled. Gracefully, she climbed the stairs and ascended to the stage again.

"Thank you, Melissa," Walter said. The lights flickered—there was deep bone-felt rumble of a gong and a strobe light on stage left that illuminated a replica and she was gone. There was something on the seat next to Glen's hand. He picked it up and raised it—it was a duplicate of Melissa's silky blouse. Glen knew how this sort of thing was done. The eyes were involuntarily distracted for two long seconds—long enough for a trapdoor to fly open and drop her out of sight. The blouse was pulled up from the seat by a black thread—still attached. If he looked for it, he'd find it. The gong masked the sound of the trapdoor mechanism. The trick was cleverly designed, but not metaphysical.

Walter bowed.

"Please return to your seats and we'll continue with the presentation."

While video snippets emphasized the words, Walter narrated a boring lecture on the historic allure of the fountain of youth. Glen tuned out. Juan Ponce de Leon. Was he looking for a vine that could be made into an aphrodisiac tea or a mythical invigorating fountain? Blah-blah-blah. He examined the backs of the heads. One woman would make a great wife—she was old, clearly wealthy and had a nasty-sounding cough. Fifty-fifty that she would survive the honeymoon cruise. Glen felt a tickle of reflexive temptation before remembering he was already married.

When Glen tuned back in, Walter was introducing a special guest.

"There's no reason for you to believe me, that's your choice. This could be another trick, that's up to you to decide. Before our young guest joins us, I want to present options to consider. First of all, I remind you that everything you hear and learn is protected by a strict non-disclosure agreement. We've gotten as far as we have by doing things quietly—under the radar. We have not stimulated governmental and societal immune systems and we need to keep it that way. This point is vital. The process is expensive, we make no apologies for that, but the expense gives you options you might not have considered. For one, you don't *have* to come back as yourselves, but you can. The legal territory is unexplored, but the new version we create can, with enough lubricating expenditures, be wholly and legally you. This avoids estate and inheritance taxes. One day you're aged and decrepit, the next day, virtually, you take over seamlessly. If you own a business, the board of directors might require convincing, but that's your problem to deal with. Families, particularly the greedy ones in line to inherit great wealth, can also be a problem. We've been through this a few times. With an add-on consulting contract, we can help with these issues, but that is one-hundred-percent optional. I will warn you, some of these problems can be very sticky, so I suggest you think through your strategy carefully. Sometimes it's better if these problems disappear, poof, like Melissa did, but I won't belabor that point."

Like the Wizard of Oz, Melissa's disembodied head appeared on the screen.

"I'm listening," she said with a wink. "Behave yourself, Walter."

"Thank you, Melissa." He snapped his fingers. "Begone again."

She disappeared in a crackle of sparkly light.

"Another option is to put your assets in a trust or assign a favored grandson or granddaughter as sole heir, then appear as your own progeny and take over. This can be easier said than done, but it's do-able. With a fully legal and registered will in place, you can come back as someone else entirely and start fresh with a new identity—while enjoying all of your assets. Wild thought, huh? Now, are you ready for something that might make you really sit up and pay attention—something you might not have thought of? Are you ready? You don't have to come back as a man or woman like you were. Ladies, have you been envious of the man's world and want to give it a try? What's stopping you? The only barrier is an easily affordable fee. Men, do you think sexy young ladies have an easier path through life? Give it a try—there's nothing to hold you back. I see your minds working through the wonderful possibilities. While you're thinking, I want to introduce the young man I mentioned earlier. As I said, you won't be sure if we're playing another trick, but I think you'll know. For obvious reasons, I'm not going to tell you this man's name. He's not taking the old identity; he chose to be his own grandson. But, who is he? I can give you some hints. In his day—which now springs forth anew—he was an actor and director you knew and loved. Alas, his day was long ago and most of you, if you thought of him at all, assumed he was dead. But, he wasn't. He signed on with us before it was too late, though barely. Need I remind you not to dawdle over your decision?" He tilted his head back and laughed. "I'm bad, am I not? Bad, bad, bad. Without further exposition, please put your hands together for a man we'll call Teddy."

Walter was the only one clapping, but he didn't seem to mind.

Teddy walked into the spotlight. He hammed it up a little, flexing his biceps. He spun in circles and did Kazakhstan spinning and leg kicks. Like Walter, he wore a microphone that wrapped around his chin.

"How long do you think it's been since I was able to do that?" he shouted. "Since forever and it feels great. Your first question might be this: is there anything about the procedure that makes me wish I had not done it?" His voice was thunderous. "No!"

Stools were brought out by stage hands. Walter and Teddy settled on them.

"I will start, Teddy," said Walter, "with my own question. The process takes six months. Was it painful or tedious?"

"Not at all, it seemed like it was overnight. One day I was on the edge of death, the next I was wearing a new body and my zest for life was fully restored. Before deciding, I took a few months to think things through and gather up the money—you greedy bastards charge a lot, don't you?"

Walter smiled and raised his right hand.

"Guilty as charged, your honor."

"But afterwards, I wished I'd done it sooner. Much sooner. What was I waiting for?" He dived to the floor and snapped off twenty-five pushups. He got up and perched again on his stool. "I could do them all day. I feel great."

"Let's take questions from the audience. Who will be first and break the ice?" He pointed. "You, sir? There's a question on your face, I see it. Let's get it out in the open."

The man Walter pointed at had a nervous condition. His head nodded back and forth and his voice was querulous.

"What's the worst thing about living a new life? Nothing is perfect, there must be a downside."

"Beyond the expense? It took nearly all my net worth to pay—there was hardly anything left to live on. Otherwise, I'm human and I still have bad days. If I drink too much, I pay the price the next day. I've had the flu a time or two, but I can't blame my friends at Immortality for that. They promised a new body, not a cure for influenza, am I right?"

"We're working on that," Walter said.

"For a small additional fee."

Walter nodded. "Right you are."

Teddy laughed.

"Other than the normal frailty of the human body, I have nothing to complain about. It's been great."

"Let's have another question," Walter said.

In the front row, a Japanese man dressed in a formal silk suit raised a hand.

"Yes, you sir," Walter said.

"Don't you miss your friends and family? The ones who passed away?"

"No, not really. I'm mad at God for creating such an ugly system—the circle of life, but I'm not going to agonize over things out of my control. What good does that do? Next question."

"I'm a religious man..."

"I'm sorry to hear that," Walter said.

The man ignored the rude quip.

"...can you comment? Did this experience bring you closer to God?"

"No," Teddy said. "Next question."

This answer did not satisfy the old man. While hunched over his ivory-handle cane, he slowly worked his way down the aisle and out of the room. Without comment, everyone watched him leave. When he was gone, Walter waited a brief moment before speaking.

"Is this like the garden of Eden? Are we biting from the forbidden fruit of knowledge when we take this evolutionary step? I can't say for sure, but I'll tell you one thing—I'm mighty hungry. We get lunch after this Q-and-A." The room echoed with laughter. "Next question."

"Did you direct a film with Brad Pitt?"

"Yes, one of his early roles, but that doesn't narrow things down. Everyone did, right?"

"Is this new life giving you a chance to do things differently?"

"Are you kidding? I grew up in the Depression years and was a slow-starter when I arrived in Hollywood to direct talkies. I was actually faithful to my first wife, can you believe it? Now I have one simple goal—to work my penis into as many starlets as possible and time's wasting, catch me? Ladies, forgive me for being blunt, but I've had more pussy in the last year than I had in eighty-plus years in my old life. I love it. Three times a night. Four. Use it or lose it. Believe me, I'm using it. Ask me which young actresses I've had. Or, make it easier and ask which ones I haven't had. Good luck."

"Scarlett?"

"Ha-ha, that's easy. Yes. Of course."

"Jennifer?"

He laughed.

"No, but I have a date with her tomorrow. Ask me later."

"Are you directing films now?"

"No, directing is too much like work. I am an agent. I know where all the bodies are buried, literally. I'm connected. I'm essential. Want to be in the hot new film coming up? Show me what you got, baby. They're eager. They're willing. I can't get enough. It's a perfect match."

"Down, big guy," Walter said. "He gets overheated. Just time for a couple more. Who's up?"

"Your life seems empty. Are you getting a billion dollars worth of sexual experiences?"

Walter wanted to speak, but Teddy waved him back.

"I'll take this one. First of all, I got in early before the price was so high…"

"If you wait until tomorrow, it might be two-billion," Walter interjected.

"…and I don't just fuck—I fight, I drink, I make deals and I travel all over the world and stay in the best hotels with the most beautiful women of the world. You can rest quietly in your grave if you like, but I prefer to live."

He jumped off his stool and threw vigorous shadow-boxing punches.

"One more," Walter said.

"I have a question," Glen said. "What happened to your old body?"

Teddy threw more punches.

"Who cares? I don't. I am me and I feel great. Before, I was dead, or close enough. Dead, do you hear me? Do you want to fight? I'll beat you silly right now. If my old body was here, I'd kill it again."

Walter quickly stepped to center stage.

"That wraps things up for this session," Walter said. "With a down-payment, we will answer additional questions via email or conference call. I hope you found this informative. Join the future and be born again. Have a great day, everyone."

The lights came up. Glen watched the elderly people shuffle from the room. Two of them were assisted into wheelchairs by attendants. It was a melancholy scene that depressed Glen.

Is it our mortality that gives meaning to our brief moments of life?

When the room was empty, Glen walked to the stage, then around to the side. There was another security guard, but he didn't raise a hand to bar Glen's way. In a plush backstage room, Walter guzzled a dripping bottle of water. With his chair pulled close, Teddy chatted with Melissa—he had a proprietary hand on her knee.

"Thanks for nothing, Glen," Walter said. "I'm not sure you helped with sales for the day."

"Bennie is nervous."

"Bennie is always nervous. I'm nervous, too. So what? We're not in this for the long haul. Here's the plan we agreed on. We build the business to profit, sell out and move on. Just hang in there for a year, no more. Is that too much to ask in return for bushels and bushels of fuck-you money?"

Glen gestured at Teddy.

"Who is this jerk?"

"You haven't figured it out? Serpico, Death Wish, Flash Gordon? Don't be a *nudnek*."

Teddy massaged Melissa's calf.

"She's falling for his line of bullshit."

Walter shrugged.

"She wants to be in the new Marvel superhero movie."

"I don't like the guy."

"So what? His money was good. We have bills to pay. Payroll to make. Your Jaguar didn't fix itself."

"I didn't like the other client either. Neel. He was a jerk."

"What happened to tough-guy Glen? Married life cut off your balls? You need mama's permission to whip it out and take a whiz?"

"Two is enough to spot a trend. What's with these characters?"

"You're way over-budget for today's questions, Glen."

Walter stood up.

"That motherfucker killed his host body. He as much as admitted it. Is my clone going to murder me?"

"They're not clones and they're not host bodies. Working in this business is painful with all the bad metaphors. We call them donors and clients and there's a reason for the semantics. The donors live on. Look at him—he's living life to the max in ways the donor never dreamed was possible."

"I'm not talking about the donors, I get that part. I'm talking about the clients."

Walter sighed.

"You're a special case. An experiment. You insisted. You wanted to eat the dog food. You wanted to go through the process. I advised you to skip it, but you made a fuss. Your donor will stay locked up, don't worry about that. He's not going to murder you. It's not murder anyway, just an odd form of suicide and rebirth. Circle of life—we put up a toll booth and people are happy to pay. We could double the price and twice as many people would want in. Don't worry, just hang on a bit longer, then we'll take the money and run." He patted Glen's shoulder. "Okay, big guy? Go home and fuck your pretty wife and let us worry over the details, okay?"

Walter drained the last of his water, sat the bottle down, then got up and left the room. As Glen got up to leave, Teddy slowly eased his hand between Melissa's knees. She was resisting, but not vigorously. MeToo movement be damned, Teddy was going to get what he wanted. Glen wondered how many other women Teddy had promised the role to.

He could not resist. Getting up, he walked over to put his hand on Teddy's shoulder.

"Melissa, he's going to take your virtue and break your heart."

"Don't worry about me," Melissa said. "I know the game."

Teddy jumped up.

"You want to go a round? You cock-block me and you'll regret it, old man."

Glen leaned over to peer around Teddy.

"At least make him buy you dinner first."

Teddy bounded like a kangaroo.

"Let's dance right now, chum. I'll knock you crosswise into next week."

"No, it's okay," Glen said. "The room is yours, enjoy it."

Glen walked out. He exchanged a glance with the security guard.

"Give them a few minutes," he said. "But if he hurts her, don't mess around—take him out quick."

The inscrutable guard nodded.

"Makes sense," he said. "I'm with you. Have a good day, sir."

Right. If only.

In the hallway, Glen got a glimpse of Emma disappearing into the women's restroom. Was she crying? It was remarkable. Smart, clever, sweet Emma was a turning into a breathtakingly beautiful young woman, like an idealized porcelain princess. She was Bennie's girlfriend and soulmate.

Glen lurked at the coffee station until she came out. It took a while, but she finally appeared and began walking the opposite direction. Glen scurried after her.

"Emma, can I talk to you for a minute?"

She turned and appeared to stifle an impulse to bolt.

What was that about?

"This is not a good time, Glen."

He put his hand on her arm. She would not meet his eye.

"Please," he said, "I insist. Just you and me for a minute."

He tugged her along the hallway. There were three people involved in an intense conversation in the Sasquatch meeting room. Glen poked in his head.

"Beat it," he said.

One of the occupants opened his mouth to complain, but then thought better of it. He gathered his tablet and notebook and pushed by Glen and out of the room.

Emma sat, but still wouldn't meet Glen's eye. Tears brimmed. It killed Glen to see her unhappy, but he wanted her to speak first. He leaned back in his chair and studied his fingernails. They were trimmed neatly and didn't need any additional work. They were beautiful—in fact, the most perfect fingernails known to man. The boring seconds stretched.

"You're trying to get me to speak first," she said. "It's not going to work."

He leaned forward.

"Once again, my dastardly plot is unveiled. What's up, Emma? We're friends, you can talk to me."

"I don't know what to do."

The fingernails on his left hand were almost, but not quite as perfect as his right hand's. He turned his hand over and studied the maze-like whorls of his fingerprints. They were beautiful too. He reached over and took her hand and caressed it. It didn't seem possible, but her fingerprints were even more perfect and lovely than his. She pulled her hand back.

"Stop it, Glen. I'll talk."

"Okay, talk."

"I want to go home."

"What? You're homesick for Anchorage? This time of year? There's something like forty-seven feet of snow up there right now."

"I talked briefly to the clients who are visiting, both of them. Dino and Neel."

"Aren't they wonderful?"

"Glen, I'm serious. There's something wrong with them—and there's something seriously wrong with what we're doing."

Glen patted her hand.

"Every successful person I know has a tough inner core.

Damn the consequences, full speed ahead, get in the way and get trampled. That's how they are."

"Glen, I've known you a long time, I know all that. This is something different. Bennie says we're glimpsing the next stage of human evolution. These people are wolves in human skin. Homo Assholeus. I'm scared and I don't want any part of this. After the semester ends, I'm going home."

"It can't be that all the clients are like this. How can you know? You haven't met all of them."

"Bennie says they are. We've done twenty-two and they're all the same. This thing we're doing—causes this. Maybe the psychopathy is already there, but we're emphasizing it or something gets lost in translation that limited or modulated their behavior in their old lives. I don't know. I think we're unleashing evil on the world."

"That's a melodramatic over-reaction, don't you think?"

"Maybe. Maybe not. I'm a girl and I reserve an inalienable right to over-react on occasion. You can flap your lips, but my mind is made up. I'm going home."

"I'm not trying to talk you out of anything. I'm just trying to understand. What about Bennie?"

She looked down at the table.

"I don't know. I want him to quit and come with me, but he's deep into this. I don't want to make him pick between me and the job, but I can't stay here."

Glen took her hands.

"Look at me, Emma. This will all come out okay, I promise. Do what you need to do and we'll figure out how to make it work."

She pulled her hands away, then fished in her handbag for a tissue which she used to blot her eyes.

"Okay, Glen," she said, "I will."

She got up and left. Glen stayed behind enjoying the lingering scent of her.

Bennie says we're glimpsing the next stage of human

evolution.

What the fuck does that mean?

Glen sat a few more minutes before his cell phone tinkled. He glanced at the screen.

Visitor in lobby. Come immediately.

He sighed.

Now what?

The usual lobby lizards were gathered in the reception area. Glen resisted their gravitational pull by avoiding eye-contact. He leaned over the front desk without looking down Lori-Ellen's loose blouse much. He whispered.

"What?"

She motioned for him to lean over closer, then whispered in his ear.

"Charles Benson. FDA. He's a weasel."

"Which one?" Glen said.

"White shirt. Necktie. Blood from his prey dripping from his jowls. I reserved the boardroom for you."

"Okay, thanks."

He turned. Charles sat by himself reading a folded quarter of *The New York Times.* As Glen approached, Charles tucked the newspaper into his valise and stood. Glen almost gave in to the instinct to put out his hand for a shake, but stopped himself.

"A pleasure to meet you, sir," Glen said. He lifted his hand to pat Charles' shoulder, but thought better of it. "Come right this way, please."

Glen badged the lock and led the way. On entry to the boardroom, the lights came on automatically. Glen gestured for Charles to sit.

"Can I get you coffee? Tea? Mineral water from the iceberg that sank the Titanic? It tastes a little fishy."

Inside, Glen cringed.

Where did that nonsense come from?

"I'm fine," Charles said.

Glen studied the man; he didn't look impressive. Short hair

slicked back from a froggy face with Brylcreem or pond slime. Thin lips, thin mustache. Pockmarked face, olive skin. Spanish? He held himself erect like a high priest of the Inquisition. He was the kind of man who would enjoy flaying the flesh from a sinner far too much. Glen shook his head. His wild imagination would do no good in this situation.

"How can I help you, Mr. Benson?"

Charles removed a business card from his brushed aluminum briefcase and slid it across the table. Glen looked at it. Charles Benson. Torturer. Murderer. Compulsive Masturbator. No, that's not what it said. Stylized FDA initials. U.S. Department of Health and Human Services. Office of Criminal Investigations. Special Agent.

Glen fished a card from his inside jacket pocket. The shiny silver card was embossed with Glen Wilson, President and nothing else.

"So," Glen said, "you spend your valuable time protecting the health and welfare of the public by investigating criminal allegations falling within the jurisdiction of the U. S. Food and Drug Administration. I'm curious, what do you think any of that has to do with your friendly neighbors here at little old Immortality, LLC?"

"Genomics, transcriptomics, proteomics and metabolic datasets."

"Big words, I'm impressed. I'm no scientist, but we work in those areas, but not in the United States. Everything here is computer work. There are no laboratory animals, in fact, no laboratories at all. No clinics. No patients. No drugs dispensed. No needles. No crazy experiments. Just computers and nerds who write the software to run the damned things. Bits and bytes. Big data pipes. Links to overseas databases. We're careful about this stuff. There is nothing done here that falls under your jurisdiction."

"I'm certain that's true and will be the conclusion I'll reach once I study your operation in infinite detail."

"Study? That implies access I'm disinclined to grant."

Charles reached into his valise and pulled out of sheaf of papers.

"Court order."

Glen reached for them and pulled them over.

"What is your probable-cause justification?"

Charles smiled.

"Exigent circumstances."

"Ah," Glen said. "I see. My careful reading tells me that this paperwork gives you a username and password to the VPN."

"No, it's specific. I get an onsite terminal, full access and whatever technical support I need to dissect your technology down to the tiniest detail."

"Oh, I didn't see that part."

They sat and looked at each other for a long minute. Charles spoke first.

"Shall I highlight the pertinent clauses?"

"No, I prefer letting the four-hundred-dollar-an-hour lawyers do it for me. I'm sure they'll get us a summary of their analysis in six months or so."

"Shall we go off the record? I'll turn off my recording device if you turn off yours."

Glen laughed.

"No need. We spent a fair amount to make sure your recorder picks up nothing but white noise." He pointed at the ceiling panels. "Scrambling transmitters."

Charles pulled a pen from his shirt pocket.

"You can beat my advanced military technology?"

Glen shrugged.

"Ours is civilian technology. Israeli."

"Okay, I concede that point," Charles said, "but don't count your IPO payout too early. This company is dirty, dirty to its core and you are going to spend a long time contemplating the errors of your ways in a federal prison."

"I disagree. We're essentially playing video games here.

There's nothing to discover and there will be nothing you can find to prosecute."

Charles raised his hands in supplication.

"Do you know how many pages of laws there are? The U. S. Code of Laws is over two-hundred-thousand pages and they were written by people like me to include catch-all clauses like *additional orders as necessary.* Take a look. Those words appear on page fourteen. What do you think that means? It means what I want it to mean. There is infinite adaptability to things like the honest services clause—Part 1 of Title 18, Section 1346, Chapter 63. *Scheme or artifice to deprive another of the intangible right of honest services.* We can take a minute while you look that up on your iPhone if you like."

"The Supreme Court gutted that one unless you have evidence of bribes or kickbacks."

"Maybe. We'll see what Congress does. Nonetheless, the average American commits three felonies before breakfast."

"What's the difference between the Mafia and the federal government?"

"Okay, I'll bite. What is it?"

"No, that's a serious question. What's the difference?"

"Funny-man. Ha-ha. I've heard that about you. I can prosecute based on the level of sophistication and planning you use to evade our jurisdiction. I can prosecute you based on any decision, recommendation, or action on any question, matter, cause, suit, proceeding or controversy. I can prosecute you for knowingly falsifying, concealing, failing to disclose or covering up anything I demand to know. I can prosecute you for aiding, abetting, counseling, commanding, inducing or procuring the commission of a felony. I can prosecute you for any material omission in response to any of my questions or demands. I can prosecute you for promoting, managing, establishing or carrying-on illegal activity. And remember, these days, a crime can be viewed as committed even if there is no criminal intent."

"Wow, I guess you got me," Glen said. He put out his hands.

"Cuff me now and perp-walk me out the front door?"

Charles studied Glen's face.

"You're mocking an officer of the court and an agent of the U. S. government?"

Glen dropped his hands.

"I suppose I am. That's a felony too, right? It must be great to stride the Earth like a God and wield unlimited power—on a measly, g-job salary. What are you? GS-9? Not even making six-figures, right? Sad, that, for a man of your skill and stature. It doesn't seem fair. Where's the justice?"

There came a knock at the door. Glen leaned over and pulled it open. He was handed a slip of paper which he glanced at after pushing the door closed again.

"Can we reverse the questions for a few moments?" Glen said. He pushed the paper across the table. "Are you Charles Nelson Benson with the Social Security Number as noted? Do you live at 1420 Deerton Street near Sand Point in a small three-bedroom, one-and-a-half-bathroom house you paid seven-hundred-and-twenty-five thousand dollars for in 2016? Is your wife's name Delores? Are your daughter's names Crystal, Hope and Charity?" Glen cocked an eyebrow. "Odd names, aren't they? Never mind, I withdraw that question. Is your wife's cell phone number as shown?"

"Are you trying to intimidate me, Mr. Wilson, by making vague threats against my family?"

"No, not at all. All this is information from public databases, your family's Facebook and Classmates profiles. The point I'm trying to make is that our relationship is symmetrical. You have the power of the law behind you in examining my sphincter and our business operations, but, at the same time, I am free to study you back again. By the way, Charity thinks she might be pregnant, but don't worry, she isn't, though you might benefit by getting around to an intimate conversation about safe sex with her sooner rather than later. That's just a helpful suggestion. Your wife had a brief affair with your life insurance agent, but you worked through it and it's over, you don't have to worry about it. I think she's got that out of her system. Pay a little more attention to her and keep up with the Friday date nights and you two will be fine."

Charles studied Glen's impassive face.

"I don't like the turn of this meeting."

"And I don't like your jackboot stomping my face forever."

"Perhaps you misunderstand me, Mr. Wilson. There's nothing personal in my line of inquiry. I'm just doing my job and if all is as you present, I'll close my investigation and shift my attention elsewhere. Shall we make a gentleman's agreement? You skip the lawyer's review and I'll skip the penny-ante, small-beer proctology exam. Just give me access. I'll do a quick overview and let you get along with your business."

"No, I don't think so. I don't trust you—there's no way you'll voluntarily rein in your zealotry. I'm not handing you a club to beat me with. Let me tell you something, Charles. In the final weighing, governance depends on the consent of the governed. That's not a lesson emphasized in public schools, but it's true. I feel no moral obligation to submit to the lash of your whip and I will do anything necessary to remove myself and my company from your servitude."

"Is that a threat, Mr. Wilson?"

"No, of course not. It's basic common sense. You can have what the court order requires: a room, a terminal and a limited-access password—and nothing more until my lawyers say so."

"Very well, Wilson, have it your way. My report will document your intransigence." He stood and gathered his papers. "One more thing. One of your customers is visiting Seattle. Who he is exactly? It's fuzzy. The background check tripped over inconsistencies. He's Dutch—named Neel."

"We call them clients."

"Fine, your client. Neel."

"What about him?"

"I want to interview him."

Glen laughed.

"Oh, Charles, that is an extraordinarily bad idea. I strongly advise you not to."

"Your advice is duly noted. Are you refusing access?"

"By all means, no, absolutely not. I'm suggesting that, regardless of what you think you'll learn, you'll regret any interaction you have with Neel, but don't let me stand in your way. Have at it."

Charles studied Glen's face.

"I can't tell if you're having a laugh at my expense or if you're trying to manipulate me again. What is your game, Wilson? I will interview your client. I will figure out exactly who he is and what mysterious *service* your company rendered. I will make sure the public's health is protected."

"I can't wait to see how that works out for you. This will be fun. I don't need the lawyers to review the request—I'll arrange a meeting right away. Today if you like. Now. If you care to hang around, stay right here. If I can track down Neel, I'll send him in." Glen stood. "In the meantime, have a very pleasant day."

Charles smiled—thin lips over crooked, yellow teeth.

"You too, sir," he said.

The Meeting

CHARLES WAS TYPING emails on his MacBook when Glen returned with Neel in tow.

"As you requested, Charles, please allow me to present Neel Baars."

Neel stretched his hand across the table to shake, but Charles waved it away.

"Please don't touch me," he said.

"As you wish," Neel replied. "You have questions? Fire away. That's the expression?" Glen nodded. "Okay. Go."

Charles gave Glen a look—as if claiming a small victory. Glen rolled his eyes.

"I'm pleased you are willing to talk with me," Charles said.

"They are paying me one-hundred-thousand dollars a day. I'll waste their time however they want, it's not my problem."

"We'll jump right in, then. What is the nature of the services Immortality, LLC rendered on your behalf?"

"Rejuvenation. Restoration. Revitalization."

Charles glanced again at Glen. It was clear he thought he was getting into a productive territory. Glen smiled.

"Were any of these services delivered in the territory of the United States, its protectorates or places where we exert legal authority?"

"No."

"Oh. Then where?"

"I don't know exactly. Brazil? Paraguay? What difference

does it make?"

"But you're sure it was not in the United States?"

To Glen, Neel said, "Didn't I answer that question? Is this man *achterlijk*? Retarded?"

"We don't say retarded anymore," Glen said.

Undaunted, Charles continued.

"What was the nature of the services? Hormonal? Stem cells? Blood replacement? Radiation treatments? Intravenous chemicals?"

"I don't know."

"You don't know what they did to you?"

"No, I don't know and I don't care. It's irrelevant. It worked. I feel *wonderbaar*, wonderful. Like a new man."

"We've had trouble establishing your identity. Who are you?"

"I prefer to not answer. It's not of your business."

"Glen," Charles said, "please instruct your client to answer my question."

Glen shrugged. "Answer his question, Neel."

"Fuck you. I will not."

To Charles, Glen said, "I'm not his mother, I can't make him."

"You're not holding him back?"

"No, he's free to say whatever he likes."

Charles turned back to Neel.

"There's a reason for our confusion. Your visa is in the name of Neel Baars, but we collected your DNA from a restaurant water glass. It belongs to a Romani from Barcelona named Roberto Hamidovic. Does that name mean anything to you, *Meneer* Baars?"

Neel shrugged.

"No, nothing."

"There are severe penalties for misrepresenting your identity."

"Then stop. You're the one who *verpest* a DNA test. You

clearly don't know what you are doing. Go fuck yourself."

"How old are you, *Meneer* Baars?"

Neel stood up.

"Old enough to rip off your arm and beat you to death with it."

"It's a serious crime to threaten a federal agent."

"It should be a federal crime to be half so stupid as you."

Charles raised his hands and made a settling motion.

"Please calm down, Neel, I'm just trying to satisfy my curiosity on a few things. There's no reason to get excited."

Neel took a deep breath. He sat down and a passive expression flowed across his face.

"Of course. I'm sorry," he said calmly. "You're just doing your job, and very well too, this I can see."

It was a remarkably fast change of mood.

"That's better," Charles said. "If you're really Neel Baars, then you're eighty-five years old. If I had to guess, I'd say you're in your thirties, perhaps early thirties. How do you explain this contradiction?"

"Maybe I'm a different Neel Baars? Maybe the Immortality treatment is halfway worth the insane cost? Is it illegal to be older than you look?"

"Immortality is impossible—it's nature's way for humans grow old and die. Anyone promising eternal life is a fraud."

"We don't actually promise anything like eternal life," Glen said. "That's God's sales pitch."

Charles searched Glen's face.

"I will not tolerate belittling of my religious convictions."

"Sorry," Glen said. "*My sheep hear my voice and I give eternal life to them* and all that. It's in the Bible."

"I know where the reference comes from, sir."

"Sincerely, I apologize."

"I grow impatient," Neel said.

From his valise, Charles removed ziplock evidence bags, cotton swabs and nail clippers—and placed them in the center of the table.

"Could I take a tissue sample?" he said.

To Glen, Neel said, "Do I have to?"

Glen shrugged. "They say it's a free country. Were I you, I'd make him get a warrant first."

To Charles, Neel said, "Get a warrant."

"That's easy enough," Charles said. "I will have it by Friday."

"Oh, what a shame. I will be on a plane back to Rio later today."

"I must ask you to reschedule."

Neel to Glen. "Can he do that?"

A wave of anger washed across Charles' face.

"Nope," Glen said.

"There's one more thing," Charles said. "Do you have any comments about a young lady named Natalie Baranquillo? She's missing and her father thinks you might know something."

"I don't know her," Neel said. "Besides, who cares about a filthy, cancerous cow-whore? There are a million of them infesting beer halls like cockroaches. They are irrelevant. Like you."

"How do you know she's irrelevant? Didn't you just say you didn't know her?"

Neel's mood changed in a flash.

"I don't know her," Neel shouted. "Stop making me repeat myself."

He picked up Charles' pen from the tabletop and pitched it at the wastebasket like a basketball. His aim was errant; he missed. Charles dived for it.

"That's government property. Why did you do that?"

Neel smiled.

"Because I wanted to," he said.

That was not the reason. While Glen and Charles' attention was diverted, Neel palmed Glen's copy of the FDA paperwork and slipped it in his pocket—as smoothly as any Barcelona pickpocket. Neither of the other men noticed a thing.

He now had Charles' contact information. He got up and slammed the door as he left.

"I don't understand the business you're in," Charles said.

"I have quite a number of questions myself," Glen responded. "Have you forgotten? I warned you against that interview. That man is a hand grenade in a china shop. Did you get what you were expecting?"

"You're cute, Glen, I'll give you that much. An odiferous fountain of hilarious entertainment."

"I get that a lot."

"I don't think your show lasts forever. In fact, I see it all falling down around your shoulders. Then, you'll be rotting in a federal prison for the rest of your life."

"Fascinating. What does your crystal ball tell you the charges will be?"

"Tax evasion?"

Glen snorted.

"I thought you'd mention something you know something about, something under the black shadow of the FDA's jurisdiction instead of shining a spotlight on your own massive ignorance. I have a clever CPA in a firm of CPAs who are paid very large sums to know the difference between tax avoidance—which is legal—and tax evasion—which is not. Whatever my future problems might be, they are not going to be related to income tax. You'll have to work harder than that."

"We're done for now, Glen. Please lead me to the computer station you promised. I have a lot of work to do."

"Let's not dillydally a single minute longer," Glen said.

Neel had an Avis rental car and an iPhone, so he was able to navigate the streets of Seattle without any problem—he found a Home Depot and bought a pair of wooden-handled machetes, a tin of machine oil and a whetstone.

At his hotel, before ordering a room service dinner, he sharpened the machetes until they were razor-sharp. They had leather sheaths he tucked in the back of his shirt. With care and practice, he learned how to withdraw them quickly without cutting himself.

After dinner, while posing in front of his hotel mirror, he perfected producing the blades and slashing with both hands until his t-shirt was soaked with sweat. With his right hand, he grunted *Natalie* and when slashing with his left hand *Baranquillo*. When he was fully exhausted, he took two more swipes, but this time his words were *Charles* and *Benson*.

His phone chimed with a text message. An online database told him everything he needed to know about Charles Benson.

At 11:00 that night, he left the room and walked to the hotel's parking garage. The streets were wet and traffic was light. The suburban streets of the Benson neighborhood were vacant, but cars lined the curbs bumper-to-grill. Neel slowly cruised—looking for the street number. He found it and left the car idling in the middle of the street. The house had a gate and a hedge, but the gate was unlocked. Security lights came on as he approached the front door. He saw the blue, flickering lights of a TV. Wearing a light robe, Charles came to the front porch brandishing a baseball bat.

"Who's there?" he said.

Neel held out his hands to show they were empty as he approached.

"You. What do you want?"

These were his last words on Earth. Neel slipped the blades from the sheaths and cut off both of Charles' arms halfway between wrist and elbow. Charles stood in shock not registering what he was seeing, but not for long. In a wide swipe, Neel neatly sliced off Charles' head and his body toppled to the sidewalk. Charles' wife was at the front door.

"What's going on, Charles?" she said.

Left-handed, Neel embedded the blade in the side of her head where it got stuck. As she fell, he had to work the blade loose, which he found irritating. Inside, there were three children, two in bunk beds and an infant in a crib. They died quietly—he left the bodies where they lay.

The light next door came on, but Neel didn't see anyone watching. In total, he was parked less than five minutes. He got in the car and slowly cruised away. Charles' body lay in the rain for hours until the newspaper boy noticed it at 4:30 AM. It was a sight that haunted the young man's dreams for a long time.

Back at his hotel room, Neel rinsed the blood from the blades and touched up their edges until they were sharpened to his liking again. Then he crawled under the covers and instantly fell asleep. When he woke up late the next morning, he ordered room service coffee.

He felt great.

At Immortality, LLC, the hallways were abuzz with the news. While sipping coffee from an insulated mug, Glen walked in late. Lori-Ellen waved him over.

"Have you heard about the FDA guy?"

Glen shook his head. "Benson? What about him?"

"Murdered. Him and his family. Horribly murdered."

Glen's face went pale. He patted his pocket and tried to think of where the paper with Benson's contact information was. It occurred to him that he hadn't seen it since the day before—in the meeting room with Benson and Neel.

"Where's Walter?"

"Vitamin K meeting room," she said.

Glen was so shook up that he walked by his bronze bust without rubbing its head. He turned around and went back to whisper to Lori-Ellen.

"We're closing the company for the day. Send everyone home." He walked away, then spoke over his shoulder. "And watch for that fucking asshole Neel Baars."

"Boss," Lore-Ellen said. Toward the front door, she poked the air with her index finger. "Too late."

Glen turned to look. Neel walked toward the building with a big smile on his face and a cheerful spring to his step.

"Oh, shit," Glen whispered to her. "I heard a rumor. You carry a gun in your purse, don't you?"

She bit her bottom lip.

"Ye-ah," she said. "Thirty-eight snubby. Wh-hyy?"

"When he gets close, shoot him in the head. I'll back you up."

"What? I'll give you the gun. You shoot him."

"It's better for me if you do it," he said.

"It's better for me if *you* do it," she repeated.

"Want to be a receptionist for the rest of your life?"

"Damn you, Wilson. Are you sure?"

"He's a rabid dog. Put him down."

Glen motioned for all the lobby-people to back away from the front door. They didn't move—they looked at him like he was loony.

"Idiots," Glen muttered.

Lori-Ellen followed behind Glen with a hand on his shoulder like she was blind. When he stopped, she stayed behind him, hiding. Neel reached the front door and pulled it open.

"Glen, good morning," he said.

"Did you hear about Agent Benson?"

Neel's smile grew wider.

"Yes, I guess we don't have to take any more of his shit. I didn't leave any evidence behind, so we're good."

Glen waved his arms.

"Everyone stand back, he has a knife."

Neel looked puzzled.

"You don't have anything to fear from me. I don't..."

At that instant, the gun roared in Glen's right ear and Neel went down like a sack of rocks.

Glen winced. Deafened, he felt dizzy and his knees were weak. He turned. The receptionist had the gun pointed at Glen's waist. He gently pushed it aside.

"I never shot anyone before," she said.

"It gets easier the more you do it," Glen said. He addressed the people in the room. "Did anyone else see a knife?"

They all shook their heads except for Paul Butler, Gerusha's friend. He raised his hand.

"I saw something shiny in his left hand," he said.

"Good," Glen said. "There are security cameras left and right. What do you have on you?"

"Uh, plastic ruler. Giveaway swag."

"Okay, slip it to me."

Glen took the ruler and knelt by the body. The back of Neel's head was a mess of oozing brain matter and blood. Glen flicked the ruler aside as if flipping it from Neel's hand. With his back to the camera, he pawed through Neel's pockets and found the paper-printout with the Benson street address on it. He stuffed it in his pocket.

He pulled Lori-Ellen to him as if comforting her and rested a hand on Paul's shoulder. They huddled.

"Think about what the security video will show—don't say anything to contradict the footage. Don't be afraid to say you don't know, that everything happened so fast. You don't have to explain why you felt threatened, you just did."

Lori-Ellen spoke hesitantly—with broken tones.

"You think he killed Benson and his family?"

Glen nodded.

"I'd bet his life on it. Let's hope Neel felt safe in keeping the murder weapons and the Benson murders get pinned on him quickly—that will short-circuit a lot of questions. What do we say to the press?"

"No comment," Paul said.

"Right, good man. No comment."

Outside, an angry swarm of blue lights gathered. Uniformed officers approached slowly with their weapons raised.

Glen lifted Lori-Ellen's chin.

"This would be a good time to drop the gun and raise your

hands," he said.

She opened her mouth, but didn't say anything. Slowly, she released her grip and the pistol dropped to the gleaming floor.

There were questions, a million questions asked over and over, but eventually the word was spread. The machetes were found under the mattress in Neel's room. They were scrubbed clean, but the pockets inside the sheaths held a lot of Benson blood. Then, the tone of the questioning changed and the detectives' demeanor grew warmer. By three o'clock in the afternoon, the last of them left. By then, there were only a few employees left in the building. Glen pulled Lori-Ellen's arm and gestured to Paul to follow. Glen led them to the boardroom. Walter was already there. Glen texted Gerusha to ask her to come.

Bring alcohol, he typed.

Walter opened his mouth to speak, but Glen shushed him.

"Any problems?" Glen said to Paul and Lori-Ellen.

Lori-Ellen spoke first.

"I have a headache from all the questions. Over and over and over, the same questions."

"That's what they do," Glen said. "They try to wear you down and trip you up with inconsistencies. Did anything come out we need damage control on? Think it through before answering."

Both Paul and Lori-Ellen shook their heads.

"We're okay," Paul said.

"Okay, Walter, your turn," Glen said.

"This is a public relations disaster," Walter said. "We've already had the Philips team pull out of the bidding."

Glen looked at him with amazement.

"We have bigger problems than that," he said. "We need a company meeting. Where's Bennie?"

Walter shrugged.

"When the news about Benson hit the net, Emma booked the next flight to Anchorage. Bennie went with her."

"What about the other client? Dino."

"Gone yesterday. Cleared out."

There was a tap on the door—Gerusha popped her head in. She dropped a bottle of Crown Royal and plastic cups in the middle of the table before taking a seat. She arranged cups and poured healthy dollops.

"This has been crazy," she said. "I'll take one too."

"What's the buzz in the hallways?" Glen said.

Gerusha sipped and gathered her thoughts.

"Most people went home. Our client, Neel, massacred Benson's family and Lori-Ellen killed him this morning when he threatened her."

"That's a good summary," Glen said.

"I can't believe we had such a brutal murderer walking our hallways. It's scary."

"It will take a few months," Walter said, "but the public's attention is fickle. We'll be back in the game soon enough."

"I don't think there is a game anymore," Glen said. "I think it's over."

"What?" Lori-Ellen said. "That's how you're going to take care of me? By making me unemployed?"

"Hold on, Glen," Walter said. "Let's not over-react. We can weather this."

"Bennie's right. There is something wrong with these clients. We can't make more of them."

"We're on the hairy edge of making a lot of money."

"We're on the hairy edge of disaster. We need to think about what we're unleashing on the world."

"Listen to yourself, Glen. You're talking crazy. The clients are mentally and physically perfect. What else is there?"

"That's the question, isn't it? What is it that does not make the transition from donor to client?"

Walter moved the bottle around the table and refreshed everyone's cups.

"We're not going to abandon the Immortality business plan

without thinking things through. This has been a traumatic experience for all of us, so let's take a few days and let things settle in our minds. The difference to all of us can be a lot of money. If we need to walk away, then we walk away, but if we don't, then that cash can be put to good use."

"How much money?" Lori-Ellen said.

Walter patted her hand.

"Think of a big number, double it twice and multiply by ten, that's how much."

"I vote for additional thought and consideration," she said.

At that moment, the sales bell echoed through the empty building.

"I love the beautiful sound of money," Walter said.

Glen finished his drink, then stood up and leaned over to kiss Gerusha's cheek.

"I need a long walk to clear my head," he said.

Outside, it was cold and wet; he lifted his collar against the wind and stuffed his hands deep into his pockets.

After an adrenaline rush comes the crash. He had a lot of experience with the black hole of depression. Ride it out, don't make any decisions that might be regretted later, don't do anything rash. Don't do anything, that was the best strategy. He walked a couple of miles, then decided *The Wild Rose* was a good place to ride out the mood. Anywhere out of the rain.

The interior lighting was dim and there was a snap-click of billiard balls. The regulars looked up to see if he was interesting, but quickly returned to their business of drinking and telling tired lies. Glen found an isolated corner table and settled in.

The portly waitress, Clara, was old, perhaps even in her 70s, but still wore a yester-years' short skirt and a tight tube top over healthy rolls of bountiful flesh. Her tinted-auburn hair was pulled up except for untamable strands framing her leathery face. She'd lived in a hot climate at one time, that was clear. He guessed at her accent, but she refused to help—she smiled and shook her head at his errant guesses.

Soon, he knew where she wasn't from.

Oklahoma City. Nashville. Knoxville. Lexington.

Her grin stretched like a clown—she'd had plastic work done a few years back and not on a large budget.

Mexican doctor in a strip mall?

However, she was not evil and brought Bass beer in liter mugs, so Glen decided to like her. If he wasn't married, he might offer to take her home after her shift and bang her hard to remind her of better days.

But, I am married, so that option is off the table, he reminded himself again and again.

His head was crowded with random thoughts competing for attention, but he wanted it all to stop and leave him alone. Sometimes the alcohol helped, but tonight, he found no solace. He flashed on the blood, the brain matter and fragments of white bone on the floor of the Immortality reception area.

I was just trying to be cute with the research on Benson and his family—trying to remind him that the government is not fully omnipotent. The relationship with its citizens is mostly, but not fully, asymmetrical. Sure, they have stockpiles of weapons and the full force and power of the rules and regulations and laws, but sometimes a desperate citizen will fight back—everyone has a limit they should not be pushed beyond. We all just want to get though our days and nights and weeks and years with minimum pain and hassle. Not zero, never zero, but the minimum. I didn't like Benson and the totalitarianism he represented. I hate oppression by the nameless, faceless bureaucratic activists who rule by chapter-and-verse regulation. When did I get a chance to vote on this stuff? Never. Where did they get the authority to enslave me?

He was headachy and there was a horrible tinnitus-hiss in his right ear that would not go away. His feet were wet and cold. He'd sit at the table drinking beer until he died except for having to get up every ten minutes to piss. It depressed him to think of the waitress as not much older than him.

In a blink of an eye, he'd be there too—hanging on with bloody fingertips to the last vestiges of a long, futile, empty life. At the end of the evening, Clara sat with him and nursed a neat glass of Glenfiddich.

For all of Glen's troubles, hers were worse—she'd outlived two husbands and all of her kids save one, a Downy young man who lived in a foster home near Macon. But, there were good times too, like making a baby under the stars on a sailboat off the coast of American Samoa and paying cash for a shiny new t-top Corvette after a score.

"Remember, any day is a good one if you're walking the face of the Earth instead of sleeping underneath it," she said.

Someone tugged his ears and would not let him rest.

"Leave me be," he complained, but they wouldn't.

He looked up into Gerusha's face. She'd washed off her makeup, pulled her mussed hair back with a scrunchy and had thrown on old jeans and one of his University of Washington hoodies.

"How'd you find me?"

Gerusha shrugged.

"Clara called someone and that someone called me. Enough already. It's closing time—time to straggle-ass home."

She managed to get Glen onto his feet. He looked at Clara.

"I like you," he said. "Give me a hug."

She seemed a bit taken-aback, but complied—she hugged him for a long moment while Gerusha looked on with a bemused expression.

"I think I'm going to spew," he said.

"Not here," Clara said, "or you'll be working the mop all night all by your lonesome."

Gerusha got him into her Volvo and then home. His memories were fragmented, but he'd made it to their upstairs bathroom before a hot torrent spewed and his stomach emptied.

In the morning, sunlight streamed though the bedroom

window to ignite his headache. Long before he got up, Gerusha had left for work. Before she left, she'd opened the drapes. Outside, it was a cold, clear morning and the brutal sunlight did a full frontal assault on his brain. Through the window, the world appeared iced over.

He dragged himself out of bed and into the bathroom and examined himself in Gerusha's bright vanity lights and mirror. If he was a city, he'd be the worst area of Detroit—a wasteland of ruin. His gray hair stood up in clumps. His eyes were pools of crimson. His skin was lax and flabby—the loose skin of his arms fell away from the bones like limp shrouds.

How did I get to this ruinous state?

She hadn't flushed the toilet and it reeked of his gastrointestinal Armageddon. She'd put a yellow sticky-note on the commode.

Look upon your good work and rejoice.

Glen moaned and pissed amber into the horror-show glop before flushing it all away. He returned to the mirror and drank two quick glasses of water, then another few ounces to wash down extra-strength aspirin. It would rot out his stomach, but would make his throbbing head feel better. Perfection was a futile illusion—everything was a trade-off.

There was no denying it—he was a worn-out, broken-down, useless antiquity. Why Gerusha stayed with him and beyond that miracle, supported him, was generally nice to him and appeared to actually, despite his best efforts, care for him, was a mystery.

I don't even like myself that much—and why would I?

He never had that much going on physically or mentally—all he had was a dauntless, relentless will and spirit which dissipated and wafted away with every new morning. It would take everything he had to get through this day. Facing up to the task was hopeless and impossible. A wry smile touched his lips. He decided to be cheerful.

Fuck it.

Just because he was a worthless piece of human debris had never stopped him before and it wasn't going to stop him now. If there was one thing he'd learned from Immortality, LLC so far, it was that he was not his body. His body was a thing that held him, but the body could be transcended. He raised his mutilated hand and waggled the ugly stubs. It was a hideous sight.

Fuck it, fuck you and fuck anything that dares to stand in my way.

He worked the electric toothbrush in his mouth and washed away the corruption and filth, then showered for twenty minutes in water as hot as he could stand.

Then, satin boxer shorts. In the closet, a perfectly fitted Italian suit he hadn't worn in public yet. He put it on. Silk socks. Italian leather shoes. A monstrous watch he hated—a gift from Gerusha that looked like a random collection of shiny gears on a giant steel plate—he put it on. He combed his hair and grinned into the mirror—it was a perfect illusion of cultured fearsomeness. The devil help anyone who crossed his path.

Kill me or get out of the way.

Those were the choices.

In the kitchen downstairs, Rose and Marcus sat at the Amish dining table sipping coffee and looking into each other's eyes.

"It worked, Glen. We're getting married. We picked a date. May fifteenth, one month from today."

Glen put a coffee capsule into the brewer and pressed the button.

"That's nice," he said while internally renewing vows to transcend any and all madness the world threw at him on this day.

"Marcus can't resist the glorious promise of my tunnel of love."

Marcus winked at Glen—Glen winced.

"I don't need the gory details," he said.

"I'm not a cold and cruel mistress—a man should know

what he's getting. I understand the idea of the test drive at the car dealership. A frigid, squeamish Victorian prude? No. Hand job, blow job, titty-fuck, no problem, all night long, but I told him my camel-purse is reserved for my precious husband—there will be no tours in the vaginal valley until the wedding ring is resting on my finger. I said it and I meant it, didn't I dear?"

Marcus kissed her rubbery lips.

"You are a woman true to her word, my angel," he said.

While eating from a yogurt container, Glen tapped his fingers on the granite countertop and watched the coffeemaker's brown fluid stream into his cup.

Was the damned machine always so monumentally slow?

"God gave woman the squishy parts to be used as gifts not to be wasted. My virginity is not a bauble to be thoughtlessly thrown away for nothing."

"That's nice, Rose. Thank you for sharing."

"We're eloping to Reno, so I'm sorry, we can't invite you to join us."

"Damn, I'm sure I'm busy on that day, but thank you for thinking of me."

"Don't worry, we'll have a big reception here at the house with drinking and spaghetti and karaoke and dancing."

At the thought of drinking alcohol of any kind, Glen's queasy stomach lurched a few inches and vibrated. His mouth filled with bile.

"I can't hardly wait," he said.

As he left, they shared slobbery tongues across the table. Their kisses sounded like rubber boots pulled from muck. If this was God's test of his willpower, he felt vindicated and strong.

What else you got, big guy? Bring it.

He got to the garage before remembering the Jag was still parked at the office.

No problem.

They had an old Nissan pickup the gardener used to haul trash to the dump. It had a fractured windscreen, rusty, battered fenders and the bed was filled with tangled branches from the winter pruning. The keys were hanging in the mud room—the truck started with a cloud of blue smoke. The exhaust rattled like coconuts in a drum.

Glen adjusted the rearview mirror and it came off in his hand. He grinned.

Perfect.

Keep it coming, Lord.

Glen walked through the lobby like he owned the place. He planted himself before Lori-Ellen and conjured as big of a confident grin as he could manage.

"Good morning, sir," she said. "You look like the canary that ate the cat."

"I feel great," he lied, "on top of the world. Once someone kills someone at my command, they don't have to call me sir anymore. It's Glen."

"Thank you, Glen. I'm not in jail yet—so far, so good."

"Don't worry, I think you're clear. I'm here to see what you want."

"I was hoping you'd ask. Some men use a woman and then forget any promises they made in the heat of the moment."

Glen smiled.

"Not me, I'm as true to my word as a flame is to a candle, as reliable as a compass pointing north, as sure as gravity pulling us toward the center of the Earth, as…"

"I get it, boss. I want to get out of this lobby and have a job as Gerusha's assistant or something. And a big raise and stock options."

"Fine. Done. Call the temp agency and get someone in here to take your place—once you've taught them the basics of the job, report to Gerusha. She'll get you an office and a laptop and get you going."

"It's not like my job is that hard. I fend off the vendors by telling them you're out of the country until Monday, though sometimes I have to shoot a psychopath in the head."

"No job is perfect."

Paul Butler appeared at Glen's side.

"Hey, Glen. Can I get an all-access badge so I can find opportunities in the hallway and not hover in the lobby like a carrion bird?"

"Fine," Glen said, "but if you disturb the programmers, you'll be tossed out on your ass." Glen turned to Lori-Ellen. "Tell Gerusha to buy something expensive from Paul."

Paul couldn't stifle a satisfied expression.

Before badging in, Glen walked over and rubbed his bronze head. He had an impulse to kiss the cold metal, but pressed it away.

Not in front of the children.

He rode the elevator and walked the hallways until he stood in Gerusha's doorway. Inevitably, she was talking on her cell phone. Glen walked around her desk and nuzzled her neck. She pushed him away, then pressed a button on the phone.

"I'm on mute—I can only give you half a minute. What's up?"

"Good morning, my sweet angel. You look ravishing this beautiful day, as usual, dear. Hang up the phone and we'll go up to my smoking room and start the day right. I'll work you out of those pantyhose and trip the light fantastic. We'll fly the sunny skies of heaven on a magic carpet. We'll…"

"I'm busy, Glen. Beat it. Go away. Scram."

He rubbed her shoulder and then slipped his hand down the front of her dress. She slapped it away.

"Begone, pest."

"I can take a hint," he said.

He walked to the doorway.

"Glen," she said. He turned. She sat with her finger hovered over the phone. "I love you."

Glen smiled.

"I love you, too, dear."

With one hand she shooed him off. With the other she unmuted the phone.

Glen walked to Walter's corner office. Walter stood at the window looking out over the canal. Across the water, the sun melted the hoary frost—steam spread ephemeral fingers of mist into the air.

"Ah, our fearless leader makes an appearance. Not to tell me again to shut down this money-printing machine, I hope. The episode in the lobby will soon be forgotten and our IPO or private buy-out will be back on track. I have the public relations spin machine working overtime. Soon a politician will get caught with his nose in a dime-bag of cocaine or a rockstar will die of AIDS or something and our minor drama will be stale, yesterday's news cycle. It was a trial, yes it was, but we're doing important work—work too important to abandon when we're so close to cashing in. We don't need Bennie anymore, he was just endlessly tweaking the process."

Glen sat on Walter's guest chair.

"I want to study more of the clients."

"I thought you might." Walter slid a piece of paper across the table. "Names, last known addresses, contact info."

Glen scanned the list.

"Where's my cop? Where's Murphy?"

Walter sat down, tilted his chair back and pressed his fingertips together.

"Murphy. Let me think. I got an email from her. I remember. She's in Mexico somewhere. Mazatlan, wherever that is. Raz is doing a charity thing for dump-orphans down there. What's a dump-orphan?"

"I don't know." Glen pointed at the paper. "Look, one of the clients is down there."

"That's an odd coincidence."

"There are no coincidences. After all we've been through, you should know that by now."

"Whatever you say, Glen."

"There's one thing an egotistical guy like you doesn't understand—that's the power of the team. On my own, I'm a hapless idiot, but the team working together with a common vision…"

Walter interrupted.

"Your vision, of course."

"Yes, my vision," Glen said. "You made me lose my train of thought. What was I saying?"

"You were talking about the power of the team and then you'd move to how the universe serves up opportunities and then tell me how Murphy being in Mazatlan with one of our clients is not a coincidence and then you'd refer to some metaphysical, hocus-pocus, bullshit, mumbo-jumbo, yoga, Buddhist, stream-of-consciousness, Kesey-Kerouac-Hunter Thompson line of completely disorganized and deranged nonsense."

Glen grinned.

"You've been paying attention," he said.

"You repeat yourself so much—it's hard to avoid your predictable themes."

"I'm calling Murphy. If she advises me to shut this company down, then that's what we'll do."

Walter studied Glen's face.

"Okay, Glen. She's an important shareholder. Her opinion deserves consideration just like all the other owners."

"Close your eyes, Walter, just for a minute—and think."

Walter sighed. "You're not going away until I humor you, so here we go. I'm blind and I'm thinking. I'm sitting here like an idiot with my eyes closed—and I'm thinking. I have no idea what your point is, but I'm thinking."

Glen followed suit. They sat in silence and the minutes stretched. Then at the same time, they opened their eyes and looked at each other.

"Okay, Glen," Walter said. "If Murphy tells us to shut it down, then we will. But, the opportunity cost will be expensive at this point."

Glen's phone buzzed. He glanced at it.

"Gotta run," he said.

Walter got up and resumed his study of the sun-drenched scene outside his window.

"Very fucking expensive," he muttered.

Glen's text message was from Lori-Ellen in the lobby.

Please come...

In the lobby, Glen saw the IRS agent, Sarah Sumner. She was flanked by two large men wearing business suits and earpieces.

"Mr. Wilson," she said.

Her tone was cold and formal.

"Ms. Sumner. How can I assist you?"

"I'm here to talk about the FDA agent. Agent Benson."

"Ah," Glen said. "What's with the bodyguards?"

"I don't intend to take any chances with you, Mr. Wilson. Your enemies appear to have poor fortune."

"My goodness, Ms. Sumner. What you must think." He leaned over to whisper in her ear. The bodyguards leaned forward with their weight on the balls of their feet. They were ready to pounce. "First of all, we're far from enemies. Can we chat privately? Here in the lobby, but away from prying ears."

She considered, then nodded.

"Okay. Give us a minute," she told the bodyguards.

They walked to a corner of the lobby by a giant palm tree in a ceramic pot—there they sat, leaning their heads together.

"This thing with Benson..."

"Horrible," Glen said. "A tragedy."

"We just spoke about him. I warned you about his warpath, now he's dead and his family..."

"That was the work of a psychopath. I swear to you—it was not by my order or wish. Benson was a jerk off, but I know the drill. He busts my balls, I fight back with the lawyers and in the end, calmer heads intervene and we work out a deal."

"That psychopath was one of your clients. Why did he select Benson?"

"I warned Benson, but he wanted to interview the client. It didn't go well—angry words were exchanged. Benson needlessly pissed off a loose-cannon—a dangerous man."

"How did Mr. Baars track down Benson's home address?"

Crap, the heart of the matter. Damn it.

"Uh, it appears there was a security breach for which I bear partial responsibility. I feel really bad about that."

"Glen, I'm going to ask and I want you to answer me straight. What are the chances of a *security breach* that ends with me as target?"

Glen studied her face. In the diffuse morning light, it was not unattractive. He considered asking her to marry him, then remembered he was already married.

"Zero. We worked a deal I can live with and as far as I'm concerned, you did your job and there's no need for ill will between us. Please honor me with the same candor. Are we okay per our meeting of the minds the other day?"

She relaxed—nervous tension evaporated from her shoulders.

"Yes, we're still good from my end."

He patted her on the shoulder, leaned close and whispered.

"I'll tell you something. I'm worried about the nature and proclivities of our clients. I strongly suggest this: if you see one of our customers coming, walk quickly the other way."

"I appreciate the advice, Glen."

She leaned over and gave him a hug. He couldn't stifle the impulse.

"Will you marry me?" he said.

"I thought you were already married?"

"Yeah, right, sorry. Take care."

"You, too, Glen."

As she walked away, there seemed to be added sway to her

hips. Glen's hormones responded the way procreational hormones do. He tingled. Without looking back, she led the two bodyguards from the lobby and waggled goodbye fingers over her shoulder.

Glen sat back in the comfortable chair and sighed. He closed his eyes—intending to rest them for a minute. His siesta was interrupted by a polite inquiry.

"Mr. Wilson, I'm Daniel Soppersteyn from the Liberty International Technology group. If you have a few minutes, I'd like to bring you up to date with regard to our hermetic dynamo wafer processing system."

"Oh, my Lord," Glen said. "Will you shut the fuck up?"

"Maybe later would be a better time," Soppersteyn said.

Glen walked across the lobby. He gave Lori-Ellen an all's-well thumbs-up.

"Thanks," he whispered to her.

At the door, he badged himself in and took the elevator to the top floor.

Soppersteyn walked to the main area of the visitor's lobby and sat back down.

Paul leaned over.

"I told you that was a bad idea," he said.

"Please let me die in peace," Soppersteyn said.

Mazatlan

"You look like you could use more sunscreen," Murphy said.

The sun had arced across the sky and was near its three o'clock location hovering over the three rocky islands floating in the Pacific Ocean. She could never remember the names of the islands, they were called something like Cockroach, Goat Scat and Flying Rat, but perhaps she was being a bad tourist—wrong-headed, judgmental and unfair. It was 85 degrees and a tropical breeze drifted over the water and cooled them to a perfect temperature. Laying on her stomach, Elke spoke without opening her eyes.

"You just want your filthy, prying hands on me again."

"No, I swear, you look a little dry."

Murphy worked lotion into her palms and rubbed the wide expanse of Elke's brown back, making sure the sides of Elke's ample breasts were well tended. Retired cop Margaret Murphy was not a lesbian because she felt no sexual desire for women in general, only Elke Rittenauer. It was a quirk of sexual chemistry—there was only one person in the world for Murphy and it was Elke.

Why?

It was a mystery. Elke liked Murphy and didn't mind her lavish attention, slavish devotion and intimacy, but the in-depth, knee-weakening passion was very much one-sided. Murphy was so smitten, she didn't mind Elke's cool acceptance of Murphy's love, she just wanted to taste Elke and put her hands on her luscious body as much and as often as possible.

Murphy was the head of security for international rock star Raz (Razor Blade) Smith, but the gala show to benefit the children of the Mazatlan dump at the Teatro Angela Peralta was over and Raz was taking a break. In the safe, cosmopolitan city of Mazatlan, he didn't need excessive security, so Murphy took some time off. Murphy was making sure the top-cleft of Elke's ass was well-protected from the sun when her cell phone bleeped. There were only a few numbers in her VIP list that were allowed through. She glanced at the screen to see if it was Raz.

Not Raz.

Glen.

Murphy considered. Should she take the call? Most likely Glen would waste her time with absurd, irritating nonsense, but after all the years of their association, they were friends. Granted, the most unusual and unlikely of friends—friends who from the outside often seemed to despise each other. Whether she embraced it or not, Glen was family. Clan. Tribe. Still, she let the call expire.

He can leave voicemail—I'll check it later.

She sighed and reconsidered. After cleaning sand and oil from her hands with a corner of her beach towel, she pressed the phone button to connect to Glen.

"Sorry I missed your call, Glen, I was in the middle of something. What's up?"

"You were in the middle of greasing up Elke's ass, Butchie."

She hated that nickname—and how did he know where her busy hands were?

"I'll give you two seconds to get to the point of your call."

"Maria Los Sanchez Cuellar Arroyo de Rodriquez. Don't bother memorizing the name, I'll text it to you."

Murphy could not resist a vague tickle of interest.

"What about her?"

"She's in Mazatlan. I want you to talk to her and give me your professional opinion. Not a background check, just a quick pass to get a gut feel."

"I need more context. Why?"

"She's a client of our company and I suspect there's something *off* about her. I hope I'm wrong. Call me back and tell me she's an angel and has dedicated her life to the benefit of orphans and I'll be the second happiest man in the world."

"No, forget it. I'm taking a few days off. Hire a private investigator."

"Thanks, Murphy, I appreciate it. I'll text you contact info and last known location."

He disconnected the call. Murphy stifled an impulse to throw the phone into the surf.

Her thoughts were a jumble.

Why should I jump at his whims—I should teach him an invaluable lesson in humility. This is stupid. I'm not doing it.

But, deep inside, she knew she would honor the favor he asked. For one thing, he'd introduced her to Elke and that was a debt which could never be repaid. Beyond that, the mad adventures of Glen Wilson were invariably interesting. She worked more sunscreen oil into her palms. She'd do Glen's bidding, but later—after a shower and siesta.

Raz's room was at the Riu Emerald Bay presidential suite. Murphy tapped on the door and one of Raz's girls opened it. This girl was twenty, maybe twenty-one and was somewhere around six months into pregnancy. On her slim frame, her belly distended as if a watermelon was hidden under her Toxic Shock Syndrome t-shirt. Like all Raz girls, she had intelligent, all-seeing eyes and a calm, Zen-like demeanor. She pulled the door wide open.

"Is the boss around?" Murphy said.

"Yes, I'll get him."

Inside, the lights were off. The doors were open and the sound of wind and surf filled the room. There were at least seven Raz girls lounging around—typing on laptop computers, reviewing graphic designs for record covers and posters on projected screens and talking on phones while wearing headsets. Raz's billion-dollar business traveled with him.

Raz himself was slender and wore his long, black hair pulled severely back from his clean-shaven face in a tight ponytail. He was in his early thirties and his body was tight and muscular from yoga and kick-boxing sessions.

"Hello, Murphy," he said. "Didn't I give you the afternoon off?"

Murphy smiled and held out her cell phone.

"Our friend Glen checked in."

"What is that rapscallion up to now?"

"I have no idea and I'm afraid to ask. He's asking about a woman who happens to be down here and I wonder, by chance, do you know her?"

Raz held out his hand and a Raz girl handed him a pair of Gucci reading glasses.

"I don't really need them," he said, "but they help with the fine print."

Murphy nodded.

Right.

He studied the message, then took off the glasses.

"Sure, I know Maria. You met her the other night. Remember? You said something about her. That she seemed cold—like a serpent."

The memory flooded back. She *did* remember. It was at the reception-gala held the day after the concert at the grand ballroom of the Crowne Plaza hotel. To fit in, Murphy wore an ankle-length formal gown and high heels. She complained the whole evening; not only was she uncomfortable, she looked like a kumquat draped in silk. She would have flat-out refused to wear the gown, but Elke commented on how lovely and elegant she looked.

The security situation was atrocious. Murphy couldn't run—she could hardly move—and the only weapon she had was a Gerber knife tucked in her tiny, pearl-adorned handbag. Fortunately, the event was hyper-calm and there were no problems, partly because at least fifty Federales wearing black masks and carrying M-16s wandered around outside and partly because Mazatlan is an inherently peaceful city. All the fashionable Mazatlan glitterati attended—drinking fine Spanish wine and eating a literal ton of fresh *camarones*. Raz met hundreds of people, including Mazatlan's Mayor and Mario Cantone Lopez, the former Governor of Sinaloa.

Raz's adopted mother was a ballroom dancer who taught him many of the standard forms when he was young, so he was surprisingly nimble and proficient while smoothly gliding along with the Spanish and classical music of the string octet. From young to old, Raz had dance partners all night long.

While Maria waited for her turn, she and Murphy shared a brief conversation.

Idly, Murphy had commented, "That's a lovely necklace."

The woman raised it to reflect lights from the ballroom's chandelier and recessed spotlights.

"A gift from my grandmother. We were very close."

The hair on the back of Murphy's neck twitched. There was something embedded in the way the woman said 'very,' but the woman's gown was skintight over fabulous curves. No weapons, so there was no observable danger for Raz—Murphy let the curiosity-tickle go while scanning the crowd for more immanent threats.

"Did that woman say anything interesting while you were dancing?"

Deep in thought, Raz rubbed his forehead.

"No, but I remember she was oddly awkward, like her mind knew moves her body couldn't quite handle. I figured it was just my brain being weird. I could have bedded her; she made her hunger plain enough. There was more friction in the pelvis-to-pelvis action than the dance called for. If I could ever take a woman for pleasure, she'd be a great candidate."

The two nearest Raz girls looked up with the faint air of amusement—like they knew why he had no energy for pleasure-sex.

"Did you size her up for being a Raz girl?"

"Of course," Raz said. "But she's too old." He gestured at his head. "Old here." He swept his hand over his body. "Not here."

Murphy walked to the wide-open French doors and watched the surf approach and recede. She had an idea.

"I'd like to get to know this woman more. Would you invite her to dinner?"

Raz shrugged and grinned.

"It would be a massive sacrifice, but I can do that for you."

Murphy walked over and patted his cheek.

"You're such a good boy," she said.

Maria agreed to meet them at the elegant Pedro y Lola's restaurant on the corner of the *machado*—a busy square near the big cathedral in the historic center of Mazatlan. They reserved a block of tables to give Raz space. Security personnel pushed the street vendors away when they approached to sell flowers, jewelry, Chiclets, scarves, woven blankets, paintings, bags of seashells, lemonwood carvings, straw hats, coconut macaroons, bags of red-pepper coated peanuts, plastic toys, painted clay pots, wooden flutes, onyx figurines, temporary henna tattoos, leather belts, city tour packages and tequila shot glasses.

Maria ordered a pisco sour while Raz stuck with cold bottled water. He trusted the local water supply, but had an endorsement deal with Nestlé's and was paid to always be seen in public with their water. In the evening, as always, the cool ocean breeze picked up, but Maria refused a wrap that would hide her tanned flesh. The V in the front of her dress nearly went to the center of the Earth.

Murphy's observation was uncharitable when she leaned over to whisper in Raz's ear.

"She might as well wear a sign that says 'fuck me raw.'"

Raz waved her away. Murphy stepped back, but stayed close enough to listen to their conversation.

"Can I call you *Raz*?"

"Yes, of course. That's my name."

"How are you enjoying Mazatlan?"

"Truly, it is the Pearl of the Pacific. I haven't met anyone who says they'd prefer to be anywhere else. That's unusual."

"Yes, generally people want to be anywhere they aren't. Especially if they're from Minneapolis or Toronto."

Raz laughed and saluted with his water bottle. As an appetizer, Maria ordered octopus cooked in garlic butter. When it came, she forked a steaming segment and fed it to him.

"It's not a problem if we both eat the garlic," she said. Murphy rolled her eyes. The woman continued, "Thank you for inviting me, I know you have many women to choose from."

"Sometimes it seems like I have *all* of them."

"Only a rare man would complain. With all the beautiful women in the world, here we are. You and me."

Raz smiled.

"Something about you intrigued me and rubbed me the right way."

"Ah, that's an expression isn't it? A little joke."

"Yes," Raz said. "You seem mature for your age. Please tell me about yourself."

"Oh, that would be a boring story compared to the exciting life you lead, Raz."

"Let me judge. Perhaps we could exchange. I will start. Did you know I was born in Mazatlan—I was one of the dump rats before a doctor and his wife adopted me and took me to the United States."

"I didn't know that. You didn't mention it at the gala."

Raz shrugged.

"If the authorities knew, that would make me an illegal alien. It's better not to give my enemies that weapon. Now you."

She thought for a minute.

"There are things I could say, but it would not be wise. How do I know I can trust you?"

"I just told you one of my deepest secrets."

"It doesn't seem that profound."

He shrugged. "Otherwise, my life is an open book."

"That's another expression, isn't it?"

Raz nodded.

"Once *Rolling Stone, Atlantic* and the *Wall Street Journal* dig deep and the profiles add up to over a hundred-thousand words, there's not much fresh material to talk about. Now you."

"I'll tell you a secret." She motioned for him to lean close. "I have an old soul."

"That doesn't seem like a dangerous disclosure. How old?"

"I'll give you an exact number. Eighty-five. I'm directly connected to my grandmother—it's as if we're one."

"Okay."

"She was famous in her day—for pleasing men, many of them with names you would know."

Groupie. Star-fucker, Murphy thought.

Maria continued.

"Richard Burton. Errol Flynn. Howard Hughes before he lost his mind. My grandmother taught me everything."

Good thing Raz is smart—he'll never fall for any of this.

Raz motioned for the waiter. They ordered—she asked for pepper-steak while Raz ordered sea bass.

Was it her imagination? Was Raz picking up the pace like he was in a hurry? Several of the Raz girls were dining at adjacent tables. Were they noticing his seduction? What would they think? It was weird how non-possessive they were. How did Raz deflate their jealousy?

"Murphy?"

She'd been drifting. That was not good.

"Yes, sir," she said.

"Sit down and join us. The street security is fine. Have a drink."

Maria did not look happy about the suggestion. Her thin, polite smile was forced. Murphy walked around the perimeter and waved away a vendor offering sloppy slices of *tres leche* cake. There was nothing notable happening. There was never one-hundred-percent security, but this was close. Murphy walked back to the table and took the proffered seat.

"Pacifico," she said to the waiter. "*Limon.*" Then she spoke to Maria. "I apologize, I couldn't stop myself from listening in. You were very close to your *abuela.* You must have spent a lot of time together."

"Yes, lots of time. You could say all the time, day-and-night."

"That's interesting. As a child, did she live with you and take care of you?"

The waiter interrupted by bringing Murphy's beer and lime.

"I forget myself," Maria said. "It's your turn, Raz. Tell me something else no one else knows."

Raz considered.

"People assume I have sex with a lot of women, but it's only been ten very special ones." He closed his eyes to concentrate. "Ah, maybe twenty."

"Few lovers, but many children," Maria said. "I don't believe the rumors, but hundreds of mothers? How is that done?"

Raz looked embarrassed.

"They hook me up to a machine, like a milker. It hurts."

"So, the women are artificially…"

"Yes," Raz said. "Exactly."

"Why?"

"No, your turn. Do you have a question, Murphy?"

Murphy considered a line of questioning. She spoke quickly and slapped the table.

"How many times have you been married?"

It worked, because Maria spoke without thinking.

"Oh, four times. No. Never. None."

"But your grandmother was married four times."

Maria nodded. *Yes.*

"My turn," Maria said. "What is the purpose of having hundreds of children?"

"Birthrates in the West are collapsing except among certain groups. Latinos and other Catholics. Mormons. Followers of Islam. In order to earn a destiny, you must have the demographics—you must reproduce. A man is theoretically capable of fathering millions. Millions make an army. Our world's social structures are crumbling. The future belongs to those who can mobilize their own private militia."

Murphy had never heard that grand plan from Raz before and her mind was overwhelmed. Derailing her brain, it took a massive effort to focus on Maria's words. Her mind made an illogical intuitive leap. She tapped the table with her beer bottle.

"I think you killed your grandmother. Why?"

"Yes, I did. No, I didn't. What kind of question is that?"

Maria seemed impatient and exasperated, but not angry. This response puzzled Murphy. After a few seconds, Maria regained her composure and spoke quietly.

"I'll cut your throat, hang you upside down and gut you like *vaca de carne.* No, I won't, I'm making a jest."

The waiter brought their meals and arranged them on the table.

"*Señora?*" he said. "*Comida?*"

"Bring me something quick. Marlin salad?" She gestured with her empty beer bottle. "*Uno mas?*"

"Of course, right away, *Señora.*"

Murphy gestured for them to eat. She helped herself to bread and butter so they wouldn't feel awkward. Maria made small talk and ignored Murphy.

Cold, Murphy thought. That's a good description. She's disconnected—she wears her emotions like clothing. Nothing sinks in. And, she's hungry, she wants something from Raz to fill her and make her feel whole. This is not unusual—many people want a piece of Raz. But, this is different. This woman is like a vampire, only it's not blood she craves, it's something else. And, if Raz doesn't meet her needs?

A disturbing image filled her mind, an image of a black widow eating her mate after copulation. In nature, cases of males eating females were rare. Cases of males eating males were even rarer. The female eats the male for nourishment for her children—to assure propagating the species. And, she'd read this in a journal, there was a version of recreational cannibalism unrelated to mating called aggressive spillover. These thoughts deeply troubled Murphy.

"Aggressive spillover," she said.

"Excuse me," Raz said. "What was that?"

Murphy shook her head. "Nothing."

"I don't want you to take this the wrong way…" Raz said.

"What?"

"It might be better if you ate your salad with the girls."

Murphy studied Raz's face.

"Is there a right way to take that?"

Raz shrugged.

"Sorry, Murphy."

"No, it's okay. I'll leave you to your conversation."

Murphy's stomach was in coils. She felt ill. Raz was smart and had such discipline.

What is going on? Did all men have a self-destruct button a clever woman could press?

She realized who it reminded her of. Glen Wilson. The stubborn, maddening wrong-headed asshole-in-chief, Glen Wilson.

There was an open spot at one of the tables. She put her beer down. One of the girls leaned over and kissed her cheek.

"It will be okay," the girl said calmly.

The waiter found her and delivered the salad—she took a forkful in silence. When she was done eating a few bites, she pushed the plate away. She looked up to see Raz escorting Maria to his rented BMW X5 SUV. She walked over, tugged his arm and whispered in his ear.

"I don't think you should be alone with her."

"Duly noted, Murphy. Appreciate your concern. Don't worry."

"At least tell me what is going on with you."

"I have a wild reputation as a rock star, but I don't generally diddle the groupies because that scene doesn't interest me. So, I don't really have that much experience with women. It's embarrassing. She's of age and willing. I'm curious. That's all there is to this. Stay here. Escort the girls back to the hotel and I'll see you in the morning."

"But..."

"Don't make me command you, Murphy. I take full responsibility. I'll be fine. I'm not worried about handling this woman. Besides, Jesus will be right outside the door listening to every stroke and grunt." Jesus was a trusted member of the security team. "Take the night off—spend some time with Elke."

She liked *that* idea.

"Okay," she said. "If this is the last time I see you, then it's been an interesting ride. Thank you."

"Don't be a fatalist, Murphy. It's a romp, not a one-way saunter into hell. I'll see you tomorrow."

Immersed in her foul mood, Murphy hailed one of Mazatlan's ubiquitous, open-air *Pulmonia* VW taxis and rode through crowded streets toward her room at the Pueblo Bonito Inn. Mazatlan was a filthy, wonderful city bustling with haphazardly parked trucks, farting buses, trilling taxis, strolling shoppers and old motor bikes sometimes carrying families of five.

After leaving the old town *Centro Historico*, the view of the emerald water of the crescent bay opened up on *Ave Cameron Sabalo.* Waves crashed on volcanic rock and powdery sand. Like an omniscient observer—not an active participant—she drifted through the mad jumble of busy humanity; joggers, sun-bathers, timeshare evangelists, dog-walkers, body surfers, street vendors, bicyclists, roller-bladers, piñata peddlers, guitarists, kite flyers, wedding parties, baptism ceremonies, jugglers, cliff divers, yoga photographers, fish-head-on-stick frigate bird jesters and gringo tourists all carefree and enjoying the sun while she fought a losing battle against despair.

Raz was making a horrible mistake, she knew it to her core, but what could she do? Throw him over her shoulder and run? Even that would not work—his other guards would beat her silly.

If he survives, he'll learn.

She grasped the thought and held onto it. It was all she had. As if there was a thousand ton load on her back, she walked the hallways of the hotel and keyed the lock on her room. Inside, Elke was wet from the shower—she stood before the window over the beach drying her hair. She turned.

"Hey, Murph. Is everything okay?"

Murphy hated the familiar truncation of her name and she bit down hard on the impulse to scream.

The name is Murphy, Murphy, Murphy, damn you to hell and may a dragon eat your spine.

The impulse faded quickly.

Elke could call her whatever she liked.

Murphy shook her head.

"No, everything is not okay."

Elke stood for a moment limned by the bright outside sunlight.

"I know exactly what you need," she said.

She shrugged and the towel fell away. To an objective observer, Elke looked like a typical middle-aged woman—healthy, but not in great shape. She was thick around the waist and her ponderous breasts sagged. However, to Murphy she was a luscious, Teutonic, Botticelli angel.

It was true. Elke did have what Murphy desperately needed. She melted into her lover's arms. They didn't leave the bed until morning when the phone rang.

A Summons

The phone rang at 10:30 AM. Murphy and Elke, groggy, were tangled in the sheets and each other, so it took extra time to fumble with the receiver and answer.

"Yeah," Murphy said.

Her mouth was dry and foul. She rubbed her teeth with a finger.

"Come, Murphy," Jesus said.

"*Now* the boss wants me?"

But, she spoke to a dead line.

She leaned over to kiss Elke, but Elke pushed her away.

"Go brush your teeth," she said.

It took a half-hour for Murphy to shower and make herself halfway presentable. She didn't bother with drying her hair or dressing up—she pulled on voluminous mom-jeans, a sweatshirt and running shoes. In the mirror, there was no denying it, she looked frumpy. She hadn't realized it until she looked at herself, but she was resigning as head of Raz's security team. She had money in the bank and didn't need to work for a year or two.

Why bother?

She walked down the hallway to the Presidential suite—there she tapped on the door. Jesus let her in. Raz sat on the deck overlooking the beach. His face was blotchy with bruises. He looked at her for half a minute before gesturing for her to sit down beside him.

Was he going to admit she was right about the woman?

His voice was incongruously filled with good cheer.

"Good morning, Murphy," he said.

When he spoke, she saw the missing incisor. His lips were swollen. A satin ascot was wrapped tightly around his neck. Suspicious, she reached over and loosened the wrap—his neck was covered with lurid purple bruises.

She yawned and stretched on the lounge chair beside him.

"I think I had a more—satisfying—night than you," she said.

"I doubt that very much."

"What are you going to do about the tooth?"

He shrugged.

"The best dentists in the world are here. We'll get it fixed by the end of the day."

"It looks like she tried to strangle you."

"She got carried away with erotic asphyxiation. There's no question, it makes for a glorious climax. What a night."

Murphy shook her head.

"You're not going to pretend it was worth it?"

Raz's lips twisted partly into a grimace and partly into a smile.

"Ever heard of a sexual maneuver called the gushing wombat?"

"Lord, no, and I hope you'll spare me the details."

"It's not something I'd ever do again, but it was intense, there's no question."

"Have we seen the last of the woman or is she hanging

around for a while?"

"You have a knack for asking great questions, Murphy."

"How about an answer?"

"Let's talk hypothetically. I'm told that if you want to dispose of a—parcel—around here, you wrap it in heavy chains and ask a shrimp boat captain to drop it in a deep trench about fifteen miles out. It's not cheap, but apparently it's effective when you want something to disappear forever."

"Was it worth it, Raz?"

Raz sighed.

"My personality is an addictive one. If I ever tried crack cocaine, I'd chase the high until it killed me. That's one of life's land mines I need to avoid. There are others. Heroin, alcohol, starchy foods—the list goes on and on. I can't begrudge myself for trying wild sex with a seasoned expert. Yes, it was worth it. No, I won't do it again. Fair enough?"

"The purpose for setting this in motion was to get a reading on this woman for Glen. Typically, the cryptic asshole didn't say what he's looking for. What did you learn?"

Raz closed his eyes and didn't open them until one of the Raz-girls came out on the deck with a steaming cup of tea. From a tray, she put a cup of Altura Tollan coffee down for Murphy. The girls were very attentive—the cream-cloudy fluid in the cup was just the way Murphy liked it. On impulse, she took the girl's hand, pulled her down to eye-level and studied her young face.

What do the Raz-girls think about last night's festivities?

As always, the girl's eyes were alert and she seemed *clear*, as if she existed on a higher plane where the troubles of the world were irrelevant. Murphy wanted to live there too.

"How are you girls this morning, dear?"

This girl was a classy Laotian or Thai with perfectly bobbed hair, blue eye shadow and creamy pearlescent lipstick. Her accent was French. It was early, but she was fully assembled for the day.

"We're fine or better. Thank you for asking, Madam Murphy."

Murphy stroked the girl's cheek, then turned to Raz.

"I always wonder—do you drug them or hypnotize them? What's your hold over them?"

Raz laughed. Due to the new gap in his teeth, he spoke softly and lisped, so Murphy had to listen carefully.

"No, it's nothing like that. I don't hold them at all. The outside clash of cultures is profoundly dysfunctional; I illuminate a vision of a better world for them and their beautiful children. They like the look of that future, that's all there is to it. Beyond that, they help and support each other. There's nothing artificial or manipulative about it, it's simply a harem-scene tuned to their fundamental nature. Look around the world. There are many thousands of ways to live. I picked through the best of all cultures and designed something new. It's not even really new, it's based on the old world of sheiks and sultans and updated for the twenty-first century. These girls put aside negativity and work together to create a better society."

"Where does it end? With an army of human robots? How many is enough?"

"No, Murphy, it doesn't end. It *begins* with a coordinated army of a million voters. Watch, you'll see."

"What about the woman? Maria. You know how Glen is. I need to tell him something or he'll harass me mercilessly until I jump head-first off the balcony."

Raz sipped his tea and thought about how to respond.

"I look for soulfulness in my candidates. There was none in Maria. She was like a reptile, all appetite with no hope for satiation. I didn't give her what she wanted, no one could. If Jesus hadn't hauled her off me, I'd be dead and she'd be out in the world looking for another man to fill her and he'd be dead too. The woman was inhuman."

"Was? You're sure about the 'was' part?"

"Oh, yes, Murphy, the woman no longer exists. That's one-hundred-percent certain."

They sat on the balcony and watched a parasailer assault the blue sky while the surf rushed in and receded.

"You're leaving tomorrow," Murphy said.

Raz nodded.

"I like it here—the sun, the people, the food, the rundown, free-spirit of the place. I'm not ready to leave."

"I understand. Take some time off. Stay here a while. There's time."

"I don't think you should count on me for the next tour. Jesus is ready—he can take over."

"I hope you'll stay with us, Murphy. You're the best."

"I'm restless. I need a change."

"What will be will be."

He reached out a hand and took Murphy's. She noticed open wounds on his knuckles.

"I have to fly," he said. "I'll be seeing you."

After he left, she sipped her cold coffee and thought about what she'd tell Glen.

Fair Warning

Glen printed the list of Immortality clients and studied the twenty names. Two of them were dead. Neel, of course, but another had also hit the news. Glen Googled and Binged until he had a sense of what happened.

In Miami, a young man named Hector Rodriquez was stopped by the highway patrol in his Porsche Carrera GT for speeding on Highway 75. It was a routine stop, fifteen MPH over the speed limit, but Hector somehow got the officer's Glock and shot the patrol cop in the head twenty times. The next officer on the scene fired once and killed Hector. The officer would be dead, but Hector was out of bullets. The authorities were having trouble building a background on Hector—his passport and driver's license appeared to be forged.

While Glen considered all this, Murphy called.

"Wilson, you're a piece of work. That young woman you mentioned? Turns out she was a psychopath."

"Hmmm, interesting. Was?"

"Why did you ask me to study her? She almost killed Raz when they were fucking."

"Raz talked to her? What did he say about her?"

"He said she seemed—soulless."

"That's an interesting choice of words. Think hard. He said that, literally?"

"Yes. Tell me what's on your mind."

"Where is she now?"

"I think she's feeding the fishes off the coast. Raz says she's gone and won't be back. I didn't care to dig in any deeper—I don't want to know. I did what you wanted, now tell me what's up."

"Thanks for checking in, Murphy, I'll chat with you later."

He disconnected the call and left Murphy cussing at her handset.

It was a familiar feeling. Many of her conversations with Glen ended that same way.

Glen leaned back in his chair and thought about the situation, then looked over the client list again. Like Hector, there was another in the Miami area, Sylvia Goddard. He decided to check—was his old boss, Steve Stephens, still stationed down that way? After a few calls, he tracked Steve down.

"Steve Stephens."

"Sarge, this is your old pal Glen Wilson calling."

"I'm old, I'm retired and you're not my *pal.* What do you want?"

"It's great to talk to you too, Sarge. Are you still lurking around Miami?"

"Yes, I'm dating a former Rockette, 74-77. Roxy. She has legs that go from sunset to sunset and where they meet at midnight, I'm telling you, it's heaven on Earth. We're happy, you should leave us alone. What do you want?"

"Grab a pen and write down this name. Sylvia Goddard. Do

you have it?"

"Yes, I have it, but why? *Goddard* doesn't ring any bells. What's up?"

"Are you on Facebook? I can message you her address."

"No, I'm not on Facebook, I don't even know what it is and I don't want to know."

Glen rattled off Sylvia's street address and repeated it until Steve had it written down.

"I suggest you call one of your cronies and ask them take a look-see. Just scope her out, okay? Uh, I suppose I should tell you—this woman could be hazardous to your health, okay? I told you."

"I'm not doing anything until you tell me what this is about."

By the time he'd finished the sentence, Glen had disconnected.

"Goddamn you, Glen Wilson," Steve muttered as he dropped the phone back in its cradle.

Roxy looked up from her *People* magazine and peered at him over her reading glasses.

"Old friend?" she said.

"Not exactly," Steve replied.

After an hour of trying to get interested in *Duck Dynasty* reruns on the cable TV, Steve heaved himself up.

"Where are you going?" Roxy said.

"Out," he said. "Lunch."

Steve Stephens Gets Lucky

Because he was comfortable in them, Steve drove a retired police car, a battered black and white, four-door Ford Crown Victoria. While sitting behind the wheel, he studied the address. South Ocean Boulevard. It was a high-end Palm Beach neighborhood with ocean-front, gated estates—home to conservative pundits, politicians, investment company perverts, retired cartel bosses and other moneyed citizens. The address wasn't on the ocean side.

What could it hurt?

He decided to cruise over and knock at the door.

The house was set back from the wide street—all that was visible through coconut palms and tree ferns was a long, curved driveway and the rear of a tricked-out, lemon-yellow Porsche. It was a nice piece of property, but neglected—the yard was a tangled mess of kudzu and crabgrass. There was a callbox—Steve pressed the button, but there was no indication it did anything. He got out of the car and looked around—the place seemed deserted. The gate was sprung and creaked on its hinges when he pushed it open.

"Hello?" he said.

The place seemed creepy and abandoned. Unconsciously, Steve checked the Smith and Wesson Police Special tucked in a shoulder holster. There were at least a dozen noisy grackles in a sprawling Royal Poinciana tree. They chattered and scolded Steve for intruding. He followed the walkway as it wound through the jungle. The house was a squat, two-story Spanish, art deco style covered in pearl-pink stucco with red-clay roof tiles. The front door was open an inch. With his index finger, he pushed it open more.

"Hello. Is anyone home?"

The curtains were pulled tight and the house was dark. The air-conditioning was off or not working and the inside air was humid and steamy. It had rank smell, musky with the underlying scent of something cooking in the kitchen, like the morning bacon had been burnt. He poked in his head and caught movement at the corner of his eye.

He pulled back—from behind the door, strobe-lit by light streaming through the doorway—a huge butcher knife flashed before his eyes. Had he not jerked back, it would have been embedded in his temple. He fumbled with the gun as he pulled it from under his wash-and-wear jacket.

"I am a law-enforcement officer. Come out where I can see

you."

"Okay." It was a female voice. "Sorry for scaring you, I thought you were a rapist. Not too many nigg—blacks—in this neighborhood and they all want a taste of the white meat. I'm coming out slowly."

The door was pulled open wide and she appeared. She was stark naked and held the huge knife at her side. She was really pretty, maybe twenty-five-years-old with blonde streaks in her long hair. Her body was perfectly toned with large, bulbous breasts and a carefully maintained landing-strip of pubic hair between her legs. Her stomach and legs were dabbed with something that looked like peanut butter. Feces? Steve aimed the gun at her chest.

"I just want to talk to you. Drop the knife."

She tilted her head back and laughed.

"It wants to talk, does it? That's nice. I'll bet a big old bubba like you has a cock like a nightstick and you'd like to stick it all up in me, wouldn't you? Well, bubba, this is your lucky day because I'm all yours. Pick any hole you want."

Goddamn you to hell, Glen Wilson. What did you get me into?

"Drop the knife, ma'am. There's no reason for this to get ugly. Let's chat a minute, then I'll be on my way."

She took a step forward. He took a step back, she took another step forward.

"Come on, Buck, let's have a few drinks and party like it's the end of the world. I won't tell your mama. You don't even have to warm me up any, I'm dripping like a faucet just thinking about getting a good pumping from your diddly-whang. Big as an eggplant, ain't it? Don't be a fraidy-cat, I won't bite you much."

There was something cold and calculating in her eyes. He took another step back, but she closed the gap. Her thighs tensed like she would jump at him. It was decision time—he pulled the trigger and shot her in the chest. The impact pushed her back a step and she stood for a moment on shaky legs before falling to the ground like a bag of cement. The knife clattered on the concrete walkway beside her.

The wound was fatal, but he'd seen the medics do miracles, so he waited a few minutes to let her bleed out. It was probably an unnecessary precaution, but who knows what this crazy white bitch might say if she survived? When he was sure she'd expired, he called 9-1-1 and asked to be connected to a friend on the local force. Paul Tinker. The conversation was terse, but filled his friend in on the whole story.

"10-61" [Isolate self for message]

"10-23" [Arrived at scene]

"10-26, S-W-F" [Detaining subject, expedite, Single White Female]

"10-79" [Notify coroner]

Paul was the first on the scene. He was a Captain and had served with Steve when local police coordinated with Steve at the DEA. He felt the woman's neck.

"Nope," he said. "Anything not like it appears?"

"No, it's the whole story. Looking for an old friend, I got the wrong address. The woman came out like this and threatened me with the knife. She refused to drop the weapon and advanced on me, so I took her out."

"Okay. I asked you to do a wellness check on a retired pal. I hadn't heard from him in a week and I was worried—his health is not good. Let's use George Collins, he lives nearby. Have you been inside?" Steve shook his head. "Okay, I'll check it out. The troops will be onsite shortly."

Paul unholstered his Glock and walked to the front door.

"Police officer. Is anyone inside? I'm coming in. Hands up, please, when you show yourself. I just want talk."

He disappeared though the doorway.

The EMS truck arrived.

"Where's the responding officer?"

Steve nodded toward inside.

The two-person crew moved briskly until they saw the body, then relaxed and slowed down—clearly there was no need to hurry. They moved aside and chewed gum and gossiped about Dolphins football until the homicide team arrived to take pictures and gather evidence. One of the arriving techs took Steve's gun and the knife and bagged them. Another took Steve's statement. Another officer arrived, took a brief look, then spoke to Steve.

"Is anyone inside?"

"My old pal Paul Tinker."

"Brass," the officer said with a cynical twist to his lips—then he straightened up from his slouch and checked to make sure his belt buckle was centered on the gig line. "I'm going in," he said.

At that instant, Paul appeared in the doorway carrying a six-year-old boy with his arms wrapped around Paul's shoulders. The kid was nude—thin and scrawny.

"Crap," Steve said. "She had a kid?"

"No, this kid says his name is Juan-Luis. I think he matches a missing-persons report out of Broward." Paul handed the kid off to an EMS tech. "Get some pictures. We might have good news for worried parents out in Hallandale." He pointed at the officer. "In twenty minutes, this is going to be a zoo. Call in the cavalry, block off the street, hold everyone back." He turned to Steve. "I think I can keep you out of it; haul ass out of here. This is going to get complex, quick."

Steve scratched his nappy head.

"Give me an overview?"

"She's been butchering neighborhood dogs and eating them and it looks like, swear to God," he made the sign of the holy cross on his chest, "she was planning to eat the kid too."

"Jeee-zuss," Steve said.

"Steve, what exactly was it that made you stop by this place?"

"It was a tip from an old—friend."

Steve stumbled over the term.

Friend? That's not the right word.

"The timing was right—another day and we'd be investigating cannibalism. Any chance I should meet this *friend* of yours?"

"No," Steve said. "You really don't want to. Besides, he's not local. No need."

Paul studied Steve's face.

"Okay, got it. Watch your six, brother."

Steve nodded and weaved through the EMTs and cops to get to his car.

By the time he got around to calling Glen, it was late on the West Coast and even later on the East. Steve had been a Master Sergeant in the Army, so he knew how to cuss. Glen tried to derail him mid-rant.

"You're repeating yourself, Sarge."

"…flea-infested, camel-fucking, human refuse…"

"I'm hanging up now."

"Wait, I'm almost done," Steve said. "You're a piss-sucking morsel of shit from a hobo's ass-crack."

He paused and took a few deep breaths which gave Glen a chance to speak.

"What about the cooz, Steve?"

"Watch the news, creep. You won't be able to escape it."

"Steve, in full disclosure—there's one more in your area. Another woman, from Atlanta, but last known sighting? Miami. She knew the woman you visited, they went through the process together. I can't emphasize enough, watch your back, brother."

Steve hung up.

Glen cradled the phone and turned to Gerusha, hugging her back to him. They fit together like puzzle pieces.

"Old friend?" she said in her sleepy voice.

"Something like that," Glen said.

Glen—Client Goddard

The next day, Glen was reading a book on his Kindle DxD tablet in his office when Walter poked in his head.

"A minute of your time?"

"No," Glen said.

"You're not answering my texts or my phone calls."

"I turn all that shit off when I want to be left alone."

Walter came in and settled on a leather guest chair.

"I assume you've heard the news…"

"I've been intentionally staying away from the news. I don't need the aggravation."

"Client Goddard."

"I don't want to hear it. I know we're fucked."

Walter laid his head back on the chair and rubbed his forehead.

"She ate a kid, Glen. They found human bones in her garbage can. Gnawed clean. She was getting ready to eat another, but the cops got there in time."

Glen studied Walter's face.

"How is knowing that going to make my life better in any way?"

"I assume that's a rhetorical question…"

"I knew it would be something sick and twisted. I'm telling you, Walter, we should track down and exterminate every fucking one of our *customers*." At that moment, the sales chime resounded. "That's great, we're creating another psychopath."

"That's not fair, Glen. A couple of them seem okay."

"I don't care how they seem, Walter. One day we'll wake up to the news that an upstanding citizen has a freezer full of human heads or has been tanning baby skins and making leather underwear—making a fortune on the dark net. We sure as hell shouldn't be making more of these abominations."

"The higher the price, the more people want it. We're hauling in cash hand over fist."

"This is my best advice. Heed it. Shut it down, Walter. Pay all the bills, refund the deposits for the upcoming clients, split the bank accounts among the team and the employees and shut the fucking doors."

"If we do that, we're not even going to end up with a billion each. Seven-hundred-and-fifty-million per person if we're lucky."

"And that's not enough? When you and Bennie dreamed up this company, I didn't even have coffee money in my pocket, now look at us."

"If it bothers you so much, you could write off your share and kick it into the pool."

"I have plans for the cash, so, no, I think I'll hold onto it."

"We were *so* close. I thought we'd cash in for, hell, I don't know, maybe as much as ten-billion each."

"Easy come, easy go," Glen said. "A fool and his money…"

"Please, no hoary maxims, Glen. You're making me nauseous."

"Money doesn't buy happiness, but neither does poverty. Idolatry of money is sinful…"

Walter plugged his ears.

"Please. Stop it."

"You're the one who came up to my private office to bother me."

"Whatever," Walter said. He looked around the cozy room. It was filled with books and knickknacks. "You have a lot of books for a guy who I've never seen open one."

"There must be something else on your mind, otherwise you'd go away."

"It just seems…"

"Spit it out, Walter."

"It seems odd that you're so eager to shut down Immortality when you haven't met your better-self yet. He's almost ready to release."

Glen stood, turned and looked out of the rain-streaked window at the channel.

"I was trying to forget about that."

"Go down south and check out the doppelgänger before demolishing our company."

"South? That reminds me. You skate around this subject and don't give a straight answer. What happens to the old version of the client? You said you don't kill them, but we don't allow two versions to run around. What's the deal?"

"We don't kill them."

"You already said that and it's not an answer."

"Have we ever talked about suicide?"

"I don't know. I don't believe we have the right to stop anyone and maybe for some people it's the logical solution to insurmountable problems, but generally it's a coward's way out. It's cruel for the family and friends left behind."

"Ah, so you're okay with suicide in some cases."

"Where are you going with this, Walter?"

"We put the client and donor in a room."

"Yes?"

"And the result is always the same. The new version kills the old."

Glen leaned back in his chair and thought about this.

"Shit, Walter, that's fucked up. After the first few times, didn't that give you a hint something is seriously wrong with the new version?"

"It solved a problem very neatly—so, no, we didn't over-analyze it. It's fully spelled out in our contract with the client. They know what happens to the old body. I admit, it's a bit weird, but this is a brave new world we're creating. The changing landscape takes time getting used to."

Glen shook his head with wonder.

"Are you hoping to get rid of me this way if I go to Brazil?"

Walter laughed.

"No. You're still relatively young and vigorous. You're not decrepit and desperately clinging to the idea of a rebirth. When you're broken down and nearly at your end, maybe the idea won't seem so alien and out-of-bounds. We're not going to lock you in a room with your new version. You're a special case. Don't worry."

"I *am* curious. We're shutting down, period. But, I'll go down *south* and check out the new and improved Glen Wilson, though how I could be better is a mystery. I am an example of a perfect man, right? My intellect, my aptitude, my generous spirit, my sense of humor, my sexual prowess, my quick wit, my sense of rhythm, my insight, my…"

"Glen, honestly, you need to shut the hell up."

"…my perfect hair, my remarkable physique for a man half my age, my style-sense, my…"

"I'm leaving now."

Walter got up and left the room, so he didn't know how long Glen continued the litany of his many virtues.

An hour? Two?

Later that afternoon, while hiding in his office, Glen got a text message from Gerusha.

Glen, I need to see you.

He leaned forward and studied the roiling water of the canal. Soon, it would be the last time he was here and all he created and enjoyed would move to another possessor. The books would get hauled off to the recycling facility. The furniture would be sold off piece-by-piece on Craig's List. The room would be gutted and refurnished to some lesser person's taste.

Isn't that the way life is?

We own nothing. Everything comes and goes in its time.

He set the dismal thoughts aside and left the room.

He looked in Gerusha's door. She was harried and hassled. There were two pencils stabbed into her ragged ponytail. She raised a finger to hold Glen off for one minute so she could finish her phone conversation.

"I don't care if it's on the truck or not—we're executing the cancellation policy of our contract. Yes, we'll pay the Teamsters. Yes, we'll pay the penalty and interest. Yes, we'll pay the restocking and reconfiguration fee so you can return it to the catalog configuration. Yes, I realize how much money that is. Okay? Okay. Let me know via email when it's done and what the final tally is and we'll do a wire transfer. Goodbye."

She dropped the phone into its charging cradle.

"Glen, help me out here. Yesterday I was buying all the equipment I could find and paying outrageous fees to expedite delivery—today I'm canceling everything, returning what I can and setting up an auction for the rest. What is going on?"

"That should be clear enough. We're shutting the company down."

"But why? It seemed like everything was in place for an IPO that would make everyone rich. Does this have anything to do with our client going mad? That doesn't seem fatal. We can weather the bad publicity. We're still signing contracts with new clients. I don't understand."

"G—, listen for a minute. Imagine this scenario—that all of the clients are as batshit crazy as the whack job in our lobby. Or," he held up his index finger to emphasize the point, "worse."

After opening her mouth to speak, the ramifications took hold in her mind. She worked the thoughts through.

"All of them?"

"Yes," Glen said. "All."

"Holy crap, I get it. Fire sale. Everything must go."

Smart girl.

Company Meeting

The main theater was filled with a hubbub of milling activity and conversation. Walter stood at the center of the main stage and simply waited for silence.

"Please hold commentary and questions for the Q and A session at the end. You've all heard the rumors—I'm sad to say they are true, we are shutting down the company. You know about the killing in our front lobby and the horrible murders instigated by our client. Due to concern over *all* the clients and the high likelihood of their future offenses, we're taking the precautionary step of ceasing and desisting all business activity, immediately. I know this news is disappointing, believe me, there is no one in this room as disappointed as me. We had great success in the palms of our hands..."

He held up his hand and three vivid laser beams converged and formed an emerald-green lightning ball in his palm. He waved his hand and the ball disappeared.

"Sorry, I couldn't resist, but this is no time for parlor tricks. We need to liquidate everything and clear the building by the end of the month. All the equipment and furnishings need to be removed from the premises. If there is anything you want, please make a list and give it to your supervisor—we'll sort through the requests and distribute everything as equitably as we can. To accomplish this task quickly will take extraordinary effort on everyone's part. From the bottom of my heart, I thank you for what you achieved. It was truly remarkable. Now I will open the floor for questions, who will go first?"

"Do the recent events explain why Bennie left?"

"Yes," Walter said. "Who is next?"

"Our stock holdings and options are now worthless?"

"Yes. As you might imagine, we have cash on hand from sales. We decided to divide a percentage of the remaining cash among all the employees. Anyone who wants to leave right this instant and be done with the horrorshow is free to do so. Sign a release and pick up a check for one-hundred-thousand dollars. You have my word, the check is good if you cash it today. So, anyone?"

The crowd was restless, but no one got up.

"What? No takers? Perhaps you're at least half as smart as you look. If you help us close up and all the equipment sells for reasonable second-hand prices, everyone in the room is now a multi-millionaire and will get something like ten million in a cash payout on the last day of the month."

This caused a great stir in the audience. Most were very happy, but some had hoped for more and were angry. There were a couple of hisses and the word "bullshit" was uttered and repeated, but these comments did not kindle anything and the room returned to silence.

"Some of you think you deserve more and maybe you do, but, in essence, the business you built failed and you are partially responsible for that failure. You did outstanding and extraordinary work, so this final result is a damned shame, but life sucks sometimes. You're walking away with something, so don't be greedy. Take your cash, start a new business and earn your billion that way."

"How much do we know about the problem with the clients?"

"This will be hard to hear, but it appears they are all psychopaths and represent a significant hazard to the public. Beyond that, I don't care to speculate. To get your payout, you will sign a non-disclosure agreement and after today, you won't be able to talk about any of this."

"What shall we tell our family and friends?"

"I suggest you be vague and say as close to nothing as possible. We've been operating on the quiet, so hopefully we can disappear without drawing much attention. Pay your taxes and don't talk to anyone, especially the press. Believe me, the more the public, law enforcement and the government agencies learn about what we've been doing, the worse it will be for all of us and our families. Shut your traps and move on with your lives."

A lab tech with an Antifa haircut spoke up.

"Senior management will get a lot more than ten-million, so, once again the little guy gets screwed while the one-percent get filthy rich."

"Thank you for pointing that out. You are completely correct. Next question."

"Can we go now?"

"Anyone can leave at any time, but we need your help in creating an orderly shutdown. Your payout depends on hanging on until the end of the month and doing everything you can think of to help us dispose of the equipment and furniture. If you don't want the ten-million, leave now, take the hundred-grand and be happy, no one will stop you. What else?" He pointed. "Do you have a question, sir?"

"What are we going to do about the clients in work?"

"All deposits are being refunded and the donors will be released back into the wild in as close to their original state as possible. For clients already completed and released? I suggest you stay far away from them. Next question."

"Will we be able to draw unemployment insurance?"

"I don't know. Next question."

"I really like my MacBook. Will I be able to keep it?

"No, it's a rental. It will go back to the leasing company. Could I get an intelligent question, please? Otherwise I'll think my invaluable time is being wasted." He pointed. "Yes, you, young lady. Cho, right? I remember interviewing you."

"I'm confused about the precise nature of the problem with the clients. We researched everything thoroughly and the transfer is remarkably accurate. The essence of the client is over ninety-seven percent transferred over to the donor and we were working with some success on the remaining three-percent. The clients are defective? How?"

Walter sighed.

"I was wondering if any of you eggheads would zero in on the nature of this beast. I don't want to go all Shirley MacLaine on you, but you deserve the best answer I can give. The right answer is we don't have enough data, so we don't know what conclusion to draw. There's a problem. It's serious. We're closing up shop and cleaning up our mess to the best of our ability."

Cho was persistent.

"What is it that does not transfer properly?"

"We don't know."

"Could it be instinctual, intrinsic morals, compassion and ethics—something we might collectively describe as the human soul?"

"No," Walter said.

Walter remembered from her interview. She was persistent. That's part of the reason she was hired.

"Do you say no because you don't want to believe it or because you know of data that contradicts the hypotheses?"

"No."

"Excuse me, Walter, that's non-responsive. Do you have data or information that disqualifies non-transfer of the human soul as a cause of what we're observing in the clients?"

Walter sighed.

"No, but listen. It looks like there is a DNA trigger or button we might be pressing. Is selfishness or cruelty a survival instinct that is potientiated under stress? Maybe. There are other theories equally plausible, so I don't see any value in speculation. We know what we need to do, so let's do it."

Twenty members of the audience raised their hands and waved them vigorously.

"Since there are no more questions," Walter said, "this session is adjourned."

Walter walked to side stage where Glen waited.

"Smooth," he said.

"I didn't see you jumping in to help out, prick."

Glen did a soft-shoe shuffle and sang a fragment of song.

"I'm a soul man—da-da-da-da-dat-dat-dat-da."

"Go fuck yourself, Otis Redding," Walter said.

After the meeting, Glen went back to his nook-office on the roof. Taking his time, he removed a Hoyo de Monterrey Sultan Maduro cigar from the hardwood humidor, carefully prepared it by dipping the end in honey and then lighting it with a gas lighter. He sat back in his library chair and watched cold rain paint the windows with sad shades of gray.

Contrary to the dismal weather, his mood was mixed—in inner turmoil, he couldn't decide if he was mostly okay or deeply troubled. The company had made him rich again and there was no question, he found being rich more interesting than being poor. There was a truism, money can't buy happiness—but neither does poverty. He was already plotting his next move—back to Alaska. The roadmap was clear and he could see the triumphant headline: Glen Wilson, the King of Alaska.

He hated the Anchorage weather and still felt the chill in his bones from being up there the last time, but north is the future. Oh, what a convoluted plan it was, but it might work and that's good enough. You can wait your whole life for a sure thing, then find, despite your care, you've paid gold and bought dung.

On impulse, he called Gerusha's super-secret-VIP mobile phone number.

"Hey, G—, what's up?"

"Glen, I'm up to ass in contracts and angry suppliers. The barracuda are ripping my flesh. Get rapidly to the urgent point of your call."

"That was a clumsy sentence, but never mind that now—I was just thinking, we still haven't properly broken in my nook. There's still time to rock it right before my flight leaves for Brazil. This is our last chance to make the stars sparkle and climb the magical stairway to knock-knock-knock on heaven's golden door."

"Have you been drinking? I have no time for nonsense."

She disconnected the call. Glen's mood took a turn to the worse.

Why do I do stupid stuff like that? She's a great woman and deserves respect—respect for her important job and for her hard-earned dignity. She is a great wife, far better than I deserve. Why am I such a fucking asshole?

He puffed the cigar and poured a drink. Before the first sip, he raised the glass before his eyes and looked at the waning afternoon light. He squeezed it as hard as he could to see if it would shatter in his hand and make him bleed the way he deserved for being such a buffoon. He could visualize the jagged wounds. They would be horrible—perhaps even fatal if the blood flow was unstaunched, but the crystal was strong and did not break.

Why do I do such stupid things?

He heard the sound of the door latch. He turned—it was Gerusha. After shutting the door behind her, she pulled off her high heels and worked at the zipper of her dress.

"You and your goddamned cigars. I'm going to smell like a fecking whorehouse ashtray."

In seconds she was completely naked.

"Where," she said. "The sofa?" She ran her hands up and down her sides. "You want some of this? What are you waiting for? You have five minutes, cowboy."

Glen smiled as he tore off his shirt and tie.

Why do I say such stupid things?

Because sometimes, sometimes, I get what I want.

Bennie asks for Emma's Hand

The Chief's house in Anchorage was solid and well-warmed by logs crackling in the fireplace. Bennie had taken care in how he dressed; he'd put on a necktie and taken it off three times thinking it might be too much, but he ended up leaving it on.

Better to be too formal than not enough.

"Sir, you've probably guessed. I'm here to ask for your blessing to ask Emma to marry me."

The Chief leaned back in his chair. He poked his nose in his glass of whiskey and sniffed it heartily.

"My daughter's virtue? Is there something, uh, gestating, that would contribute urgency to your request?"

"So far as I know, sir, her—virtue—is intact and nothing is gestating."

"Good, Bennie. That was tactfully said."

Bennie looked puzzled.

"If you say so, sir. I can only report what I know."

"She's young—not even out of college yet."

"That's true, sir."

"You said you quit your job. How will you take care of her?"

Bennie pulled a copy of his bank statement from his shirt pocket. The Chief smoothed it out and held it out to capture light from the fireplace. He ran his index finger over the grand total.

"Uh, really?" he said.

Bennie shrugged.

"So I'm told, sir."

"So, taking care of her needs is not a problem. Anything else I should know?"

"We fit together well, Chief. She is good for me and she says I'm good for her. I love her."

"What are your plans?"

"I don't know, sir. Start a business? Work at the university on some research ideas? If Glen has a new plan and I like the look of it, he might invite me to take a role—that's an option."

"Ah, Wilson. That man is an odd piece of work." The Chief sighed. "I'm not sure I'm ready for this. My little angel is all grown up."

"Sir…"

The Chief interrupted him with an upraised palm.

"Let me think this through."

He slouched back in his chair and closed his eyes. Soon, his chest raised and fell and he appeared to be asleep. Bennie reached out to touch him, but thought better of it and withdrew his hand. He sat and stared at the flames. Then, suddenly, the Chief sat up and looked Bennie in the eye.

"Em said you might ask and told me she'd flay me if I said no. But, know this, young man…" he pointed at the massive moose head on the wall, "…if you mistreat my daughter in any way, it will be *your* head mounted there. Don't worry, I'll find another place for the moose. Do you understand?"

"Yes, sir."

"That said, a woman needs a strong hand on occasion, I know that."

"I'm not sure Emma would agree…"

The Chief shrugged.

"Right, modern women. I know, whatever. The bottom line is, yes, you have my permission to ask. If she'll have you, then we'll welcome you into this family with open arms."

"Thank you, sir."

The Chief closed his eyes again.

"Feckless Wilson," he muttered. "I wonder what he'll dream up this time."

Glen Wilson—Primeiro—The Chase Scene

IT WAS A circuitous route that took over thirty hours. Seattle to Vancouver, BC on Alaska Air, then to Toronto and finally an endless ten-hour haul to Sao Paulo on Air Canada. The long trip gave me a lot of time to think, but instead, I used the time constructively to drink free booze in the first class cabins. Did I miss anything about the old days of traveling to South America in rattletrap DC-3 goony birds? No, nothing. Those barbaric days can stay dead as far as I'm concerned.

I watched several movies, so I felt updated on the degraded state of modern pop culture. Things blew up in the most incongruous ways. Running. Car chases. Pretty young plastic women wearing scant scraps of clothing. I liked that part.

In the Toronto to Sao Paulo leg of my trip, I was catered to by a stunning flight attendant named Rosalind. With the smell of Gerusha on my skin and the taste of her lingering in my mouth, I was able to remember my marriage vows, so I only proposed twice. I think Rosalind turned me down both times, but I mentioned I was drinking, right? What do I know?

After Sao Paulo, there was an AirBus hop to Porto Velho with a short layover in Brasilia. Porto Velho is in the remote state of Rondonia.

A remote location in Rondonia, is that an oxymoron?

I didn't know anything about Rondonia—despite my travels in South America, I'd never heard of it. Porto Velho is Rondonia's largest city—Rondonia's population density was 6.7 people per square kilometer. For contrast, compare that to Manhattan with a population density of 27,000 people per square kilometer.

I imagined Porto Velho as a muddy village with natives running around in loincloths puffing on blowguns all day, but of course it was a charming city of 400,000 on the muddy Madeira River with high rise buildings, multi-lane highways, a modern airport and black-haired women wearing stylish shoes with wedge heels. I was sure there would be no Starbucks coffee shops there, but, praise be to the limitless ambition of Howard Schultz and his successors, I was wrong, as it turned out there was one just off Avenue Jose Viera Caula.

I insisted the helo pilot, Zeka, join me there for a latte. Who knows when I'd get my next chance? The drink was well-prepared by a perky barista. The pilot and I ate chocolate croissants and chatted about the weather (hot, humid, rainy). He mentioned it had been half a day since the Immortality facility security team checked in, but that happened sometimes—the radios died or the power went out—they could be too busy fixing the problem to check in.

Did I feel a tickle of warning in my spider-sense?

It would be nice to imagine I did, but I had a steaming cup of coffee and a French pastry in front of me. Life is good. What could go wrong?

I was strangely excited about meeting myself. Who wouldn't like to get to know themselves better and get an outside, more objective perspective? I imagined a joyful union where we talked like soul mates while I told him about the secret parts of my many adventures and he, being me, would soak it all in—understanding me fully and entirely. We could puff on cigars and have a few drinks. I could teach him my tricks for seducing women. He'd be the son I never had. Did I think about the psychotic madness of the other clients? Of course I did, but I assumed my boundless spirit would dominate. I am an irrepressible man of tremendous strength and will—and humble too. I was simply certain any version of me would be completely charming and wonderful. I didn't have any misgivings until an hour into our helicopter ride when Zeka pointed out plumes of black smoke on the horizon.

Oh, shit.

We made a pass before setting down. The air smelled of diesel and the place was nothing but rubble. There were bodies everywhere. How did he do it? Here's my speculation based on something I read in a book many years ago: he figured out a way to vaporize diesel from the backup gennies in a sealed concrete enclosure, then set it off from a safe distance with a detonator via time delay or remote trigger.

What's a good detonator?

Something that takes time to heat up, but bursts into intense flame on ignition. Make a long trail of steel wool with one end lit by an open flame? Or, use jumper cables to connect a magnesium wheel rim across AC power? Make a massive pile of wooden matches and set them off with a short section of small-gauge copper wire soldered to larger wire plugged into a wall socket? Who knows what could be found in a Brazilian workshop. He needed to run fast or buy a few minutes, because this bomb was massive—it leveled trees a hundred yards in every direction. The facility was literally a smoking hole in the ground.

Zeka radioed back to Porto Velho. Help would be coming soon.

There were other clients who might have done this, but I knew it was me. I knew it. This was my work, a pissed-off, no-holds-barred, take-no-prisoners Glen Wilson on the rampage.

There were survivors, but not many. A nurse died in Zeka's arms. Slowly, from the trees, a few injured, shell-shocked victims emerged. They didn't like the look of me, so I stayed back while Zeka talked to them in Portuguese and translated for me. With the help of the ambulatory, he patched up the worst victims and staunched their bleeding the best they could. Slowly the story emerged.

They said there was a madman who looked vaguely like me,

though much younger, of course. He convinced an assistant, Rosa, to loosen his handcuffs, then he got one of the guard's guns and shot the guard, then Rosa. All the clients were dead, the madman made sure of that. He fired until he ran out of bullets, then did something in the underground backup generator vault. Then, an hour later, the place exploded. Of 80 staff, there were eight left with a couple barely hanging on.

"Where did the man go?"

The nurse pointed and I walked down a muddy path to take a look. The trail led to a river. On the bank were marks from the keel of a boat. I looked down the meandering river where the chocolate water churned around a bend and disappeared.

Zeka pleaded with me. I should fly back to Porto Velho with him. But no, there was only one person who could do this. Me. I needed to follow the man down the river. Find him. Kill him.

I grabbed my backpack—Zeka tossed me his emergency kit bag too. I waited on the riverbank for another boat. Soon, one appeared—a motor-scow powered by an ancient Volvo diesel engine. I waved them over and handed over a wad of cruzeiros reais until the captain nodded. The equivalent of ten dollars or a thousand? I don't know. It didn't matter. The boat was not fast, but it was headed in the right direction. I shared the squat boat with canvas bags of soybeans—the boat was so loaded down, the river water came right up to the gunwales and lapped over on occasion.

It's impossible to cruise down a muddy river in a jungle on a rusty old boat without thinking of old movies like The African Queen or classic art films like Anaconda. This was not much like the movies because there were many signs of civilization—places where the rain forest was cleared and beef cattle grazed, for example. And, the depressing rain was relentless and unphotogenic. The endless scenery was repetitive and boring. For miles, I stared a few yards into the mist from under a canvas cover, thinking dark thoughts and feeling sorry for myself. What would I do if I'd killed a bunch of people and went on the run?

The port would be watched, so, as my elusive alternate self, I'd slip into the river a few miles before the city and walk to the nearest bus stop. The boat would be found drifting—the crew would be weighed down and sunk in the river.

The first thing is to be unpredictable. The river led to Porto Velho and if my ultimate destination was Rio, then the options were to stay on the river, take a multi-day bus ride or try to catch a flight with a private pilot who didn't require paperwork if the cash looked right. Maybe Rio is too obvious. Bolivia is not far away and I knew my way around there a little. Or, it might be better to pick someplace at random, then I'd have to follow a trail of dead bodies while getting farther and farther behind and while his trail grew colder and colder.

Did he have papers? Maybe he found identification that was close enough. It didn't matter if he had money, because coshing a few tourists and dragging them into dark alleys would solve that problem in a hurry.

Does this sound arrogant? Many people consider me to be a world class buffoon, but I was capable of terrible things. I'd killed a few people in my life, but each, in their own way, deserved it and the world was a better place without them. I wasn't an evil person, but it was in me. It's in everyone. If you take away the empathetic restrictions of a capable man like me, the result won't be wholesome and peaceful, let me put it that way.

I probably should have taken Zeka's offer to fly back to Porto Velho because that's certainly where my clone was headed, but I wanted to follow the trail accurately to make sure nothing was missed. The tedious journey gave me time to inventory everything I carried. My backpack had the usual stuff, a Bowie knife, matches, candles, Mylar space blanket, rain cover and a dozen Snickers bars for sustenance and trade. I looked through Zeka's jump-bag.

He was more sophisticated.

He had cash in three currencies. Trail mix. Water bottles and purifier. A well-thumbed magazine with pictures of mostly naked women. A battered Taurus .38 revolver, and, thank the many Gods, bug repellent. I sprayed the nasty-smelling stuff all over and the relief was instant. The mosquitoes still buzzed, but stayed six inches away. That was a compromise I could live with. He also had an Iridium satellite phone and spare battery packs. I called Walter to check in so he'd have a general idea where I was last seen when and if I disappeared somewhere.

I asked him to email pictures of the new Glen to me—and copy Murphy and Steve while he was at it.

"Uh, Glen, while I have you on the line—there is something I should tell you."

I didn't like the sound of this.

"What," I said.

"Most of our clients are very old, in their 80s, even 90s in some cases..."

There was a pause. "Yes?"

"In your case, you're not nearly that old and we found a donor in his thirties with a remarkable resemblance. The new Glen looks a lot like you. After we reshaped his face, the effect is eerie. We were going to surprise you with a nearly identical version, only thirty years younger."

Oh, shit.

"He looks like me?"

"Very much so."

No wonder the clinic staff avoided me.

"Great. What else should I know?"

"He was originally from Rio, so he might be drawn that way. The old memories are mostly subconscious—we can't completely wipe them out. His main motivational drivers will be yours. For example, if you have vivid memories of someone doing you wrong, that might be something that influences his behavior. The desire for revenge can be very powerful."

Enemies? Where do I start the list?

"Any physical weaknesses?"

"In grade school, he was a fútbol player until a knee injury

took him down. He didn't come back one-hundred-percent after a year of physical therapy—this fed a downward spiral. It's a typical story; he was addicted to painkillers which led to a heroin addiction we had to deal with. He's off the black horse and the knee is mostly fine now, but if you get a chance, kick him in his right one. I don't mean to imply he's broken. Compared to normal, he's fast and strong and in great shape. He spent time working as a soldier for a Rio cartel, but we don't know much about those years of his life."

"Send me pictures of what he used to look like—there might be pull in that direction, or the opposite. Give me a phys-des I can visualize until I can check my email."

"I'm looking at a picture. Handsome, a lady killer."

"That goes without saying if he looks like me."

"Are you going to shut up and let me talk?"

"Go."

"Dark, glossy hair, almost black. Bangs. Close-cropped beard. Diamond earring. Hard partier. Ferrari. Had a taste for coke when he could afford it. Nasty temper when he was doing well and after the injury, it got worse. A two-year sentence for beating the snot out of a policia officer—we pulled him out of prison. The initial psych report said he was manic depressive and should be on a suicide watch. The money we paid went to a couple of estranged kids by three mothers. What else can I tell you?"

"How far along was he in conversion?"

"Almost ready. Eighty-five percent, maybe more. Strong personalities take extra time and effort."

"Okay, I think I have it. Call me if anything else comes to mind. Oh, and Walter, you are truly a world class asshole."

"Coming from you…"

I'd heard enough.

I disconnected the call.

Glen Wilson—Segundo

HE MOVED SLOWLY and smoothly like a contented house cat and tried to emit a quiet, comfortable strength that would tempt Rosa to take him home where she could love and pamper him—where he would comfort and protect her from the harsh realities of the cold world. Her eyes lingered on him and she flicked them to the dish of tapioca pudding on the tray held in front of her.

What does that mean? Did he imagine the glance?

He was trapped. Was any hope an illusion? He smiled while waiting for the guard to remove the chains. Everyone cleared the room and the chains were released. He ate slowly. Again with the extra carrots. He didn't care for them, but he pretended they were delicious and radiated love for them and anyone who would give him such a lovely treat. He loved them more than anyone or anything in the world.

In the pudding was a metal key and something small wrapped in plastic. The key was an odd shape, but he didn't study it—he spooned it up and raised it to his mouth, holding it in his left cheek and subtly exploring it with his tongue. Then, after spooning up the plastic bundle, he moved it with his tongue to his other cheek. At the bottom of the bowl, there was writing on a scrap of paper. Without blatantly looking, he scraped it clean and read it as he used the spoon to get the last blotches of congealed tapioca goo.

Wait until the power fails.

After a few more minutes, the spoon, the bowls, the note and the tray dissolved into water, then the water evaporated, but not the key and plastic bundle which remained cold and solid in his mouth—as solid as the hope coalescing in his gut.

On his bunk, he turned so the security cameras could not see what he was doing and unwrapped the bundle.

Bendix King SD memory chip card. He didn't know anything about electronics.

What is it? What did you do with a card like this?

Plug it into a phone? A camera?

He slipped the memory card into his shoe.

When the power failed, which it did every couple of weeks, the lights flickered while the batteries took over the emergency loads and again after the backup generator spooled up and took over.

His mind raced.

Was the security system vulnerable when running on batteries? If so, that was a bad system design, but what other conclusion could he draw? How did Rosa know this? Was she right? The transfer to full power function took about forty-five seconds while the motor started and the generator rotors spooled up to speed. He knew the generators were diesel-powered because he could smell the vapor and hear their characteristic rumble.

He guessed the strange mechanical key would only work when the emergency power was on. That didn't give him much time—barefoot he could run through the hallways, slip out a door and run for the nearest fence. Would Rosa be waiting with a vehicle so they could race away into the night and be passionate lovers for the rest of their lives?

His mouth curled into a smile.

No, not while there were accounts to be settled. You don't trap Glen Wilson like a rat in a cage without consequences.

The waiting was additional, delicious torture. His mind worked through all the permutations and possibilities he could conceive. Through the fractured mirror-glass, he studied what he could see of the hallway and settled on a plan.

Would it work?

He was eager to find out. A day passed. Then two. All the time he appeared super-casual—as if he had all the time in the world, but inside, his thoughts over-boiled. Mentally he was on tip-toes waiting to spring into action. Finally, on the third day—several hours after the evening meal—the lights flickered.

In a second he was at the door. He inserted the key. It didn't turn, but the red light turned green and he hauled on the handle. As if there was residual magnetic flux, the door would not move and his heart sank. With desperate energy, he pulled harder and the door eased open. One plan was to just go—run for the nearest exit and hightail it to freedom outside the compound.

He grinned.

No.

In the hallway, there was a utility closet. There was no time, but Glen needed something. In the closet, he found a claw hammer. That would do.

He looked in the security ports for the adjoining rooms. To hell with the women, they could rot in their cells, but the men, they could be useful. He pulled open a door. The man inside looked vaguely familiar.

Movie star?

He handed the man the hammer.

"On the way out, smash all the security cameras," Glen said. "We have about thirty seconds."

The quick-witted man nodded, then wasted no time—he ran down the corridor stopping every few seconds to smash ceiling-mounted cameras with uncontrolled glee. As Glen worked at another lock, a security guard rounded the far corner. Quickly, he too was smashed with the hammer. The escapee worked the pistol from the guard's holster. Glen made eye-contact and sent the message with everything he had.

Go forth and foment mayhem.

The man nodded. Message received.

Glen shoved a mop into the hands of the next freed inmate. He pointed the opposite direction down the corridor.

"See if you can kill a guard with this," he said. "Get his gun if you can. Disable all the security cameras you see."

The man nodded. He ran down the hallway.

Glen worked the little key to release a third man.

"Help me with the others," Glen said. "Tell them to destroy the security cameras—as many as they can."

They ran down the hallway where Glen worked the locks and moved on while his new assistant released inmates. His assistant was working on the fifth door when the lights flickered again. Glen tapped his shoulder.

"Forget it," he said. "The key only works while we're on battery power. Run for it."

The man did not hesitate. He sprinted down the corridor.

They expect me to run.

"No, not yet," he muttered to himself.

For some reason, he felt no particular need to hurry. He heard gun shots from two directions and that made him smile. With cheer in his heart he walked toward the fallen body of the first guard. Though there was a nasty indentation on the front of his head, the man still breathed, though labored as if he was choking. Shoeless Glen was dressed in paper-thin garments. This would not do. The guard was smaller in stature, but his clothes were baggy.

They were certainly better than wearing paper.

On his belt, there was one big key. A master key.

Glen grinned and stripped the man naked. A clasp knife fell out of the man's boot. Glen opened it and admired the blade's razor edge. A lot of care had been taken in sharpening it. Glen pulled on the man's underwear, they were still warm. His t-shirt smelled musky and rank. Glen pulled on the boots—they too were snug, but would do.

He almost forgot the chip card, but fished it out of the shoe and buttoned it into his new shirt pocket.

Standing, Glen looked down on the guard. He would have an ugly scar and perhaps brain damage. It would be unfair and cruel to leave him in such a pathetic state. Glen leaned over and stroked the man's neck on either side with the knife's blade. Initially, blood spurted vigorously, but only for a few seconds until the flow died to a trickle. Glen watched the man die. He thought he should feel something, but he didn't. This was a better outcome for the man—dying peacefully and avoiding the unpleasantness of a damaged life.

You're welcome.

Why did he feel like he had all the time in the world? He strolled through the hallways as if he was master of the place. He tried the door of the electrical room. It was unlocked. Inside, there were several huge breaker-switches—he hauled on them and shut the place down, then followed the corridors toward the sound of the generators. He shut them down too. Just inside, there was a small 2KW Honda generator, an air compressor and a hose. In the gym, there was a shower with an adjustable-flow shower head.

He smiled.

Now all he needed was a large enclosed area which he found under a metal utility plate. It was like divine providence wanted to make sure he had everything he needed close at hand. Cheerfully, he set to work making the facility into massive fuel-air bomb.

From a box of wooden matches and duct tape, he fashioned an igniter at the bottom of the generator room door. When the door was pushed open, the matches would strike and if all went well?

Kaboom.

The hallways were dark. Back in the inmate's hallway, he peered into a cell. There was a contorted face pressed against it. Glen smiled and held up the big key.

He mouthed the words.

Want out?

Yes, the woman replied by vigorously nodding.

Glen pantomimed turning the key and pointing up and down the hallway.

You'll help the others?

He didn't care about them, but they would increase the chaos and confusion.

Yes, she nodded.

He let her out, then he explored the hallways going the other direction. There was a small dining room; the coffee was still hot. He helped himself. A shadowy figure stood up. Glen turned. It was Rosa. Glen smiled and gestured for her to join him. Slowly, like a robot, she came forward.

When she was close enough, Glen reached out and slowly cut her throat—she collapsed on the floor like a bundle of rags.

Stupid girl.

From the buffet table, Glen found bacon, bread and a stainless steel bowl of steaming scrambled eggs. He assembled a hearty breakfast. He felt invincible, but why? He did not know.

With a full belly and no heed for the massive bomb which would explode at any second, he strolled the hallways one last time. Off the surgery, there was another room—a small one he missed on his earlier scan. It had a wire-mesh window about twelve inches square. Peeking in, a ghastly face drifted into view.

The face was a horror-show of wrapped gauze painted with surgical lines of crimson blood. This man looked like the human equivalent of one of Eddie Van Halen's spray-painted guitars. Glen assumed the character was a man. He was at least six-feet-tall and husky.

This must be a recovery room. Clearly, this man had major reconstructive surgery...they hacked up his face real good.

Patchface.

Glen grinned. Hideously, Patchface grinned back and, nodding vigorously, pointed at the door's lock.

Glen could not imagine a more perfect agent of mayhem. If

released, this quilted monster would forever haunt the dreams of children he encountered. Still, his first impulse was to leave the creature trapped—to be blown to pieces when the clinic exploded.

Why?

He did not know.

While walking away, he heard the man's muffled voice.

"Don't be a chopsy, I'm absolutely hanging this morning, boyo."

Thinking about the accent, Glen turned back to the window.

"Welsh?" he said.

The man nodded.

"I hate the Welsh," Glen said.

He turned to walk away.

"You know your onions, Mate, I can be toff if that's more your ace."

It was a perfect, upscale, London accent.

Glen laughed and turned back yet again.

With the bloody knife, he pointed at himself, then one direction down the hallway, then at Patchface and the other direction. He held the knife up to the glass.

The message was clear, they would go opposite ways.

Or I'll cut you.

Patchface nodded with enthusiasm. While Glen watched, more blood soaked into the gauze. Smiling, he turned the door's handle, then stood back with the knife ready. The man walked out, nodded once to Glen, then walked off the other way.

Good.

Continuing his exploration, he wandered and found a garage. In the garage was a tiny four-wheel-drive Mitsubishi pickup. The keys were not in it, but they hung nearby on a nail. He tugged the garage door's quick release latch and hauled it open. The truck started instantly.

Outside, it was dreary and rainy and the air smelled of rot-

musk and decay. He engaged the four-wheel-drive and eased the truck onto a mud and gravel track. He was about 150 yards away when the facility erupted. Immediately, the truck was battered with debris, including a chunk of concrete that burst throughout the rear window, bounced off the dashboard and plopped on the seat beside him. That was okay. What was not okay was his arm hanging out of the driver's side window. A chunk of jagged metal grazed it and opened a deep, six-inch-long gash.

Shit, that was unnecessary.

After a few seconds, it felt like his arm was on fire. Then he noticed it was. Calmly, he let the truck steer itself for a few seconds while he batted at the weak flame. The truck teetered on the edge of a chasm where hungry brown water cascaded and surged. He fought with the wheel and managed to stay on the track, but there were a few seconds where things were dodgy—he could have easily gone over. The truck would then be on its roof and he'd be trapped in deep, swirling water. To die that way after what he'd been through would be ironic.

His mouth twisted into a smile.

Not today.

He punched the accelerator and the knobby all-terrain tires clawed the earth. The pickup slewed back onto the muddy trail.

Where was he going?

No map. No GPS.

He did not know. It didn't matter.

Away from here.

Anywhere.

He drove for several hours while blisters on his arm swelled and the blood coagulated. He staunched the flow with the security guard's rank t-shirt, but at some point, he'd need medical attention. Cleanup. Stitches. Salve. He felt light-headed from the pain and the blood loss.

With the front wheels over the apron, he stopped at a bridge over a cleft, then got out to look at it. He must have taken a wrong turn because this bridge could not be on the right path—it was made with rotted logs and crumbling concrete and looked like it would fall any moment under its own weight. Surely the truck's weight would be too much.

Fifty yards below, dirty water churned over a ten-foot waterfall-ledge. It was a bleak sight in the torrential rain.

Glen was startled by a figure who emerged from the lanky trees. Logger? The man wore a vivid yellow slicker—his brown eyes peered from under the dripping hood. He carried an odd implement with a sharp, curved blade like a half-moon on a thick, long-handled shaft. The man made a driving gesture and pointed across the chasm.

Right, pal. Better you than me.

Glen gestured in return.

You do it.

The man shrugged, tossed his tool in the bed of the truck, then worked himself behind the wheel. His teeth were brown and gappy—his smile was a memorable one. As he eased away, Glen grabbed the tool from the truck bed.

Would the man wait on the other side?

No way.

Halfway across, the left side of the bridge lurched. The man braked, then got out to have a look. A hundred-pound hunk of concrete dislodged and floated down to the raging river. The man turned, shrugged his shoulders and grinned. He stood for a moment at the open door—thinking—then gave up on the truck. Shuffling his feet, he sidled backwards.

The middle of the bridge sagged and the truck slid forward over the edge. For an instant, it floated on the water, then disappeared.

The man turned and briskly walked back. Glen waited until he was near, then embedded the blade of the man's tool in his chest, then kicked him over the edge.

Idiot.

He turned. Follow the road or try to find the track of the

logger through the rain forest?

You'll never get anywhere if you follow the path of morons.

Road.

Glen glanced at his blood dripping from under the sleeve of his jacket. His arm was in bad shape. How long could he survive without medical attention? A day? Half?

He trudged through the gloom of falling night to see if he could find where he'd taken a wrong turn. He made it a mile before falling first to his knees, then face-first into the mud.

He woke with the blinding sun in his eyes. Lifting his head, he saw a clot of cows grazing while steam drifted in coils from a field. He was on a two-wheeled cart being slowly pulled down a muddy track by a blinkered dray horse. The horse was driven by a young, brown-skinned boy with a switch he flicked when the horse showed interest in stopping for a mouthful of tasty crabgrass. The boy wore sandals, cut-off jeans, a Pittsburgh Pirates t-shirt and a 76'ers flat-billed gang-cap.

Sports fan.

Glen was so weak, he could barely sit up. He grasped the edges of the cart and lifted himself as if peering over the edge of a life raft. The cart was filled with hairy, stinky bean pods stuck to his clothes and skin—he picked them off and flicked them aside like vermin. Whatever they were, he didn't like them. He fell back into the crop in a faint, so he didn't know how long the journey was.

Trapped like a bug in a spiderweb, he woke with his arm on fire—he opened his mouth to scream, but a filthy rag was stuffed in it and his head was held down. Back into the void he went.

He woke again and looked at a low ceiling. The air smelled smoky and he could hear rain beating on the tin roof. A leak dripped into a clay pot. In the corner, heat radiated from a barrel-stove. He lifted his arm. It was covered with clean, white gauze. The logger's tool leaned against the wall in the corner.

An old woman smoking a pipe rocked in a chair. She watched him from under hooded eyes. His feet were strapped to the kitchen table with blankets and tie-down straps. He could move his head and arms, but was going nowhere. The woman got up and leaned over a black pot of burble on the stove—she stirred it with a long wooden spoon that looked like a camp shovel. With a ladle, she spooned gruel into a bowl and set the bowl aside to cool.

She rolled up a blanket and used it to prop up his head. He reached out to grab her arm—he held it with as much strength as he could muster. She nodded downward and he noticed her other hand. It held a long, curved blade like a sickle. With a stroke, she could take off his hand.

He let her go and held up his hands in supplication. The blade went back into a woven belt around her waist. Propped up, he was able to eat the hot soup she raised to his lips. It was saltier and spicier than he liked, though there was a part of him that recognized it and like it. The name drifted into his mind.

Moqueca.

Once he'd had enough, she pulled the bundle from under his head and he fell back into deep, black sleep.

People came and went—he didn't know how long he was there. They swathed him in a diaper—it was embarrassing, but he was going nowhere and there was nothing he could do. The old woman changed his diaper like he was a baby and cleaned his penis and ass with a damp cloth. He could have grabbed the blade from her belt, but there was always someone else nearby with some kind of weapon at hand—a club, an axe or a gun; it was as if they didn't trust him.

Why would that be? They didn't know him.

The bandage on his arm was changed daily with gauze soaked in something pungent and astringent. He didn't know what it was, but the pink edges of his wound closed up and his arm healed. It itched something terrible, but he ignored it.

In the evenings after more soup, they gave him a thick, dark liquid that helped him sleep. It grew to where he craved it and slurped up all he could get when it was offered. What was in this potion? Some kind of opiate, obviously. It troubled him that his body craved it so much, but still, after dinner, he counted the seconds to the next dose.

One morning when he woke, an old woman painted something foul on his cheeks and brushed him with a bundle of colorful feathers—as if dusting evil from him. He couldn't move, not even an inch, and she was lucky because if he could, he'd twist her wrinkled head clean off her slumped shoulders.

These people didn't trust him.

Was that a nasty prejudice against all foreign interlopers or was it just him?

They were right to keep him restrained because he spent much of his waking hours thinking of the proper and most efficient ways of killing each and every one of them. Not to maximize the pain or anything like that, but to efficiently dispatch them with the least effort and the least risk to anything going wrong. It would be ironic if they killed him while he was in the process of killing them.

This was not personal. He'd kill anyone who inconvenienced him. He had the vague thought that this was wrong, but he didn't feel anything. They were inconsequential.

While he was lashed down, he had plenty of time to think.

Where was he going? What would he do when he got there?

It amused him that they tried to drive the evil spirit from his body. If they wanted to do something useful, they should try to drive a good spirit in. It wasn't what was *in* him that was the problem, it was what was *missing*—empathy, compassion and love for his fellow mankind.

Finally, his release day came. They took no chances—there were seven inside the hut and another twenty or so outside. The seven were all armed, including a young man with a small bow made of black wood. The arrow was notched and ready to fly. There was a stain on the arrowhead—with the right kind of Amazonian poison, even a scratch could be fatal.

The old woman held the logger's tool he'd been carrying. The rest of their weapons were a motley assortment of old axes, knives and a hammer with a head made from an oblong rock. His bindings were loosened and he was allowed to remove them. Once he was standing on weak knees, he crouched and stretched.

It took a long time before he felt stable enough to walk. He put on the clothes he arrived in and laced up the boots. He reached for the bladed tool, but they were having none of that—the old woman gestured with it. If he took a step closer, she was going to jam it into his chest.

Okay, I get it.

They'd assembled a pack for him, a bundle wrapped in filthy canvas with a length of rope for a shoulder strap. Clenching and unclenching his fists, he looked all the natives in the eye slowly, one-by-one. He owed them for taking care of him, but if he ever came this way again, he'd kill them all.

What were the chances he'd ever be here again?

Zero.

After slinging the pack on his shoulder, he stood outside the hut blinking in the sunlight. The village was in a clearing with tall trees leaning over and crowded around. For no reason, he started walking toward the sun, but a teenaged boy pointed a spear in an alternate direction. The boy made a gesture.

Keep the afternoon sun to your left.

Glen turned. They opened a space in the circle and he walked toward it. Outside the circle was a path.

Glen took it.

Within minutes was alone with the chattering birds and monkeys.

He didn't look back.

Glen Wilson—Primeiro—Rio Branco

ON THE SECOND day of drifting on the river, I saw a stretch of paved highway and a rickety wooden dock. I stood out in the rain and pointed.

"Señor," I said. "What's that?"

The captain looked up from the tiller.

"Landing," he said.

"Does the bus stop there?"

"Sim," he said. Yes.

I gestured. "Let me off here."

He cocked his head and looked at me as if I was loco.

"Yes, I'm sure." I grilled the captain. "Where does the bus go?"

"Depends on the which way. Porto Vehlo, probably.

"What about the other way?"

The captain shrugs. "Rio Branco."

"Is there an airport in Rio Branco? Bus station? Train station?"

"Yes."

The fake Glen would have money from the crew of the boat that picked him up. The fucker was on a bus to Rio Branco.

I knew it.

The bus stop was a muddy fringe where the bus could get halfway off the highway. There were people waiting to go the other way, but I was alone waiting on the other side. I was covered by my dripping, yellow parka and it was not cold, but every part of me felt damp. I could feel the fungus growing between my toes and planning a full offensive on the rest of my body. There were scattered trucks and tour buses headed my direction—I poked out my thumb to see if anyone would stop. I wouldn't, but someone might. As it turns out, a silver Range Rover caked with mud stopped a hundred yards away and stayed there with its hazard lights blink-blink-blinking in the rain. Was it stopped for me? I wasn't sure, but it was worth a try, I had no idea whether to expect the bus today, tomorrow or the next.

Remember, mañana does not mean tomorrow, it means not today. I humped my pack and ran up the highway.

The driver was a Brit, Suzy Hutchson, a pretty girl in a wholesome, save-the-Earth, no-makeup way in her mid-thirties. She had massive thighs—which look terrible in jeans but are great for the double-backed procreation dance—and vivid black eyebrows, streaks of gray in her auburn hair and really large breasts—I'm talking about prodigious, juicy melons under a WWF t-shirt.

They were so bountiful that I actually paid attention for a while as she started her World Wildlife Federation rap about Chico Mendez (the Gandhi of the Amazon) and how the toreros (wildcat loggers) were destroying the important, irreplaceable diversity of the virgin rain forests and how important it was to support the native Surui primitives and riberinhos (riverside dwellers) against the relentless encroachment of modern society. In her opinion, anyone that would trade a tree for a McDonalds hamburger patty should have a Candiru catfish swim up their bum and open its famous gill-spines.

I did not completely disagree with this sentiment. However, I have a low tolerance for posh activists in Range Rovers flying halfway around the world on commercial airliners to save people from themselves. Shouldn't she stay home in jolly olde England and save the starving indigenous teds, suedeheads and mods? I'm all for voluntary associations and self-funded activism, but she was supported on her noble mission by taxes levied from the

Beeb and contributions from the near-monopoly Sky Television.

The way the world halfway works is truly a natural wonder.

I don't care how rare the purple Amazonian tarantulas are. If one touches me, it's going to get squished into goo—I'm admittedly prejudiced and intolerant of spiders: giant, rarefied or otherwise.

I tried to engage her in a conversational exchange but she wasn't leaving many gaps to fill, so I tuned her out and slept while watching the endless miles of green forest stream by, sweeping curve after sweeping curve.

She drove like a terror, gunning the V-8 and passing the other traffic: slow-motion semi trucks bearing shipping containers, Porsche SUVs with kayaks strapped to their roofs and VW buses bearing grinning, bearded, high-on-life hippy-freaks. I began liking her a bit more when she threw a reusable, ecologically conscious container of homemade gorp on my lap. It had dried blueberries, squares of dried mango, mulberries, raisins, cashews, granola clumps, cranberries, almonds, pumpkin seeds and in what seemed to me a horrible cliché, Brazil nuts.

I liked her even more when she pointed to a cooler in the back and made the drinking motion. In the cooler were ice-cold bottles of Brahma beer. I popped the top and handed her one, then opened one for myself. After the first heaven-sent sip, I asked her to marry me, but she pretended not to hear.

After an hour, her sales pitch petered out and it finally occurred to her to ask…

"What exactly are you doing out here, Wilson?"

Hmmm, how to answer? I could tell her I'm on a contract for Archers-Daniels-Midland or Monsanto and get dropped off here in the middle of nowhere. I couldn't tell her I'm tracking a psychopathic version on myself that has killed approximately 80 and will kill a lot more if I don't stop him. Is there anything worse in her mind than working for Monsanto?

"I'm scouting for locations for a possible Mel Gibson film about the plight of the Amazonian Indians."

Weighing the moral balance between the juxtaposition of evil, anti-Semitic, wife-abusing Mel with the merit of promoting the native Amazonians kept her processing and silent for a while. When she seemed about ready to declare judgment and speak, I added, "it's a sensitive love story—a Romeo and Juliet romance between an alien warrior from Mars and a beautiful Amazonian princess. We're leaning toward Dwayne Johnson for the Martian and Katie Perry for the princess. What do you think?"

That kept her silent until we reached the outskirts of Rio Branco. She stopped to fuel up at a Petrobras station and when I came out of the toilet after a lengthy session on the throne, my backpack was on the concrete apron covered with my yellow parka—and she was gone. I settled the backpack on my shoulders and hiked toward the city center.

I had built an image of Rio Branco in my head: a river village connected only to the outside world with a small airstrip, but the reality was more modern and sophisticated. Of course, it was intimately connected to the muddy river, Rios do Acre, a tributary of the mighty Amazon, Rios do Amazonas.

Take a piss anywhere in central South America and it will likely end up in the Amazon.

With the backpack weighing heavily on me, I strolled along the brick walkway and stopped for a few minutes to watch brown-skinned kids leap from a bridge into the mucky water.

My mood was hard to decipher. What was wrong with this little city? I could find myself a deaf Ka'apor bride, learn her sign language, open a tattoo parlor and spend the rest of my life raising parrots to be smuggled into the USA. There are many ways to live and who is to say one lifestyle is better or worse than another? I could see me smashing the satellite phone and dropping out. Who needs the complexity and hassle of modern life?

These thoughts disappeared when I saw the Cafe do Teatro and smelled the aromatic coffee. I ordered a triple Bourbon Santos espresso and a horseshoe shaped pastry called

Ferraduras—instantly, all was well in the world.

I had a decision to make—I needed to change my appearance to look as different as possible from GW2. Which way would he go with his disguise? Would he be instinctually drawn back to looking as he was or would he go the opposite direction? That's a decision he'd probably struggle with too.

I walked by a literal hole-in-the-wall cranny with an old adjustable chair. Dentist or barber? It didn't matter. If he was a dentist, I'd replace an implant with a gold tooth—that would draw attention and help with my disguise. If it was a barber—I made a snap decision—I'd have him shave my head.

José was a barber. He pressed me into the chair and asked me twice to be sure. Si, cabeca raspada. Take it all off. Two days ago, did I think I'd have a Camponesas running an ivory-handled razor over my head so I'd intentionally look like a prison camp escapee?

Life can throw weird twists your way.

He handed me a hundred-year-old mirror so I could admire his handiwork. My beard was an itchy stubble, but I told him to leave it. My white head needed some sun to blend with my face, but good luck with that in the rain forest. Outside, the rain was steadily intermittent which might not make sense unless you've been there to experience its dripping glory. Anyway, the point was to look like someone different and José earned a big tip because he did his job well—I looked like a doomed cancer patient.

As a new man, I carried on walking toward the central plaza. The city was typical of South America with metal beer signs, sidewalks warped by ficus roots, squatting vendors, chugging diesel buses, charming multi-colored, pastel-painted houses, the cheerful vibrancy of the bustling street culture and the irresistible optimism of having children around to make ugly faces at, but for all of the positive traits of these great people—and they are many—picking up trash was not one. The place was filthy with discarded plastic bottles, food wrappers, broken glass and cigarette butts.

The architecture was the usual mix of shanties, Catholic churches and crumbling old buildings side-by-side with modern glass-faced office buildings and refurbished colonial style mansions. In the Centro, there was a sales pitch every three feet including a persistent, black-skinned young man who was sure I'd like my picture taken with a huge copper-and-black rainbow boa snake for a just a few reals, señor.

No, obrigado. No-no-no.

I checked into the Inacio Palace Hotel. I shouldn't complain, but this was no palace, not that there were a plethora of options in Rio Blanco. I was desperate for a shower and a place to sleep. In the middle of the night, in a dream, I figured out where he was going. I was sure. While I was not mistreated at the La Paz prison, the experience left a sour taste in my mouth—there was a score to settle. That's where he-I would go.

In the morning, I had a vague sense of epiphany, but it was fleeting, like life itself. Did I have a breakthrough thought about finding my alter ego? If so, it was gone—I felt empty-headed and clueless.

What would I do if I was me? I didn't want to go anywhere.

I felt paralyzed.

And hungry.

Downstairs, the breakfast buffet was a wonder with flan, rows of sliced pineapple and melon, fresh hard-rolls, cheese and jet-black coffee from a tarnished silver urn. It was there I stopped first, pouring a cup and dropping in sugar cubes and pouring clotty cream. It was so beautiful, I made a vow not to complain about anything all day. A vow I violated almost instantly, of course, while waving away a cloud of annoying fruit flies.

I picked up a newspaper, Cruzeiro do Sul, and tried to make sense of it. A teenager in starched jeans, a yellow Team Brazil Ordem e Progresso t-shirt and putrid Michael Jordan shoes that looked like someone had vomited up fruit salad on them walked through the room with a spider monkey on his shoulder. He made a motion like taking a picture.

I damned well did not want my picture with a filthy macaco aranha, so I waved him away.

He was persistent.

"Maconha bomba, Bob Marley do diablo, senõr? Prostituta? Virgem meretriz? Poeira?"

He worked his index finger in the circle of his other hand, the international symbol for love in a peaceful world. His monkey reached over and took two pieces of my pineapple. One went into his own mouth, the other he fed to the teenager. If you have a monkey, you need never go hungry.

"I don't want to meet your irmã."

At the mention of his sister, he stopped chewing and looked for a reason to be offended. I waved my hand and handed him the newspaper.

I don't know why I do some things. I made the sign of the cross on my chest.

"Christo Rei." Christ the King...

The boy looked at me for a moment before a light went on in his head. His face erupted into a full grin.

I raised my hand before he could say it.

"No niños," I said. "No."

Now he was really confused.

The security guard, leaning back in a chair against the wall, sleeping, woke and adjusted his hat. He noticed the teenager bothering me and started to rise, but I waved him away.

"Relaxar," I said to the teenager. I patted him on the shoulder. "Just tell me if there were any murders last night. Assassinato."

After studying my face for a moment more, he looked at the paper as if it was a dead rat until I pulled a fifty-real banknote from the front pocket of my trousers. That captured his attention. After examining it carefully, he stuffed it away and shrugged. He shuffled through the pages.

"Transito acidente?" he said.

"No. Murder, not a traffic accident. Do you speak English?"

He shrugged his shoulders. The English literacy rate in rural Brazil was 3%, so it was unlikely. He folded the paper and pushed it across the table.

"Nada," he said.

Whether that was the number of murders or his English fluency, it didn't matter. I waved him away and returned my attention to my coffee. He seemed mystified and stood there thinking. Surely I must want something. I focused on my coffee until he wandered away.

Almost instantly, a black wave of melancholy washed over me. Sometimes this happened. I could not move. I was stuck. I was certain the alternate me would come this way, but I was wrong. Dead wrong. I was used to being wrong, it was not something that troubled me. Would you rather do a hundred things and get sixty right or do ten things perfectly? Everyone has their own path to tread.

Now what?

If I could just move a finger, I could break the spell of depression, but I could not do it. I wondered if this was it. Here I'd sit until it was time to bury my sorry soul. Rio Branco, Brazil, who would have guessed this would be where I took my last breath? I had a premonition. This was not it for me, I would die someplace much colder—where the air was thin. Space—hovering above a spherical Earth like an astronaut.

It was a stupid vision, there was no way I would ever strap myself to a rocket and launch myself into space.

I reflected on my life—growing up poor in Eagle Point, Oregon. Playing poker in Saigon. My life on the alpaca ranchero with Linda. Smuggling cocaine and playing cat-and-mouse with the DEA and the Nazis. Running for Congress. Trapped in a mental hospital in North Dakota. Dealing with the bums in Seattle. Acting as security agent for a rock star. Being poor. Being rich. Chasing immortality.

All those adventures ending here in a lost corner of South

America.

If I could pick up my coffee cup for a sip, that might break the curse, but I knew, as long as I was thinking of moving, I would not be able to.

The sad realization came to me.

I would never achieve success with this mission on my own. I was better with my team, my glorious, dysfunctional, ragtag group of supporters—my friends. Bennie and Emma. Murphy and Elke. Steve. Walter. And Gerusha, beautiful Gerusha. If I had a heart, it would ache for her. The tick-tock machine in my chest pained me—as if it was on fire.

And, what exactly was this mission? When I saw the smoking ruins of the Immortality clinic and the bodies, I knew there was only one way to stop a renegade Glen—he had to be killed, and by me. But, to find him and get to him, face-to-face, I would need help. The team might not like me much, but when I needed them, they would be there.

How did I know this? It simply was. They would complain and insult me and pretend to not care, but when it came to it, they would be there for me—I was as certain of that as I could be of anything in life. If I could move, I could call Murphy and get her working her network.

What was I going to do now that my instincts had proven themselves wrong? My problem was obvious. If the alternate Glen was like me, his actions would be unpredictable. That's the way I was, taking advantage of every random opportunity that came my way. Was my mission doomed? Would he find a quiet corner of the world and disappear?

I realized I was sipping. The coffee was good and was an excellent reminder of the simple joys of life. The little things. A compliant woman. Good health. Fine coffee. Nearly a billion dollars in the bank.

There was no way the alternate Glen would fade into the woodwork—he would want to make a mark, or at least settle a grudge with his enemies.

Our enemies?

Perhaps my black depression was a sign from the universe—should I sit here in a remote corner of Amazonia and wait for him to surface?

No, sitting and waiting was not my style, I would move, but to where? I remembered something Walter said. The donor was from the shantytown of Rio. Like a homing pigeon, would he go there? The idea felt right. I was unfrozen, I knew where to go next. I would make some calls—I would set the Glen Wilson machine in motion.

But first, a drink.

Glen Wilson—Secundo

GENERALLY KEEPING THE sun on his left, he walked on the game trail until his legs gave out. There was a patch of bright sunlight ahead and it piqued his curiosity, but he could not take another step. His arm was throbbing.

He found a pile of leaves and leaned against a deadfall tree. It started to rain harder. Warm drops dribbled through the overhead canopy. He pulled the canvas bundle open and rooted through the contents. Inside, there was a patched nylon poncho—a hideous fluorescent yellow. He pulled it over his head. He also found a greasy baseball hat, emerald green with a proud yellow 'Brazil' emblazed across the crown. He pulled it on.

He didn't feel alone. On the bottom of a fern frond, he watched a round beetle crawl; its shell was black with red and yellow bands. It didn't look dangerous; he wondered how many deadly things were nearby. The air was foggy and the dripping rain rattled the greenery.

He looked around, taking it all in.

A tree had a green skirt of hula vines hanging around its base—its roots made it look like it was walking. He watched a brick-red spider with long legs on the prowl, its body looked like it was attached upside down. The spider stirred something in his gut. He didn't like it.

Another spider—crawling on spiky legs on a web protected by a large leaf—looked like it had a Catholic cross on its back. The living forest was not a scene he was used to, his mind was filled with images of crowded streets and ill-intentioned people lurking in alleys. He craved *esfiha*: breadroll stuffed with escarole greens and Minas cheese, so hot you could not hold it in your hand.

His mouth flooded with saliva.

He rooted around in the bundle. He found a gourd filled with milky fluid. After pulling out a wooden plug, he sipped it—it tasted foul, but he would not waste it. He took a bigger sip and replugged the gourd. He fished around more and found twists of dried meat.

Lizard?

He wasn't going to over-think it. Protein is protein. He took a mouthful of the salty meat and slowly chewed. It was disgusting, but might keep him alive. From the direction of the brightness, there were sounds—mechanical sounds. Machines, big ones. He put his hands down to lift himself and spotted a huge ant—nearly as big as a finger. Its massive jaws worked in his direction while its antennae vibrated.

This is a bad place.

With a stick, he flicked the monster away. Exhausted or not, he needed to keep going. If he stayed here, the bugs would eat his flesh and leave nothing but bones. He brushed leaves from the bundle, reslung it across his shoulder and walked toward the sounds of the machinery.

The light grew brighter and he found himself in a clearing where raw red dirt was being molested and chewed. A logging team, guarded by a fat man in a cowboy hat holding a lever-action rifle, worked at pulling down the tall trees. Trying not to look threatening, he picked his way carefully along the forest's edge. A tractor dragged a tree with a cable while men with chainsaws set on its limbs like ravenous beasts.

The open area was a wasteland—it went on as far as he could see. Skirting the workers in intermittent rain, he walked all afternoon. Along the muddy road, he tried to flag down a ramshackle logging truck, but it would not stop.

Ahead, as the truck slowed for a washout filled with rapidly running brown water, he simply hopped on the passenger-side running board. The driver scowled and waved him away, but didn't do anything when Glen refused to jump off. The fractured window was up, the rusty door was locked and the juddering truck did not appear to have springs or shock absorbers. The only way he could hang on was by hooking his arm through the mirror. It was faster than walking, but with the slow passage along the rutted road, only barely. As the truck swayed, the logs, retained by flimsy steel cables, shifted and groaned.

Through the window, the passenger seat held only the driver's lunch—a crusty *bauru* sandwich resplendent with tomatoes, lettuce and thick slices of ham. This stirred something in Glen, a feeling of discontent. It was unfair, he could be riding in comfort and the sandwich was plenty large enough to share. From street vendors, he'd eaten hundreds of sandwiches like this. But, the driver ignored him and would not unlock the door.

The roadway improved; it was still rutted and rough, but more and more covered with crushed gravel. The truck's speed slowly increased—on straight-aways, the wind tugged at his clothes and canvas bundle and threatened to dislodge him. Glen held on tightly and looked at the sandwich. It seemed to symbolize everything wrong in his life. Some people had more than enough, while others struggled to hang on to nothing. It ate at his gut.

The driver peered through the windshield and geared down. Glen looked ahead. At a bend, a chain had been raised and a group of men stood defiantly brandishing a banner.

PARE! STOP!

The driver slowed until the truck lurched to a standstill with the diesel engine clattering—he peered through the dirty windshield to study the scene, then reached under the seat to pull out a sawed-off shotgun which he rested on the window—pointing sideways.

One of the protesters wore a head piece with red and blue

plastic feathers and a leather patch hanging from a string over the front of his blue jeans, he was a half-assed, fake Amazonian native. The others were more honest. They wore sports jerseys, baseball hats and skateboard shorts. They were not serious, just local punks practicing amateur extortion.

With the truck stopped, Glen jumped off and waved at the protesters as he walked around the front of the truck to the driver's side. Was the driver smart enough to keep his door locked?

He wasn't.

The driver had a chance to shoot him, but hesitated. Glen didn't, he pulled the shotgun from the man's hands and beat his head with the duct-taped grip. He pulled open the door and tugged on the driver's arm until the man fell out on the ground. Glen cocked the gun and shot him in the head—it made a gratifying boom and left a mess of splattered blood and a clumpy mush of brain matter. The protestors shared a look between themselves, then ran off toward the woods. In a few seconds, their motorbikes started and they putted off in clouds of greasy, two-stroke smoke.

The driver was dead, but Glen kicked him anyway.

This is what happens to men who don't share their sandwich.

He heaved himself up into the cabin and ground at the gears before the truck would move. In a low gear, he floored the accelerator and thundered toward the chain. The heavy truck had no trouble breaking through. A mile farther, frustrated at the slow pace, he stopped and walked around the load, loosening the binders on the logs' wrapper cables. They creaked and shifted, but did not spill over and kill him.

On the next curve, the logs broke loose of the cables and slewed off the truck onto the roadway. Lightened, the truck was instantly capable of ten more KPH. At 40, Glen's face broke into a smile. He liked moving and liked moving faster even better. He reached over and picked up the driver's sandwich, holding it before his nose and breathing in its aroma. It smelled good and the crunchy bread, butter and thick slices of ham tasted better.

The gravel evolved into patches of asphalt, then into a rural road and then into a highway. With the engine roaring and giving all it had, he drove it for five hours until it sputtered and ran out of fuel. He pulled off, but there was no room. It blocked half of the highway.

Too bad.

Without looking back, he climbed out, stuffed the shotgun in his bundle and walked away. West, with the sun on his left.

Glen Wilson—Primeiro—Rio Branco

WHEN GRAPPLING WITH the black dog of depression, drinking did not help, but that was my most common strategy—a futile attempt to drown my sorrows.

The Vernadas do Porto bar and restaurant was across the Acre River from my hotel and high above the river's surface, but on the building walls, there were still signs of flooding. The river, when it reached this depth, was probably something to behold. Instead of a gentle meander, I imagined a raging flood.

During the rainy season, this region of the Amazon rain forest got eleven inches of rain per month.

That's a lot of angel's tears.

Why did I think that?

Sitting on the wooden deck looking out over the river, I ordered a bottle of dark cachaça liquor, a pair of Itaipava beers and salty, fried manioc to munch on while I waited for the strong cachaça spirits to kill me and put me out of my misery.

The waitress, a plump, very-brown-skinned young lady named Desidéria, stood over me and made me pay for my drinks before she'd take them off the tray. I tried stimulating conversation.

"Desidéria. It means yearning, craving, pining. That's not a common name."

"My father is Swiss," she said in perfectly understandable English as if it explained everything.

Hell, what do I know? Maybe it does.

She had cute dimples, black, shoulder-length hair and I could see a section of tattoo under the sleeve of her blouse, but she slipped away from my reach when I tried for a closer look.

Pouring the pungent spirit into my shot glass, I reflected on how that was the story of my life.

All the secrets of life, eternally slipping out of reach.

I was three fingers into the bottle when I caught glimpse of something headed toward the back of my head. It looked like a white, athletic sock filled with something weighing it down in the toe.

Probably damp sand.

That makes a great cosh and rarely causes a fatal blow.

If I was smart, I would never sit in a public place where someone could sneak up behind me.

If only…

Hung-over, I woke with a terrible headache. My joints were stiff and sore—my spine felt like it had been tenderized, twisted like a pretzel and left in the sun to dry.

I tried to think.

Had I ever before woke up handcuffed to a bathroom sink's drainpipe? My brain was not working well, but it seemed like this was a first. At my advanced age, unique experiences were something to be relished and appreciated.

Right?

I rotated my head and my neck complained.

How long had I been in this position?

I didn't like this new experience one bit.

From another room, voices. There were at least three playing a game. From all the screaming and insults, it sounded like a lively game of Truco Mineiro.

I needed to apply my prodigious brain to escape. Looking around the bathroom, I examined a window cracked open. That was an easy way out, no problem there. The handcuffs were cheap and flimsy. I looked around for something to unlock them with, but didn't see anything promising.

It looked like the the old cuffs were made from melted-down tin cans, but I could not pry them open.

Would I be stuck here forever?

What did they want?

Ransom?

Quickly, I realized these kidnappers must have been the most inept ever. All I had to do was unscrew the elbow joint of the sink's drainpipe and slip the cuffs through. Gray water spilled out and pooled on the floor. It took less than two minutes before I was upright and looking at my sorry visage in the bathroom mirror—fingering the lump on the back of my skull.

Through a gap in the crudely fashioned door, I studied the players and memorized their faces.

Handcuffed, it wasn't easy to work myself through the window—and I fell into an untended patch of broad-leaf Philodendrons. It made a hell of a racket, but the card players were screaming at each other. It would take a riot to get their attention.

I wasn't sure where I was, but I could see church spires, so I headed that direction. In ten minutes I was walking on a busy avenida trying to get my bearings. My hotel was a kilometer away.

The walk would do me good.

My first impulse was to avoid the policia, but when I saw one strolling, I hurried to catch up.

"Señor," I said, brandishing the cuffs.

He looked at me with suspicion.

"Afogar o ganso," I said. It meant knocking the boots, doing the nasty.

He shrugged and worked at the lock with a key from a ring that held at least a hundred.

"Gracias, señor," I said, rubbing my wrists to stimulate circulation.

I'm not sure what he thought—was this a common thing

with the gringo touristas?

I patted my pockets. I still had my wallet and hotel mag-strip card. I was not robbed.

Now what?

To my hotel room to get cleaned up. Shave. Brush my moldy teeth. Water and three or nine aspirins. Then I should be as good as new.

It only took an hour in the room before he was bored. There were three free channels on the TV, but all they showed was *futball*, so he clicked the TV off.

Fuck this.

He decided to go back the Vernadas do Porto and see if his bottle was still available. It had better be. In the hotel lobby, he grabbed a copy of the local, English language *Folha de Sao Paulo Agora*, folded it and tucked it under his arm.

It was a long walk, almost two kilometers, but as the aspirin kicked in and his muscles loosened, he started feeling more human.

When he got to the restaurant, Desidéria was there—sipping from a steaming mug of yerba mate. He caught her eye and stood expectantly.

He couldn't read her expression.

She inclined her head and ushered him to the same table.

No way, not this time.

He seated himself with his back against the wall so he could see who came and went and no one could sneak up behind him.

She returned after a minute with two beers and the remainder of the cachaça bottle. She stood, waiting for payment and he shook his head.

"I'm not paying for the same bottle twice," he said.

With a plump, brown finger, she tapped the beer bottles, both of them.

He shrugged.

Okay, fair enough.

The beers he'd pay for.

He handed her a pair of *reals*—folding money—waved away the change, and unfurled the newspaper.

Sipping, he paged through. There were murders in Rio and Sao Paulo, but there was always violence there. Nothing jumped out at him. However, on page five, a report caught his attention. Down river, brutal murders.

Five days ago, a bloody killing in *Novo Aripuanã*, a hotel maid found dismembered. Four days ago, four hardwood loggers slaughtered in *Manicoré*. Three days ago, a *tourista* couple from Australia in *Humaitá*. Two days ago, a mutilated nun found in Porto Velho. The vector was plain—this monster was headed his way. He studied the timeline. Something nasty was clearly headed right toward him.

He sat back in his chair and thought about it.

He was exactly in the right place at the right time.

Of course, I am right.

I always am.

Glen Wilson—Secundo

IT WAS EASY; Glen lurked in a shadow and waited for a macho driver to leave his woman in the car with the engine running while he went into a BR Mania convenience store to buy fried snacks and beer. Pointing the stubby shotgun at the passenger, Glen told her to move over and drive to the east, always east.

Movimentação.

The first young lady claimed she could not handle the *transmissão manual*, but she figured it out quickly when Glen jammed the shotgun in her jaw and broke a tooth. She spent the rest of their time together pressing on her jaw with her free hand and projecting hatred toward him for nearly 250 kilometers. Over and over this plan worked and depending on how much gas the hijacked car's tank held, he covered a hundred to three-hundred kilometers per car, before stopping near a new convenience store, sending the girl on her way—driving on gas tank fumes—and starting again.

The second girl was at an AM/PM store at an Ipiranga petrol station, but after that he lost track. Hop after hop, car after car, kilometer after kilometer, it took three days to get to Brasilia…including some time for sleeping at an Accor hotel or whatever flophouse he could pay for with money lifted from girl's purses. They never had much. He could not trust the girls, so he tried not to sleep in the car.

There was no point to any effort to kill them, so he left the girls alive.

What was memorable about these endless thousands of miles? Torrential rain. Two-lane highways and two-thousand or so construction delays. Roads washed out. And, a tree that had fallen across the road that turned out to be the biggest snake he'd ever seen.

The anaconda was too big to drive over, so they waited for it to slither off—and it was in no hurry at all.

Otherwise, the trip was long and dull.

Sometimes the girls would try to engage him in conversation or turn on the radio, but he put an end to it by waving the shotgun. It might have been better if he had shells for it, but it did its job anyway, so it didn't matter. None of the girls showed any inclination to challenge his authority, so there was no problem.

During the long miles, he had time to think, but did not straighten anything out. He knew who he was, Glen Wilson, King of the Universe, but he still felt disjointed and confused. It was like there was another man living inside him, a man to whom his weak knee made sense. He spent hours examining his mutilated hand and knew the injuries intimately, one from a flashing machete, the other from a pair of bolt cutters along the shoreline of a massive, flat lake, but still, it often felt like these things happened to someone else.

And, he remembered being older. Not decrepit older, but slowing-down older. Tired older. In the passenger's makeup mirror, he studied his face. He was himself. A younger version of himself and maybe similar to someone else. It was a puzzle and his mind worked over the possibilities.

The clinic was an odd thing.

What did they do there?

It was not ramshackle; it was modern and clean and a lot of money had been spent to create it, but why? Thinking about it made him angry, blindingly angry, but it seemed everything did that. Everything his mind touched on made him furious and want to break something or kill someone.

The things that happened to him were not his fault, but he had no one to blame but himself. Logically, he should then hurt himself, but that was not going to happen.

How can I hurt myself without hurting myself?

It was a dilemma, a brainteaser.

There were people he knew, people he thought he should care about, but didn't. He wanted to smash their faces. One-by-one, with great satisfaction. Of all the jumbled things in his head, only this made sense.

A cop and her lesbian lover. Bleeding and begging for mercy. A tall, elegant man with flowing white hair swept back from his face like a tosh twat, slashed across the belly with a short knife, trying to hold his bloody guts together. A beautiful blonde, oh, the fun he would have with her. Feeling an urge, he looked over at the driver. With black hair and a round, cocoa-colored face, she was the opposite of the fine-featured blonde of his fractured memories.

The impulse for brutal sex faded.

After the blonde of his dreams, there were others he would get to in his own sweet time.

He would kill them. Kill them all. But, he needed money to make that happen. Money. He needed it, a lot of it, to make his plans possible. In Brasilia, who had money? Cash money. That was an easy answer. Only the drug dealers.

In Brasilia, where were the drug dealers? All over the place, really, but the bad neighborhoods of Valparaíso de Goiás were his best bet—but not directly. He would go to Goiânia first, then catch a bus in Barra do Garças so he could slip into Goiânia legally and quietly. Then another bus to Valparaíso de Goiás. Indirection, it came natural.

And, it felt better to have a destination and a plan, no matter how faint and ephemeral.

Glen Wilson—Primeiro—Rio Branco

GLEN HAD WORKED his way another inch into the cachaça and enjoyed a beautiful *Chaba Brasil Autênticos mata norte e mata fina* cigar. Apparently, Desidéria felt she owed him something; she brought him the free smoke, a book of matches and a carved coconut husk to use as an ashtray. He waved two fingers to get two more beers.

It took him aback when the kidnapping crew entered the room—but they were more surprised than him. They looked at each other and tried to think of what to do.

Attack me again?

No, not with me onto their game.

Without the element of surprise, these fools had nothing.

Leave quickly, hopefully unrecognized?

Glen speared them with a glare and pointed at the chairs arranged around his table. Spewing a cloud of aromatic smoke, he waved at Desidéria to bring more glasses, then spoke in a commanding tone—something he hoped would be interpreted as an invitation.

"*Bebida alcoólica.*"

They were frozen, undecided.

When Desidéria appeared bearing fresh glasses, she explained the situation to them.

"*Amalucado norte-americano ter macaquinhos na cabeça.*"

Crazy Yankee with monkeys in his head.

Glen grinned. That was funny.

"One of you must speak some English…" Glen said.

Desidéria looked at them, each in turn, then pulled up a chair for herself.

"I will translate for you, Señor," she said.

"*Maravilhosa,*" Glen said. Marvelous.

He folded the newspaper and pointed at the article about the murders.

"I want to hire you. *Fortuna, papel moeda.*"

A fortune in paper money. This got their attention.

All of the sudden, they were all smiles.

They toasted again and again as Glen explained what he wanted them to do.

American dollars were like gold—they would kill their grandmothers for a ten-thousand BRL reals, something like USD $2,500 each.

Desidéria pointed at herself. She felt that she deserved a payout too. Glen laughed.

Sure, why not.

By the time the bottle was empty, they were lifelong friends. *Irmão.* Brothers.

Basically, Glen would hang out, smoking and drinking at Vernadas do Porto while his new friends would monitor the incoming roads and watch for the intruder and report to Glen—who would formulate a plan to capture the escapee.

This was a great plan. Glen didn't know the ins and outs of the area and he could hardly be in three places at once.

That thought amused him.

Three places at once—he was already in two places at once.

He tried to make it clear. *Em perigo.*

This creature is me. That's a dangerous person.

Looking at each of them one-by-one, including Desidéria, he stared into their eyes and tried to communicate the degree of risk.

Watch. Be careful. *Em perigo.*

Glen Wilson—Secundo

HE KNEW WHERE to look, but wasn't sure how he knew. As he walked and walked, the Valparaíso de Goiás neighborhoods grew more and more ragged and rundown. The right place would be an old shop; auto repair, car body painting, a windshield shop, some legitimate, drive-up business that failed. The signs would still be in place and there might be old cars still arranged as cover, but there would be nothing being actively worked on. Barbed wire would be strewn all around, but that was common for these neighborhoods.

There would be a roll-up garage door and eyes, eyes everywhere, watching. Cameras. Vans that rolled in and rolled out—only inside ten minutes or so—not even enough time for an oil change.

In modern parlance, the place would be repurposed.

He found the place…a used tire shop. There were old tires scattered all around, but they had been in place for years. They were cover, not inventory.

Without looking too closely, he made a pass on the opposite side of the street with eyes flicking over, then kept walking.

After slipping around a corner, he found an Internet café where he ordered a *Guaraná Antarctica* soft drink which he sipped from the can while swiping left on the Tinder application on the rent-by-the minute Internet terminal the previous user left open for the few minutes remaining of his purchase. The slender, five-foot-tall young man Glen glimpsed while he was leaving had a predilection for black women with extraordinarily large butts.

Whatever floats your boat, man.

He counted his money—he had the equivalent of almost four hundred U.S. dollars in Brasilian reals.

What else?

Not much. A canvas sack. A sawed-off shotgun, but no shells. The clothes on his back. The intellect and skill of Glen Wilson.

It was more than enough; he had everything he needed.

The only thing missing was a plan.

He'd rent a room for the night, have a few drinks and the plan would come to him—there was no doubt.

He tilted back the soda and finished it, then set back out on the street.

After a mile of ramble, the room he found was in a rundown house. Outside, a hand-painted sign.

Quarto para alugar.

Room to rent.

An old woman appeared when he knocked. 75 reals a night—about US $15. He had his choice of the six rooms—all were vacant. The old woman seemed very happy to get his 500 reals for the week. With one tooth left, she seemed very proud of it—her grin was a wonder.

Fabiola.

Her name meant *bean farmer*. It seemed appropriate.

She was a shade over five-feet-tall and round like an apple covered in a cotton dress that had been washed a hundred times too many. Her thin hair had been dyed an incongruous black, but not recently—a solid two inches of gray had grown out.

After handing over cash, he waited for a key, but apparently this wasn't a key kind of place. He walked down a hallway—the flimsy door was not locked. It didn't even have a lock.

At one time, the room had a TV, but all what was left was a pale square on the wall and hanging cables. Looking out through the ragged curtains to the back, he saw an open-air bar made from crumbling concrete blocks and broken tiles. The washed-out sky was visible through gaps in its palm-frond roof and there were bottles on a crude wooden shelf, but they were dusty, dry and empty.

He walked out the back door and brushed off a rattan chair.

Fabiola seemed surprised he was interested in the bar—he patiently waited until she came out to see what he was doing.

"Brahma Chopp," he said.

She shook her head.

"*Nada de cerveja, señor,*" she said, raising her hands as if to show that no bottles of beer were hidden up her sleeves.

After pressing back a wave of murderous anger, he spread his arms in response. He decided to give her twenty minutes—if he wasn't enjoying a beer by then, she would die. That wasn't accurate, everyone died and she was old and near death's door. She would die within the hour. Quietly hacked to pieces with a dirty washcloth stuffed in her mouth to muffle her screams.

"*Jardim de cerveja.*"

Beer garden.

He must have scared her because she went back inside and hollered for someone named Lourivaldo.

Sixteen minutes later, she appeared with six one-liter bottles of Brahma beer, ice cold and shimmering with condensation in a five-gallon paint bucket filled with ice—along with a clean glass and church-key bottle opener.

"*Eu que agradeço,*" he said. I thank you.

Lourivaldo was a husky kid, maybe 14. Mixed race, he had nappy hair and dark skin. He looked lanky and strong, but perhaps not too bright.

"*Filho?,*" Glen asked.

Son?

"*Adotivo,*" she said.

Adopted.

Like me, a stray in a whole country of strays.

There was someone else in the house, someone like a ghost who was careful not be fully seen. He could feel the eyes on him and hear the muted footsteps in the old house.

The click of high heels. The faint scent of perfume on the intermittent breeze.

Quem é ela? Who is she?

Fabiola shrugged.

"Alana," she said. "*A princesinha.*" Alana, the little princess.

Glen felt a stirring in his gut.

"*Ela é bonita?*" Is she pretty?

Fabiola frowned.

"*Ela não é para você.*" She is not for you.

Glen laughed.

We'll see about that.

The sky threatened rain, but held off. He enjoyed the relative peace—the city was near and urban noise was everywhere. Outraged air horns, bass-heavy booty music and trucks blaring political slogans, but they seemed a world away. He enjoyed the solitude of the abandoned bar.

After a half-hour, Fabiola appeared with a plate of *pastel de queijo* pastry-pies, an ashtray, a short-box of Final Blend Robusto cigars and a butane lighter.

He had the impulse to ask for her hand in marriage, but was mystified about why. Oddly, it seemed like something he did.

Eating, puffing and drinking, his life was good. From a canvas bag he liberated from one of his rides, he pulled out the sawed-off shotgun and studied it.

It would be better if I could load this thing.

He caught Fabiola's eye—she came out to see what he wanted. He didn't expect anything from her.

"*Cartucho de espingarda*?" he said. Shotgun shells?

She studied the bore, shrugged, then went back inside.

After a few minutes, she reappeared with a leather sack—she poured the contents out on the bar.

He laughed, grabbed her by the shoulders and planted a kiss

on her cheek. He had another odd impulse to ask for her hand in marriage, but he pressed it away.

It was a collection of old, tarnished shells of various gauges, .22, .32 and 7.62mm, but there were shotgun shells in the mix, 16-gauge, 20-gauge and six battered 12-gauge shells. It didn't look likely they would all fire, but the shotgun had a double-barrel, so he'd double his odds by firing both chambers at one. He cracked it open and loaded it—then put the four remaining 12-gauge shells in his shirt pocket. He waved to dismiss the rest. She scooped the remaining shells back into her bag and waddled off.

While she was gone, he practiced ejecting and reloading. He wasn't fully smooth about it, but he could fire, then be ready to fire again in about five seconds.

Too long, but what could he do?

Make sure to be a moving target, that was about it.

He closed his eyes and tried to figure out if today was the day he would die.

He felt like he would know.

There was no doubt. This was *not* the day. Today, he was bulletproof. After studying his mysterious, mutilated fingers, he felt sure.

This was not the day.

Glen Wilson—Primeiro—Rio Branco

THE KIDNAPPING TRIO was clearly excited. Abandoning his research, Glen folded his newspaper looked up at them. Apparently, there was news. Desidéria brought him a fresh beer and, like babies, gathered the empties in her arms.

"They found something?" Glen said.

Desidéria shrugged.

"They want you to go with them."

Outside the bar, under a drizzly, overcast sky, they'd illegally parked an old Datsun flatbed truck. It was in rough shape. Mud splattered, the fenders were barely hanging on and the windshield had more cracks than glass. Luis ushered him into the passenger seat of honor and helped him get settled in. He instinctively reached for the seatbelt, but there was none, of course. The other two climbed onto the truck's bed and standing, grabbed the light rack. The truck was a diesel. Once the engine was running, it rattled and rumbled. At least three of the four cylinders were firing and in the Amazon rain forest, three out of four ain't bad. With elaborate choreography, Luis worked the stubborn gearbox and they were under way.

The under-powered motor was not speedy, but Rio Branco was not a metropolitan city. In fifteen minutes they were rumbling through a patchwork of farms clawed out of the rainforest. Luis kept up a continuous patter in Portuguese—Glen caught maybe one word in twenty.

Along the way, Glen tried not to get too excited.

What were the chances these fools actually found the fake Glen?

Near zero, of course.

A few miles away from the city, they turned off on a muddy spur and drove by a greenwater pond toward a grove of trees. There, they stopped and jumped out.

A few yards in the grove, they stopped before a figure tied to a tree with strands of rusty baling wire. In bad shape, one of the man's legs was twisted at an unnatural angle. One arm was broken and tied to his chest with a dirty rag. He head was covered with a canvas sack. Glen kneeled while Luis worked off the sack and exposed the man's face.

"*Estrangeiro,*" Luis said. Foreigner.

The man was alive, but barely. His face was wrapped in dirty, blood-soaked bandages. Luis unwrapped his eyes first. From deep inside, the eyes blinked, expressing pain and hatred like a snake. Slowly and with pride, Luis unwrapped the man's face.

"*Contemplar,*" Luis said.

The stranger's face was a patchwork of ragged skin. Raw incisions were infected. He barely had a face at all. Glen wracked his brain for something intelligent to say.

"*Laboratorio*?" he tried.

"Water," the man said.

He speaks English.

"Get him some water," Glen said.

Greedy, the man slurped from a bottle. Mixed with blood, water streamed down his face.

"Okay, enough," Glen said. "Did you come from the laboratory?"

"Fuck you," the man said.

Luis upended the man's sack. A blood-stained hatchet and cloth-wrapped bundles tumbled out. Glen unwrapped a bundle and dropped the content with disgust.

A thumb.

There were six.

This disgusting creature collected thumbs.

Glen recoiled.

"No," he said. "Nada."

He kneeled and lifted the man's chin.

"You've seen me. Which way did I go? Upriver? Downriver?"

"Eat shit," the man said through broken teeth.

There was no doubt this was one of the creatures from the lab, but was no version of Glen.

No way. No how.

"Okay," Glen said. "So be it."

Slowly, he drew a finger across his neck and stared down his companions—they started to complain, then gave up. With quick strokes of a clasp knife, Luis opened the wretch's throat and he gurgled for a few seconds before dying.

"Now what?" Glen said.

A hundred meters away, a backhoe worked at a trench. Luis whistled and like a wallowing beast, the backhoe lumbered across the field. Neatly, the body was picked up and in minutes, the backhoe tamped raw Earth on the fresh grave.

In five minutes, the man had gone from being a living, breathing human on the face of the Earth to an anonymous hole in a muddy field. It was as close to not existing as Glen could imagine.

Would it be this way for me?

Fighting off waves of black depression, Glen trudged back to the truck.

Now what?

Glen Wilson—Secundo

GLEN FOUND CREATIVE ways to walk to the market and made wide pedestrian loops going back and forth in front of the tire shop—trying to get a sense of the activity without drawing attention to himself, but there wasn't that much foot traffic and there was little he could do for disguise beyond wearing a different hat or t-shirt.

A hundred meters away, in an overgrown park, someone had planted and cultivated a rubber fig. For a few hours in the afternoon heat, Glen rested behind the massive, flowing, free-air roots and watched the comings and goings. He felt invisible, but apparently was not. Coming the back way from the hotel, Lourivaldo brought him a plastic chair, a pack of Hollywood lights cigarettes, a *Beirute* and a cold liter of Brahma beer.

The Lebanese *Beirute* was roast beef, cheese, lettuce, tomatoes with herbs and spices stuffed between slabs of pita. It was a feast for kings. Lourivaldo was happy with the crumpled reals Glen paid him with. With nothing else to do, Lourivaldo stayed, passing the hours leaning against the tree and reading a militaristic comic book with the lurid title *Comandos em Ação.*

After three hours, Glen stirred—if nothing else, he needed a piss.

"Roubo?," Lourvaldi said.

Robbery.

Glen looked at the kid. There wasn't much bulk to him, but he was just as tall as Glen. They stood eye-to-eye.

"Quê?" Glen said.

"*Mucho grana—terça-feira.*" the kid said.

Glen's first impulse was to smack the kid upside the head—then stomp him to death. The kid sensed something and took a step back. Glen took a deep breath and reined in his rage.

Lots of money on Tuesday.

Glen worked out the calendar in his head. Tomorrow is Tuesday.

"*Tá bom*?" the kid said. Alright?

Despite trying to keep a low profile, Glen was obviously drawing attention. In this neighborhood, strangers stand out. He couldn't lurk for another week.

"*Que beleza*," Glen said. That's beautiful.

Glen Wilson—Primeiro—Rio Branco

AS IT TURNED out, Luis and Desidéria were an on-again and off-again item. For now, they seemed on. Between customers, she sat with Luis talking quietly with their heads together over a table covered with photographs and documents.

Glen couldn't imagine what they might be talking about. Maybe they intended to kidnap him again. The way he felt, it would be welcome. He was tempted to go back to the rundown house and tie himself back to the sink. He couldn't shake the dark mood. When he was tired of watching the kids play in the mud of the lazy river, he pored over *A Tribuna* and tried to make sense of the world.

Desidéria found that he was interested in crime stories in the tabloids, so she made sure he had the latest Veja and whatever other lurid, crime-oriented weeklies she could find. This cost a fortune, but at the rate of his spending, he figured to run out of money in about 500 years, so he wasn't worried about it.

Finally, Luis, with a sheaf of papers, stood expectantly in front of Glen.

We're finally getting down to business.

Glen gestured for him to sit.

With Desidéria standing behind him, Luis spread the papers across the table. She wore a silk blouse he'd never seen before—unbuttoned more than he was used to. Her ample brown skin stirred something in him. They were really pouring it on.

It took a minute to figure out what Luis proposed—he wanted Glen to 'invest' in a paddle-wheel river boat. In the photographs, the boat listed to port and looked like it was barely floating.

Glen laughed and touched Luis' shoulder when he looked offended. This would clearly be the single worst and stupidest investment decision he'd ever made. 20,000 Reals. Something like 4,000 US Dollars.

Perfect.

I'm such a loser. This is exactly what I deserve.

He could see himself dropping out and working as a Blackjack dealer on a riverboat casino. If he paid the bills, Luis would be forced to give him a job. As a bonus, maybe he would drown in the next flood when this decrepit wreck inevitably sank in the muddy water.

"Si," Glen said.

"Si?" Luis responded.

"Yes, si," Glen said, shrugging.

Luis leaned over and kissed Glen on the left cheek, then the right. Desidéria pressed herself on his arm. She was very soft and warm.

"Will you marry me?" he said.

She pulled back and looked at him with confusion.

"*Quê* ?" she said.

"Nevermind," Glen said.

Glen Wilson—Secundo—Tuesday

BREAKFAST WAS A crusty loaf of seed-bread, a funky, pungent yellow cheese, strawberries and rich, black coffee—a meal fit for a king. The shotgun was loaded and the four spare cartridges were in his pocket.

Lourivaldo dropped something heavy and wrapped in canvas on the table.

"*Quê?*" Glen said.

"Facão," Lourivaldo replied. Machete.

He studied the young man's face.

Was the mission so obvious? So obvious that the trabalhadores would be expecting him?

He unwrapped the blade. The hilt was wrapped with old leather and the steel was black with a silver streak on its freshly sharpened edge. It looked hungry for blood.

Glen emptied his pockets and studied the pile of cash on the table. It wasn't much, but if his day was successful, he wouldn't need it. If he failed, they could have it, he'd be dead.

"*Isso é tudo.*" That's all there is.

After a moment of reflection, Glen added the plastic-wrapped SD chip card to the pile, then stood and stretched his back—it cracked as the bones in his spine aligned. He was ready.

Lourivaldo picked up the chip card and unwrapped it.

"O que é isso?" What is this?

Glen shrugged his shoulders.

"Eu não sei," he said. I don't know.

Lourivaldo slipped it into his shirt pocket.

Glen reached for the shotgun.

"Esperar um minuto." Wait a minute.

Now what?

In the corner, there was a bundle wrapped in old burlap. It was heavy. Lourivaldo dragged it into the room's center.

The first thing he pulled out was a roll of duct tape.

What the fuck?

The Portuguese name appeared in Glen's mind. *Fita adesiva.* That struck him as funny.

Was there anything in Brazil that could not be fixed with duct tape?

The shuffling Fabiola appeared with the mysterious princess. Glen was immediately smitten.

In this young woman, everything was mixed perfectly. Her tanned skin was golden like honey. Long, dark wavy hair. Hoop earrings. Often, young Brazilian girls wore too much eye makeup, but not this princess. She didn't need fake eyelashes and just used a minimum amount of shade around her eyes. A bright-red flannel shirt was tied around her waist to show off her slightly pudgy belly. Skin tight blue jeans. Bare feet with nails painted a vivid red.

Every cell in Glen's body craved her.

Fabiola scolded him.

"*Eu te disse, ela não é para você.*" I told you, she is not for you.

Oh, no, you are mistaken, she is one-hundred percent for me. When I get the money, she's coming with me to America.

This thought surprised him.

I didn't know I was going to America.

Maybe he did know deep inside, but not consciously.

I'm getting a lot of money and taking the princess to America.

The thought filled him with wonder.

Lourivaldo poured various lengths of cast iron rebar across

the floor. Glen was puzzled.

"*Eu não sei o que está acontecendo,*" he said. I don't know what is happening.

Fabiola shushed him and the trio set to work. They started with the front part of his shins—duct-taping lengths of rebar over his trousers. Then his thighs. Then his chest. Then a few bars on his upper arms. They left his joints free to move. Soon he looked like a robot from a no-budget scifi movie. It was heavy and he could barely move. It was the stupidest thing he'd seen.

These people are crazy.

Over the top, they pulled on a voluminous, bright-yellow rain slicker. With a straight razor, the pants were slit and pulled back together with tape. When he moved—which was barely possible—he clanked. Lourivaldo strapped a helmet like an old bucket on his head and they stood back to admire their work. They nodded in approval, then loosely taped the machete to his left arm and the shotgun on his right. Lourivaldo fished the spare shotgun shells from Glen's pocket and taped them to his chest.

Maybe the trabalhadores will die laughing and save me the trouble of killing them.

The princess spoke for the first time. The tone of her voice was lush and heavenly and she enunciated with educated precision.

"*Se você cair, você está morto.*" If you fall down, you're dead.

Thanks for restating the obvious.

"I can't hardly move. How the hell am I getting there?"

Fabiola silenced him with a finger on his lips.

"Não se preocupe, meu amigo." Don't worry, my friend.

Out front of the house, the earthy rumble of a diesel truck could be heard. He could barely see anything from under the loose helmet. Like a blind man, they led him through the house and out the front door. The old Toyota stake-bed truck had a Maxon vertical lift. Two men in work clothes and straw hats helped him into position. One worked the lever and the lift motor groaned as Glen ascended.

These people are loco, loucas.

"*Segure firme*," the shorter worker said. Hang on tight.

Glen felt somewhere beyond foolish.

"*Pare*!" he shouted. Stop.

They ignored him. With a jolt that nearly toppled him off the back of the truck, the Toyota lurched forward. In a few minutes, they had stopped in front of the tire shop. Quickly, they worked the lift and Glen stepped out onto the street. In seconds, they were gone, leaving Glen coughing in a cloud of greasy blue smoke.

It was more of a shamble than a walk, but, feeling like a complete asshole, he slowly moved forward.

He shuffled forward 10 meters. The first guard coming out looked at him briefly, then raised his AK and shot Glen in the head—he toppled like a sequoia.

Everyone came out and stood in the driveway looking down at him. *O chefe*, the boss, did not agonize over the decision before rattling off instructions.

"Get this shit off him," he said.

With six of the men working, it took about two minutes to hack off the yellow slicker, then cut the tape and pull off all the rebar. With a gesture, the boss told them to keep going. Soon Glen was naked on the on the greasy concrete. He bled profusely from the head wound. They studied his motionless body and tried to understand what they saw.

It was a mystery.

Glen didn't look like much. He was wiry and lean with not much in the way of bulk or muscle. There were ugly scars on his knee. The boss poked at him with the toe of his vaqueiro boot.

Glen moaned.

O chefe kicked the bucket-helmet down the driveway.

"Enterre-o profundamente," he said. Bury him deep.

Mazatlan

"What are we going to do if we stay here?" Elke said.

Their pueblito suite overlooked the pool and the ivory sands of the Mexican Gulf. Kids splashed in the emerald water. They were finishing a shrimp cocktail washed down with cold Pacifico beers.

"I could spend the rest of my life exploring your nooks," Murphy said.

Elke flicked icy condensation onto Murphy, who cringed.

"Hey."

"I'm serious. I'm not going to find a job selling electronics down here."

"Sell something else or retire. We have money."

"I don't want to retire. I like to work. And, you? You'll retire in your urn."

Murphy sat up.

"I can do private security. Bodyguard. I can drive one of those armored Mercedes. Raz can link me up with the Banda and Norteño rockstars who perform here. You can start a business, something fun like a high-tech startup. I don't think Mazatlan has a Bill Gates yet." She stretched out her arms and legs and wiggled them. "We can talk this through after our nap."

"Is this a sleeping nap or the other kind? Do you promise to keep your hands to yourself?"

Murphy feigned shock.

"I have no idea what you're talking about."

"You're damned lucky I don't have anything better to do."

"And," Murphy said, "I intend to keep things that way as long as I can."

Bennie and Emma

After walking through the spacious lobby, Bennie pressed the elevator button.

"Are you sure about this?" Emma said.

Bennie turned to look at her. He took his time and examined her from her feet to the top of her head. Like everyone else in Anchorage, she wore boots, but not everyone can pull off black rhinestone, ankle-height hiking boots with fluffy pink socks peeking between boot top and Kelly-canvas Capri pants topped off with a lurid, multi-color Coogi mercerized cotton sweater decorated with a LSD-kaleidoscope of 3-D art. As if losing interest while walking out the door, her toque was a flat-black cable-knit, but rescued by psychedelic rainbow pom poms on top and hanging down from the ear flaps on knitted strings.

He tugged the braids hanging from under the toque's ear flaps and planted a kiss on the end of her broad nose.

"Sure about what?"

"You're going to ask me. Are you sure you want to do it here?"

"I don't know what you're talking about. Glen said buy a building. This one is for sale. You were bored hanging around the house. That's it."

"Oh," she said, disappointed. "Shouldn't we wait for the realtor?"

"Why?" Bennie said as the elevator doors slid open.

Inside, he pressed the button for the top floor.

After ascending, the doors opened and they walked into a spacious open area. There were two odd-shaped designer chairs with round, bright red cushions. Emma flopped into one and spun in a circle.

"I like this," she said.

Immediately losing interest in her surroundings, she started playing a game on her phone. Bennie walked to the windows and looked out over the parking lot and the Anchorage skyline. It was a clear day and the fringe of surrounding mountains were stark, like prison walls.

An Inuit woman stood up from her desk, smoothed her knit dress, and then, walking briskly, approached Bennie.

"Young man, I'm Ataksaki. Can I help you?"

"Attack Saki? What's that?"

She sighed. "You can call me Elizabeth."

Across the room, she caught sight of Emma squinting into her phone. She stopped and froze.

Unconsciously, she whispered, "I know you."

She bit her lip in concentration.

A man in a business suit and necktie with very dark skin, wispy mustache and black, slicked-down hair approached Bennie from his corner office.

"We're expecting a realtor, so we don't have time for visitors right now, young man. You could make an appointment, though. We welcome visitors."

"I'm just looking around," Bennie said.

"I'm Juatan, but you can call me Jordan. That's easier. Your father is here somewhere?"

His gaze zeroed in on Emma. Forgetting about Bennie, he walked up to stand by Elizabeth.

"I know her from somewhere," she said.

"That's Chief Eddie Kleedehn's kid. I haven't seen her in a wolf's age—she's all grown up."

"What shall we do with her?"

Jordan looked at her as if she was daft.

"What we do with all VIPs. Settle her in the boardroom and see if she'd like a diet Coke or something. I'll see what her friend wants."

The Inuit woman scurried off. Jordan straightened his tie and walked back to Bennie.

"Can I inquire about the nature of your business?"

Bennie made a snap decision. He liked the building. If there were problems, they'd be Glen's, not his.

"My name is Benjamin Franklin Jackson, Junior, and I'm buying this place."

The elevator doors slid open and a flustered man carrying a valise entered the landing area. He walked over quickly and handed Jordan a business card.

"Larry Evans. I thought we were meeting in the downstairs lobby. We need to make sure you have the, uh, financial wherewithal, before scheduling a thorough basement to roof tour."

Jordan pointed at the slender Bennie, who was striding toward Emma in the boardroom.

"I think that's your buyer."

"The kid?"

"Yes, the kid."

In the boardroom, Emma was already sipping a diet Coke. She looked up at Bennie as he came in.

"She says Byron Nicholai is her nephew."

"Who's that?"

"Yup'ik rapper. *Agayutem yui*, Children of God? He has beats." She turned to Ataksaki. "For all of his alleged genius, he knows nothing about music."

Bennie protested. "I know about Bach and Mozart."

"See what I mean?" Emma said.

"She's my fiancé."

"Hold on, mister. You haven't formally asked me yet and your proposal better not be anything casual. I expect to be swept off my feet."

"I thought we'd skip all the nonsense, fly to Reno, get hitched and jet back. Easy."

Emma rolled her eyes at Ataksaki. "His manners need a lot of work."

With Jordan trailing behind, the realtor, Larry, entered the room.

"Before scheduling the grand tour and getting the inspections going, we can start with your financials—letters of credit and the like."

"Fourteen-five is the asking price?" Bennie said.

"Yes, but between you and me, there is wiggle room. Once we complete your qualification paperwork, I will convey your reasonable offer and get the back-and-forth going with the Native Village Corporation owners."

"We'll pay the full price."

"Which bank are you borrowing from?"

"No borrowing. Cash, bank draft, gold bars or digicoins, whatever the sellers prefer, we don't care. Draw up the papers." To Jordan, he said, "What is the status of your lease?"

"We're on month-to-month while the owners seek a buyer."

"We don't want to inconvenience you, but can you be out by the end of the month? Draw up an invoice if you like, we'd like to keep your décor and furnishings. We'll buy anything you care to leave."

"I don't understand what is happening," Larry said.

Bennie tapped him on the chest with a skinny finger.

"Right now you get full commission, but if you irritate me, I will punish you. Get the paperwork ready—I want to sign on Friday and get this done. Go."

Larry looked at Jordan with imploring eyes.

Help?

Jordan shrugged. "I suggest you get busy," he said.

"This is highly irregular," Larry muttered as he left the room.

"Please let me ask once and I won't bother you about it again, but you have the resources?"

"Yes," Bennie said.

"Okay. Yes, we can be out quickly. Most of the staff is already at the new building." He pointed at a similar, glass-faced building 200 yards across the parking lot. "We're not going far. We'll be neighbors. Can I ask another question? What will you do here?"

Bennie sighed. "When I asked Glen, he said we're taking Alaska into IPO. He said it like that explained everything and refused to elaborate. I will be doing computer work for him—assembling a database of teachers to start. Why teachers, I knoweth not. Do you mind if Emma and I hang out here for a few minutes? We have business to discuss."

"Take all the time you like," Jordan said. At the door, he hesitated. "Door open or shut?"

"Shut," Bennie said.

As the door closed, Emma spoke.

"No way, Benjamin. You ask me now and the answer is 'no.' Irrevocably no. If you can't think of something more creative, then at least steak and crab legs at Club Paris with wine, candles, red roses, sweet potato pie for dessert and a ring with a diamond big enough to choke a muskrat."

Bennie shrugged. "I already have the ring. But, if you don't care to see it..."

"Right you are, mister. I don't want to see it—this is not the time or place."

"Duly noted, princess. Let's get out of here. I need to get busy moving cash around."

"I don't suppose a peek would hurt."

"You made yourself very clear. Crab legs need to be involved."

"Damn you to hell, Benjamin Franklin Jackson, junior. I don't even believe you. I bet you don't have the ring, liar."

Bennie patted his pockets. "It was around here somewhere," he said.

She punched him in the arm. Hard.

"Already the spouse abuse starts."

"If you have it, then I want to see it. Now."

It was not in a box. He produced a small, tan craft envelope sealed with a heart sticker. He kneeled and handed it to her.

"It probably doesn't even fit."

He tried to tug the envelope from her fingers.

"I can take it back to the Walmart Supercenter and get a refund."

She opened the envelope. The ring was not fancy, just a simple white-gold band with alternating channel-set diamonds and deep-blue sapphires. Inside, 'James Allen' was engraved on one side. 'Emma' was engraved on the other.

She opened her mouth to say something rude, but could not do it. She could not speak at all.

"Let's make sure it fits before we break up and find new soul-mates," Bennie said.

He gently placed the ring on her finger.

"Oh, Bennie, it fits perfectly."

"Don't act so surprised," Bennie said.

Glen Wilson—Secundo—Tuesday

THE *TRABALHADORES* WEREN'T much interested in digging. Despite their instructions, they did not bury Glen deep.

A few kilometers out on highway 280 between Samambaia and Santo Antonio do Secoberto, they pulled off on a stub of dirt road and stopped by a grove.

There, they took a half-hour—including cigarette breaks—and scraped a hole a half-meter deep, then unceremoniously hauled Glen's body into it. They piled dirt back on and tamped it down and were done. Eager to get to a cantina they passed on highway 060, they did not notice the dusty Fiat Bravo parked on the highway shoulder a hundred meters further along.

When they were out of sight, the Fiat waited for a break in traffic, then made a U-turn. In the front, Alana. In the back with a shovel, Lourivaldo. With only a few nicks of Glen's skin, they excavated him. After making sure he was still breathing, they hauled his filthy body into the Fiat's hatchback and drove back toward the city. They did not go back to the hotel. Instead, they turned off on highway 080 and arrived at a house by the lagoon in the village of Brazlândia.

There, they hauled Glen into the bathroom and washed him off with a handheld showerhead. With cold water pouring on him, he was semiconscious and moaning. They hauled him out, dried him off and put him in bed.

Glen Wilson—Secundo—Wednesday

SLOWLY, GLEN DRIFTED into consciousness—finding Alana washing his genitals with a sponge and cold water from a bucket. His first attempt at speech was a croak. She ladled water and he swallowed some, but more dribbled down the side of his face to soak the pillow.

Everything in his body ached.

"You could be more gentle," he said.

He tried to raise his hands to explore the bandage on his head, but could not move. Inclining his head, he looked.

Damnable duct tape.

They didn't trust him.

His arms and legs were trussed.

From a bullet that bounced off the rebar they taped on him, there was an open, seeping wound on his belly. Like he was an old sock, she had laced the wound closed with a needle and black thread.

"Nurse?" he said.

She smiled. "*Veterinária.*"

Fucking great.

Hearing their voices, Fabiola and Lourivaldo leaned in the room to look at him.

"*Bandeja de cama?*" Fabiola said.

It took a few moments for his frazzled brain to translate.

Bed pan.

"No," he said.

Fuck, no.

From the way the room smelled, he'd been shitting plenty already. He didn't want to think about it. He didn't want to think about anything.

He drifted back into the dark land near death.

Glen Wilson—Secundo—Thursday

WHEN HE WOKE, his mind felt clearer. Straining, he could remember being shot in the head, but nothing else. The room was crowded; all four of them were there.

At a small table, while the *Chocolate com Pimenta* telenova played in the background on a tiny TV screen, Fabiola and Lourivaldo played a sedate, listless game of *Conquian*, South American Rummy.

How did I get here?

While I'm at it, where is here? This is not the hotel in Valparaíso de Goiás.

Estou muito confuse, he said. I'm very confused.

The three exchanged glances.

Is it time?

Si.

They put the cards away and placed a large suitcase on the table. Once opened, he saw that it was filled with cash, mostly US dollars, but also bricks of cellophane-wrapped *reals.*

Lourivaldo took the role of spokesman. He spoke quickly, but Glen was able to absorb most of the information.

While Glen provided the spectacle in front of the tire shop, Lourivaldo crept through a window into the main room and lifted the suitcase filled with cash, then absconded with it.

They used me as bait.

"Cut me loose." Glen said.

They looked at each other and laughed. This infuriated

Glen, and he struggled against the tape. But, it was hopeless, he wasn't going anywhere.

While Glen watched, Lourivaldo divided the proceeds, 50:50. Glen's portion was stuffed into a garish Brasília Futebol Clube sports bag, which he then zipped closed. Their portion was stacked back into the suitcase. Glen estimated how much there was.

Something like $75,000 or slightly more, not including the *reals*.

It was enough, though barely.

Lourivaldo left for a moment, then came back with the bucket helmet. It had a deep crease at the left temple.

"*Isso salvou sua vida*," he said. It saved your life.

He placed it on top of the sport bag. He left again and came back with a sheaf of papers. He set them down by the helmet, then showed Glen the chip card. He placed that on the table too.

Glen didn't understand any of that. He addressed Alana.

"*Vamos para a America*." We're going to America.

Fabiola leaned over and smiled.

"*Não, eu te disse, ela não é para você*." No, I told you, she is not for you.

She cupped his genitals and squeezed.

"*Pequeno*," she said. Small.

"*Não me deixe assim*." Don't leave me like this.

"*Tchau*," she said. Goodbye.

After dragging the suitcase off the table, Lourivaldo said it too. Then Alana said it and they were gone. He heard the sewing machine motor of the Fiat start up and listened as they drove off until the sound of their car was absorbed in the faraway traffic.

Great, now with the money within reach, I starve to death.

He raised his head and looked down his body.

Fabiola was right; he was small—a helpless, pathetic mess of wounds and bloody bandages.

After an hour of feeling sorry for himself, he realized that the tape on his left wrist was loose—not a lot, but a little. He could move a quarter of an inch. In ten minutes, it was three-eights.

An hour later, he was free.

After a session on the toilet, he washed up and studied his stash. The papers were a mix of medical records and other documents. He didn't think too much of it—he'd sort through it later. For now, he needed to get away from here. Far away from here.

It was a miracle; they'd left him a car. The key was in the front room with a basket of bananas and bottled water. Weak, he sat, ate and drank. This gave him enough energy to take a look outside.

The car wasn't much—an olive drab 1960's era VW Fusca. Beetle. There was a miracle. It started.

He tapped the fuel gauge. They left him nothing.

Fuckers.

There was an even bigger miracle. When the gears engaged, it rolled. Would it make it to a petrol station, then 600 miles to the airport in Rio?

There was only one way to find out.

He stopped at Petrobas and filled the little tank. On a whim, he checked the oil and it was off the stick. Would he have made it two more miles?

Who knows?

It made him angry. They had half of his money and left him with a crappy car in bad shape with no fuel or motor oil. If he found them, he'd kill them, one-by-one, but probably save the luscious Alana for last.

They'd see how *pequeno* his rage was.

It was a nice fantasy, but he needed to get away from this city before the tire shop boys found him with half of their money and no weapons. They'd finish what they started.

Miles.

He needed to cover some miles.

Glen Wilson—Primeiro—Rio Branco

THE DAYS RAN into each other while Glen spent his days at the cantina reading the tabloids and waiting for divine inspiration. Almost immediately, once the paperwork on the river boat was signed, Luis presented estimates for repair. The $4,000 boat needed $20,000 of work. Glen laughed. That was typical.

He should make it look hard, otherwise Luis would come back again for more and more money, but Glen did not care. They laughed at him and called him *Senhor Sacos de Dinheiro* (Mr. Moneybags) behind his back, but he couldn't take offense. He deserved to be exploited and insulted. They should piss on him too while they were at it.

All day long, watching the lazy river and drinking until he felt like stumbling back to his hotel room to sleep, he would do it all again the next day.

Then, one day...

In a lurid tabloid famous for in-depth stories like a pregnant bride killed in a helicopter crash on the way to her wedding, a teenage suicide when the local futebol team was humiliated by a European team and 300 missing when a dam collapsed, a low-resolution picture caught his eye. He glanced at the headline.

Space Robotman Landed in Valparaíso de Goiás.

He studied the photograph. There was something about it.

But what?

Luis was always playing with his laptop computer.

Glen called out to him and pointed at the photo.

"Video?" he said.

Luis shrugged, but a half-hour later, he had it.

The blurry video was not quite a minute long—taken by someone on the street with a cell phone.

Glen watched it over and over and asked Luis to stop on one frame. The "robot" was clearly just a moron with a sawed-off shotgun taped to his chest walking stiffly in a rain slicker with a metal bucket on his head.

"Zoom in," he said.

Zooming did no good, but Glen thought there was something wrong with the robot's hand. It looked mutilated...like fingers were missing. Glen looked at his own hand.

Fingers missing like mine.

"Where is Valparaíso de Goiás?" he said.

Luis shrugged. "Brasilia," he said.

There must be more...

"Use your Google searcher and find more news there."

"*Mecanismo de busca.*" What is wrong with me?

He decided to call Bennie.

It took some fumbling around with Luis's phone, but he finally got through.

"Who is this?" Bennie said.

"Your boss. Wilson. I need something."

"Why are you in Rio Branca? When are you coming to Alaska?"

"Nevermind, none of that matters. I need a news summary...anything weird in Brasilia city and that area. Anything that seems odd, particularly if it has any relation whatsoever to the robotman in Valparaíso de Goiás. And, I need it now."

"I'm in Anchorage. You bought an office building."

"Don't distract me with non sequiturs and trivialities. News. Brasilia. Anything quirky. Sooner is better than later. Got it?"

"Yes, I got it. Emma and I..."

Glen disconnected the call.

He handed Luis back his phone.

"Give them a chance and they will talk all day instead of working."

Luis did not understand a word, but nodded anyway.

Bennie and Emma

After snagging an unused corner office and computer in their new office building, Bennie scoured a week's worth of Brasilia's online news, but did not see anything that caught his eye beyond the bizarre robotman video which was trending on Twitter and generating thousands of memes—except for three presumed *traficante de drogas* hanging from an overpass near Valparaíso de Goiás.

Emma claimed the adjoining office to play her endless Mario Super Smash Brothers Penultimate video game. She poked her head into Bennie's room.

"Find anything?" she said.

"Three drug dealers hanging from an overpass."

"How odd are those kind of murders in Brazil?" Emma said.

"There are a lot of murders in Brazil, but they don't have the cartel wars like Mexico. A public execution like this, particularly in Brasilia, is noteworthy. Plus, it's only a kilometer from where robotman was filmed."

"How are you going to get him the information? He's unattentive to email."

Bennie thought about it for a few moments.

"They probably still use FAX machines—I'll FAX him at his hotel. Inacio Palace. He'll probably get it."

"I assumed FAX machines went away with the dinosaurs."

Bennie shrugged.

"If that doesn't work, I'll try something else," he said.

Glen Wilson—Primeiro—Friday

AFTER A WEEK, the Inacio Palace breakfast buffet was boring. Glen looked over the selections and took his usual mango and crusty bread roll with slices of ham and cheese. The black coffee was the saving grace.

There weren't many guests, so he was able to snag his usual table along the wall. He was eating and reading the Sao Paulo newspaper when the desk clerk came up and placed a few sheets of paper on the tablecloth.

"Sir. A FAX message."

"Okay, thanks," Glen said.

FAX? Are the carrier pigeons on strike?

It wasn't much—three drug dealers hanging from a pedestrian overpass and a map that showed how close their hanging bodies were to where robotman was filmed. The proximity was curious, but probably a coincidence. There were three pages of printed photos of the tire store screen-captured from Google streetview.

What am I supposed to do with this useless nonsense?

On the last page was a handwritten note in Bennie's precise, cramped handwriting.

The robotman's tire shop doesn't appear to do much tire business.

He looked closer at the photos.

Bennie was right. At a tire shop, the used tires were bought and sold quickly enough that they don't get dusty and look abandoned.

His mind toyed with the possibilities.

Why would the *Primeiro Comando Capital* cartel execute its members?

Stealing, of course. However, what if there was a heist?

What would I do if I was desperate for money?

I'd steal it from drug dealers.

If I was successful, there would be consequences.

A picture formed in Glen's mind. The fake Glen was headed to Rio and robbed a drug cartel along the way. This locked into place. It was obviously true. However, something niggled at the back of his mind. Something troubling. It took a few seconds to drift into focus—then it shook him so much that he spilled his coffee.

How did Bennie know how where he was?

I didn't tell anyone. I don't have a cell phone.

Are they tracking me?

He ran to the front desk and scribbled Bennie's cell number on a pad, then waited impatiently for the call to be placed.

He grabbed the phone from the concierge's hand.

"Bennie, you fucking weasel, how did you know where to find me?"

"It's no big deal, Glen," Bennie said. "We embedded a tracker during the Immortality process."

"How the fuck does it work?"

"Once a day, if the implant *finds* a wifi connection, it sends an IPV6 packet. It's not an accurate location service, but we know what wifi connection is used. For you, it was usually the hotel access point, so I assumed that was your hotel. What's wrong? It worked, didn't it?"

"Bennie, you creepy little fuck, listen carefully and think. Is it possible the fake Glen has a tracker like this?"

Bennie was silent for a second.

"I don't know," he said.

"Well, you miserable waste of human DNA, find out. Find

out yesterday and let me know now. Get busy."

"Okay, Glen, I'm on it. By the way, while I have you on the phone, Emma and I..."

He was talking into a dead connection.

Glen Wilson—Secundo

THE STEERING WANDERED, so driving the VW bug was brutal work. Noisy, it could barely do 60KPH. By the time Glen reached Sete Lagoas, it was pitch dark and he was exhausted. Extracting a bundle of *reals* from his bag, he paid cash for a room at San Diego Veredas Sete Lagoas, then promptly ordered two meals and a bottle of Lagosta white wine from room service.

When he woke, the roller-tray was there. At least it was a good meal for the flies—he didn't see anything he wanted to eat.

He brewed coffee from the in-room service and looked through the bag had stuffed under the bed. He did a quick count of the money. It was more than he expected. Over USD $100K in American hundreds and more in *reals*. The chip card didn't mean anything to him, so he tossed it in the waste basket. The stack of printed papers was over an inch thick.

Was this all from the tiny chip card? Why did Rosa think it was important?

Sipping coffee, he paged through it all.

It was a combination of medical records along with photographs and biographies of...himself...and others who, it seemed, were supposed to be important to him. The prominent character was Glen Wilson and there was page-after-endless-page of his ridiculous adventures—which he skimmed.

Boring.

The other people included Margaret Murphy, Elke Rittenhauer, Robert "Steve" Stephens, Walter "Doctor Zalooq"

Crowley, Benjamin "Bennie" Franklin Jackson, Gerusha Wilson and a few assorted others.

Looking over these names reminded him of how much he relied on a team to support his efforts. In fact, on his own, Glen was a loser. Hopeless.

Fat lot of good the team in Brasilia was.

They used him as a decoy, nearly got him killed and then tossed him aside like garbage. His head felt packed solid with rage. If he believed in going backwards, he'd go back and find them. He would spend the rest of his life if that's what it took to make things right.

The fat old woman.

Murder.

The kid?

Torture. Murder.

Alana?

Rape. Torture. Murder.

But, Glen Wilson does not go backwards.

How can I pay this forward?

He looked at the photographs.

Murphy?

Rape. Murder.

Elke?

Rape. Sodomize. Murder.

Steve?

Slow torture. Murder.

Doctor Zalooq?

Murder.

Bennie?

Murder.

Gerusha?

Rape. Rape again. Slow torture. Murder.

And what about his namesake? Glen Wilson.

Flay. Dismember. Amputate his hands and feet, but over days if not a week. Then start with his leg stubs and pour acid on him slowly until he died, screaming. That might be enough.

The images of mayhem gave him comfort. It was good to have a purpose. He found himself staring deeply into Gerusha's photographic eyes. She was so, so pretty.

What was she doing with a dried out lizard like the old Glen?

She deserved firm, young flesh and a rock-hard cock.

The dossier included current locations, so he needed to decide. Miami first to take care of Steve—or Mexico first to take care of the women? First, he had to get out of Brazil. There were kilometers to go.

He decided he'd had enough of the old bug.

Fuck it.

It could rot in the hotel's car park.

He packed up and walked to the concierge, who stepped outside and whistled for a taxi.

For that, she expected a tip.

I'll give you a tip. The tip of a sharp dagger in your liver.

He heard her mutter.

"Filho da puta."

She was a pretty one, though a little heavier than he preferred. Shoulder-length black hair with blond streaks. Tattooed. He didn't care for tattoos. Regardless of her imperfection, in an instant, his rage subsided.

Being cursed by a pretty girl buoyed his spirits.

The taxi took him to *Carmo Veículos* where he quickly picked out a bright-red, three-year-old Peugeot 207. After the transaction, his bag was 20,000 *reals* lighter, but he had power steering. Air conditioning. Navigation system.

Cheerful as he accelerated through a *rotatóri* and then merged onto the highway, he decided the women in Mexico would be first. He needed a woman. He'd fuck Elke while Murphy watched. Murphy was an ex-cop. She wouldn't like that.

The Peugeot also had cruise control. He engaged it and

drifted down the highway, weaving around trucks while thoroughly immersed in his daydream.

Glen Wilson—Primeiro

After a half-hour of tapping his foot and drinking four cups of coffee, Glen called Bennie with the hotel's lobby phone. Bennie wouldn't let him speak first.

"Yes, we're tracking him all the way from the lab. He's been heading straight toward the coast. San Diego Veredas Sete Lagoas—that's where he was at last check-in—a day's drive from Rio."

"Okay, I'm rolling," Glen said.

"Hold on a minute. There was a security breach at the lab before it blew up. Someone downloaded your background files. We're worried that the client might have contact information for the team. Steve, Murphy, Gerusha, me, everyone."

Glen pondered.

"Shit. Okay. Warn everyone. Make sure they know this could be serious. After all, this is a clone of me we're talking about. I'm like a walking army. A walking nuclear bomb. A walking weapon of mass destruction."

"Yes, Glen, we know how dangerous you are."

"Tell them not to do anything regular or predictable. Let's not panic, maybe he'll whore around in Rio for a while. We could get lucky. Maybe he'll get shivved in an alley or something. But, that doesn't seem likely, does it? Glen Wilson is not the kind of guy who gets killed in random street violence. We'd better discard that possibility."

"What do you think he'll do, Glen? What does your gut tell you?"

"I think he'll go for the women first—the closest. Murphy and Elke are still in Mazatlan?"

"Yes."

"I think that's where he will go."

"Okay. I will spread the word."

"I want Murphy and Elke out of there. Tell them to meet me in Seattle. If Murphy resists, then we'll protect her in place. Call Ovidio Guzmán in my secret contact list. Tell him I want 24-7.

"Okay, got it. Glen, this isn't so important right now, but Emma and I..."

He stopped.

Glen was already gone.

It took only a few minutes for Glen to stuff everything in his travel bag. Then he took a taxi to the *Plácido de Castro International Airport.* In an hour he had arranged a private flight to Rio and they were underway. In his mind, he plotted the route. Private jet, Rio to Miami. Then again, Miami to Seattle. He'd be in home in 24 hours.

They flew over the river and Glen had a last look at his boat. It was listing hard to port in the muddy water and it appeared that the workers were on siesta.

Glen Wilson—Secundo

RIO WAS A city of vivid contrasts. Many of the poor people were in the hillside favelas. The beaches were for tourists. The rich people lived in Leblon, Gávea or Lagoa. He needed paperwork—passport, visa, driver's license and credit cards. For a price, you can get anything in Rio.

He knew of a place near the São Conrado Mall—expensive, but fast and their work was the pinnacle of perfection. That's what he wanted. The front was advogado, legal services, Garcia, Kümin and Maragoni. He didn't say anything, just opened his bag and showed the plastic-wrapped bricks of cash to the receptionist. Security was a round, humorless man in a tan business suit who looked him over from head to toe.

Though he'd showered at the hotel, Glen realized what a mess he was with open wounds, bloody bandages and ragged clothing. The man gestured. Behind the reception desk was a maze of offices, then a doorway, a corridor and then a large, claustrophobic room with concrete walls. One-hour service, USD $20,000.

You do what you gotta do.

What was left of his cash stash was split 50:50. Half of the money would go into a bank account. They'd keep the rest for "financial services rendered." Easy come, easy go. Which bank? Santander. He'd get a check book and a debit card.

The round man left him with a teenager—that's how the young man appeared to Glen. He looked like he was 14. Shorts, leather sandals, open collar Hawaiian style shirt and a gold chain. Black hair cut short and sculpted with a straight razor. The black hair on his head was dyed. The stubble on his chin was auburn. His knuckles were swollen and scarred. His ears looked like they'd been smashed with a hammer, then glued back on.

Tough kid. MMA.

After seating him before a white-screen and taking his picture, the young man tut-tutted.

"You'll need a lot of retouching," he said.

Glen was surprised. The young man's English, though there was an accent, was crisply enunciated and excellent. And the accent wasn't Brasilian or Portugese.

"You speak English."

The kid shrugged.

"My name is Gavin," he said. "Ireland by way of Singapore. Now here. If you're traveling soon, we should have a nurse clean you up and make you more presentable."

"Cost extra?" Glen said.

"We'll throw it in," the kid said.

He gestured for Glen to move to a folding chair in front of a rusty metal desk.

There were decisions to make. What nationality? American. What name? Something very generic. Paul Thomas Smith. Visa or Mastercard? Both. Profession? Consultant. On what airline did he want to be a frequent flyer? The best choices were American, United and Delta. He picked American. Admiral's Club. What generic hometown? Dublin, Ohio.

After typing in the information, Gavin tapped his watch. "*Uma hora.*" One hour. He pointed toward an espresso machine. "*Gratis.*"

In seconds, the young man was gone.

Apparently, the printing operation was on another floor.

After brewing a double espresso, Glen opened the door and looked out. A uniformed security guard stared at him impassively. This one was no joke; he was huge—with hands that could crush a coconut.

"Care for some coffee?" Glen said.

The man stared holes into Glen and did not respond.

"Suit yourself."

He wandered around the room and picked up and discarded old magazines. He simply could not drum up interest in Brazilian football or tourist brochures. At the same time, he could not sit still. There was not even a window to look out.

There was a tap at the door and the nurse entered. She was huge and squeezed into a uniform that did not fit. Her skin was as black as coal. She carried a bag. After looking him over, she got to work cleaning his wounds, gluing shut the small ones and replacing bandages. She handed him a mirror.

He looked a lot better.

"Diga a eles que você foi assaltado." Tell them you were mugged.

He nodded. That happened a lot in Rio. Anyone would believe it. Without another word, she packed up and left.

He paced. The hour seemed like twenty.

When Gavin returned, Glen looked everything over. All the holograms, bar codes and security features looked good. Somehow they made the American passport looked well-used—it was creased and stained and had various country stamps: Belize, Italy, Canada. It would need renewing in three years. He looked at the kid with the question in his eyes.

"It's better if you look like an experienced world traveler," the kid said.

The wallet had his initials embossed. PTS.

How did they do everything so quickly?

Where there is cash, there is a way.

Glen tossed him the Peugeot key.

"Have fun," he said.

73 minutes after arriving, he was back on the sidewalk blinking in the sunlight. He walked down the street looking for a clothes

store, but there was not a lot of shopping here on the avenue.

He hailed a taxi.

"Shopping Village Mall," he said.

The first place he saw at the mall was a Tommy Hilfiger, so he ended up with a green-and-yellow, open front hoodie over a powder-blue dress shirt, relic jeans and pale-blue Skecher deck shoes. The outfit was completed with a Hilfiger Decker watch and cherry/red-gradient sunglasses. He also got a pink watchcap to cover his head wound. His papers were stuffed into a trendy leather shoulder bag. He looked like a spoiled, over-aged frat boy who had a tough weekend. Or, maybe the best weekend of his life.

He felt ready to travel.

Outside, he waved to the next taxi in line.

"Aeroporto," he said.

At the American airlines counter, the young ticketing agent, Clarita, took an interest in him. As he approached, her toothy smile got wider and her posture straighter. Her English was immaculate.

"Your best bet to get to Mazatlan is to connect in Miami—the best I can do is a 13-hour layover. You'll have to go through customs twice."

After what I just paid, the least of my worries is customs.

"First class?"

"Of course, sir, with your Platinum Pro status, that's no problem. You could even take a companion. I can take two days off, that's no problem. Traveling is easier when you have someone to share it with, right?"

He scooted over so he could take her in from head to toe. Long, black hair. Maybe 29, so she was experienced. Healthy, not too fat. Hoop earrings. She even smelled good, musky with a hint of floral.

"You smell great. What scent do you use?"

She blushed.

"It's mostly me with a dab of Coffee Man Seduction behind my ears and...."

How long since he'd had a woman? Too long.

He could see the whole scenario as if it already happened. She'd cock tease him for nine hours on the plane, then he'd fuck her raw and murder her in a luxury hotel's bathtub when he was done with her.

But, no. The universe was offering Steve Stephens as a free gift. It would be better to sleep on the plane, take care of Steve quick-like, then check back in at the airport.

"It doesn't work for me now, but give me your card and I will make a point to come back through and we'll do things right."

She printed his ticket, slipped it in a cover and then added her business card.

"Safe travels, sir," she said.

"Until we meet again," he replied.

Then he turned and was lost in the crowd.

Once through security, there was time for a quick meal. He ordered a bowl of gnocchi with white beans at Spoleto and gobbled it down without tasting a bite. While eating, he studied the Steve Stephens mini biography. The man was old and fat. Diabetes. Congestive heart failure. Going deaf and blind.

This would be no challenge. Glen decided to dispatch him with a thin blade to the heart and let him drown in his blubber. He could feel the blade slide in and could hear the old man whimper and beg for mercy. It looked like the man only had six months left, so it would hardly be worth the effort, but he was doing it anyway.

To be safe, he should have a gun as a backup and he debated the merits. He'd have to get rid of it before getting back on the plane. He decided not to decide.

I will let the universe decide for me.

On the plane, he accepted a glass of white wine, but didn't finish it before he was asleep. He didn't wake until the plane's wheels hit the ground in Miami.

Being first off the plane, he beat the rush at customs. The drug-sniffing dogs ignored him and the agent barely looked up before stamping his passport and collecting his disclosure form.

"Have a great day, sir," the agent said.

"You too," Glen responded.

Rental car.

Fighting traffic.

Overtown used to be called Colored Town, but that name was no good these days. While driving around, he liked the look of Overtown Gun and Pawn. Inside, the pistols and the knives on display were next to each other. He like the look of a walnut-handled, Tac Force spring-assisted folding stiletto. The blade popped out crisply and looked thirsty for a fat man's blood.

Perfect. Making sure the clerk saw his wad of cash, he put a fifty on the counter.

"Keep the change."

The clerk liked that. He licked his lips.

"Is there anything else we can do for you, sir?" he said.

"I was toying with the idea of buying a handgun. Nothing too heavy, maybe a 32 revolver and a box of shells. But, sad to say, I am not a Florida citizen."

The man's eyes flicked left and right.

"That requirement is easily waived with an expedite fee," he said. "Two hundred in cash."

Glen laughed.

Expedite fee.

That was good.

Ten minutes later, Glen walked out.

In the car, he loaded the .32 pistol. It was tiny in his hands, a Charter Arms snub-nose.

Thank you, universe.

Better to have it and not need it.

He thought about stopping at a drivethru for a greasy Cuban sub, but he wasn't hungry.

Let's get this done.

Steve and Roxy

THEY HAD THEIR daily routine. A light lunch in front of the TV for their daytime drama, *The Guiding Light* streaming on Hulu. They were determined to watch all 57-years of the shows before they died.

Steve pretended to be above it all, but the intersecting Bauer story lines and personalities were addicting and it gave them something to argue about—usually about police procedure.

"Even in the 50's, they didn't do things that way."

"It's a dramatization, Steve. Get your anal retentive head out of your ass."

"What does that even mean?"

"That's my point, Steve, I was speaking figuratively. Don't be so literal or you'll never enjoy anything in life."

He reached out his hand. She brushed it away.

"I enjoy debating with you, dear."

"Shut up and pay attention or you'll never keep up."

The short shows they watched were still in black and white. They had a long way to go if they would finish 57 years of shows.

"What's the schedule today?" Steve said.

"You say that everyday. Tuesdays are Bridge. Wednesdays are the ballet for seniors class I teach. Today, it's fencing. Foil techniques."

"I don't know why you do all that stuff."

"Alice Cooper said it best. If you stop, you die. Now, shush and try to follow along."

They watched for a few minutes, then the doorbell chimed. Surprised, they looked at each other.

"Are you expecting anyone?" she said.

He shrugged. "Nope."

"Okay, I'll get it."

"No, stay put, I need a pee anyway."

For him, it was a chore getting out of his recliner, but he struggled, out of breath, to his feet and waddled toward the door.

"Damnable nuisance," he muttered.

Out of habit, he reached under his bathrobe and stuffed his Smith and Wesson Police Special service weapon down the back of his pajamas.

Glen Wilson—Secundo

Under a palm tree, he found a place to park a hundred yards beyond their address. After parking, he studied their pictures. Steve was fat and at least ten years older than Roxy.

What does she see in him?

Steve had been an Army Sergeant, cop and DEA agent—then an independent security consultant, whatever that is.

Now on this hot, humid day under blue skies with puffy, scattered clouds, it comes to an end with a knife in the heart.

These people did not matter. The only man who mattered was Glen himself. But, Glen had to suffer as one-by-one, the people he loved died horrible deaths. He shut off the engine and released his seatbelt.

Time to get busy.

These people were not going to kill themselves.

Steve and Roxy

Steve hauled the door open. The woman was about 30 and dressed very elegantly. White blazer over white satin blouse. White dress pants. White flats on her feet. Her sculpted hair was pulled back in a French roll with a diamond-encrusted clasp.

"Whatever you're selling, we don't need none," Steve said.

"Steve?" she said.

"Yes."

"You killed my sister-in-law. Now you die."

Swinging widely, she jammed a hunting knife under his arm and into his chest.

"Oh," he said as he fell backwards like a beached whale onto the tile of the entryway.

Along with him, the umbrella stand by the front door toppled, too.

Now standing, Roxy said, "Steve?"

The woman fished around in her shoulder bag. She'd brought a spare knife and felt fortunate that she had. After pulling out the new knife, she unsheathed and held it up.

"Now you," she said.

Steve was bleeding out, he could feel it. However, he still had a little life left. He looked to his left and saw Roxy's fencing foil laying on the floor. He pulled off the protective rubber tip and backhanded it—Roxy neatly snagged it out of the air and assumed an attack stance.

Then with quick left-right sweeps, she opened wounds on the intruding woman's cheeks—which immediately streamed blood onto her satin blouse.

The woman dropped the knife.

"Fuck this," she muttered.

She reached into her shoulder bag and brought out a pink Ruger 388 LCP.

Light. Compact. Powerful.

As she aimed at Roxy, Steve, with the last of his strength, pulled his pistol from under his backside and, aiming up, shot her in the chest six times.

Still standing for a moment, she was dead.

Almost immediately after, Steve was dead, too.

Glen Wilson—Secundo

Thirty feet away, Glen heard the shots ring out in quick succession. He stopped.

What the fuck?

He continued, then turned at Steve's sidewalk. A woman all dressed in white lay in the doorway. Blood was splattered everywhere. Behind her, like a man mountain, lay Steve. Kneeling by Steve, he recognized the girlfriend from Steve's dossier.

Roxy.

Looking dazed with blood dripping from her fingertips, she stood with the fencing foil at her side.

"Roxy," he said. "What's going on? Is Steve okay?"

"Steve's dead," she said.

Noticing the knife in his hand, she raised the foil and pointed it at him.

She will use that thing to keep me from getting close enough to use the stiletto.

He dropped the knife and reached for the revolver, then raised it.

Roxy lifted her other hand and he looked deeply into the barrel of the tiny pink pistol.

"He might not have seemed like much to you," she said, "but we had plans."

Her aim was steady and true. He put his pistol back in his pocket and raised his hands.

"Get the fuck out of here," she said.

He was sorely tempted to call her bluff, but a thought filled his mind.

Regardless of the method, the mission was accomplished.

Steve was undeniably dead.

And I have a plane to Mazatlan to catch.

"Okay, Roxy," he said. "I'm going."

Headquarters

In Gerusha's office, amid toppling stacks of paperwork, she and Lori-Ellen juggled telephones. Return Authorizations, online auctions, marketplace listings—they were even using Craigslist to sell office furniture. The volume of correspondence was staggering.

Walter appeared at the door.

"Stop," he said.

Gerusha pointed at her headset.

"I'm on a conference call," she whispered.

Walter pulled off her headset and then Lori-Ellen's.

"Stop," he said.

Annoyed, Gerusha said, "We're busy following *your* instructions. Let us do our jobs."

"I sold everything left to Pheyer. They are taking over the leases, they get everything. Patent applications, paperclips, servers, cables—even stuff not delivered we can't cancel. Package price, all-in-one deal. They'll even take employees if any of them want to work after their big pay-out."

"This is nonsense, Walter. We're doing really well. The economy is strong and for some reason, people want our stuff. We even turned a profit on the AI engines—you can't get them anywhere without waiting a year."

"Anything not already sold or under contract stays put."

"This does not make sense," Gerusha said. "We were on track to clear over a billion." She looked at printed spreadsheet. "One-point-three. I don't understand."

"Four-point-seven billion. Cash."

Lori-Ellen could not hold back. "What the unholy fuck?" she said.

"Bidding war," Walter said. "That's what it took for them to beat Kagami Oshubushi. The team from Munich will be here in the morning to take the reins. Quick transition. By five o'clock tomorrow afternoon, you're done."

"What do they think they are getting?"

"Beyond the patents and the talent we assembled? I don't know. Maybe they think they can recover data from the wiped drives, though I wish them good luck with that. They get any and all lawsuits, too. If you can beat that deal, then I'll call it off."

Gerusha reflected.

"No, with what we're getting, we're not even in the ballpark."

"Setup a voicemail response, settle everything we're committed to and blanket cancel the rest with an email blast. Then turn off your phone and take the rest of the day off. You'll have a busy day tomorrow, but at five o'clock, you'll be done and we'll have a dinner party."

With that, Walter was gone.

Gerusha leaned back in her chair and looked at Lori-Ellen.

"This place is one surprise after another," Lori-Ellen said.

"Tell me about it," Gerusha replied. She cleared her desk by dropping a stack of papers in the recycle box. "We will break a lot of hearts."

They got busy with their automated responses to email and phone calls. In an hour, they were done. Standing in the doorway, they looked back into Gerusha's office. In tears, Lori-Ellen put her arm across Gerusha's shoulders and pulled her close.

Gerusha flicked off the lights.

"What are you doing tonight?"

Lori-Ellen shrugged.

"I thought we'd be working all night. I don't have any plans."

"Come to the house, I'll throw something together. Don't bring anything, we have plenty of wine."

"Sounds good to me," Lori-Ellen said.

Gerusha scribbled on a scrap of paper.

"Here's the address and code for the gate. You'll miss it the first time you pass by, everyone does. Huge hedge Glen won't let the groundskeepers trim. Come by about 6:30—it will be fun."

Lori-Ellen's Dinner at the Wilson's House

For Lori-Ellen, Gerusha's offhand invitation was a very big deal. At the company, there was a tight-knit inner circle of people who knew each other for years and shared legendary adventures — while she was a receptionist not even halfway though a community college associate degree. After two years of smiling at Glen as he crossed the lobby and watching as he habitually rubbed his bronze bust, she'd murdered at his request and had then been promoted to be his wife's assistant.

Glen's wife who had been the fulltime receptionist before her. The tangled weirdness of it all made her lightheaded.

Now, she was on the frontier edge of being a multi-millionaire and had not yet absorbed that fact. It didn't seem real. She expected to wake up and be eternally paycheck-to-paycheck -poor once again.

Once again and forever, like she deserved.

She admired the mysterious Gerusha—the stunning Gerusha who barely applied any makeup and wore casual clothes, but made them look stylish, classy and wonderful. Gerusha who wore canvas sneakers and a rose gold Piaget watch.

I could buy a BMW for what that watch cost—and not a cheap one. A good one, at least an X-drive 540.

Instead, she drove a four-year-old Toyota Yaris with a crumpled fender.

Overwhelmed, she couldn't walk. She sat down to catch her breath.

Next week, I can afford to get the Toyota fender fixed.

The news from Walter began to sink in. She was getting a full share. 1%. One-percent of Pheyer's 4.7 billion buy-out.

Assuming there must be some error in her thinking, she did the mental math over and over. Ten percent of 47 billion is 470 million. Ten percent of that...

47 million. Plus another 8 million from the liquidation effort.

Holy Mother Magdalena.

I'm rich. Or, I will be shortly. And I'm going to Glen and Gerusha's house.

Unless something happened along the way.

With my luck, I will get hit by an asteroid on Elliot Avenue.

Her life had changed so much over the last month.

This can't be real.

A month earlier, she'd used a cash advance from a tortured credit card to keep her checking account from going overdraft. Even today, she had maybe $75 in her account depending on what bills were auto-paid.

She was afraid to look at the balance.

After all the money waved around, they'd probably screw her and give her a $500 severance check and a pat on the head. That's what happened at her previous job working for a Lynnwood accounting firm.

Sign here or you don't even get the $500.

I needed the $500.

Because of the brutal commute into Seattle, she almost didn't take the temp position at Immortality. Driving into the city every day was a huge pain in the ass, but she couldn't afford to live in Ballard or anywhere close. 90 minutes in the morning to go 15 miles. Two hours in the evening. It really sucked, but there was nothing else.

She shook away her dark mood.

They weren't going to screw her. Say what you will about Immortality, LLC, but they paid their bills—Gerusha made sure of it.

She thought about Gerusha and how casually elegant she was.

I am such a frump.

But, Gerusha did not look down on her. She was open and friendly, though they had little time for chit-chat or gossip.

Gerusha who was married to the legendary Glen Wilson.

Trying to stand, her knees were weak. Like a drunken

sailor, she held onto the stair railing to steady herself.

I am an insider with their address and gate code.

She wondered about the dress code. She didn't know any other rich, powerful people.

Did they go full formal for a dinner party?

Should she stop at a hair dresser—have her eyebrows and nails done? Overwhelmed, she toyed with the idea of canceling, but she recalled words from Glen.

"Always go forward, never backward. The simulation punishes you for what you *don't* do."

As always, what he said made little sense. He was always saying obscure, stupid things.

What's the *simulation*?

It didn't matter. She was invited and was going. To hell with fear and second thoughts.

There was no time for going home and no time for a visit to the salon. The way Gerusha knew her at work, that's how she'd go.

Except...

There were yoga sling sandals in the Toyota's trunk.

She was ditching the high heels.

Gerusha was right, Lori-Ellen drove by the house, then had to double-back when the house numbers went past the numbers on Gerusha's note. The driveway was narrow and unmarked. The mailbox and gate were hidden by an unruly, overgrown hedge. Lori-Ellen did not know what to expect. A vampire castle? A Hollywood-modern chrome and glass party pad? An old-money mansion?

It was none of those. It was brick two-story house—vaguely English Tudor with a slate roof and ivy growing around the windows. There was nowhere else to park, so she stopped in the middle of the cobblestone driveway and sat for a minute looking at the house and yard.

Would they be formal with a cook, maid and butler? Or,

would Gerusha have a big meal catered from one of the fancy restaurants downtown? Would there be caviar and champagne in fluted crystal glasses? Lori-Ellen's apartment was 800 square feet in a rundown complex only a half-step better than public housing. The idea that in a week, she'd be able to buy a place like this made her dizzy.

This can't be real.

The front windows were dark. The massive entry door had a brass knocker—a crudely fashioned owl, huge and heavy. Hesitantly, she let it tap-tap—ready at an instant to accept that no one was home and the invitation was a forgotten mistake. She stood for five uncomfortable minutes too scared to knock again.

Gerusha, dressed in a bathrobe and fuzzy slippers, threw open the door. With a scrunchy, her tousled hair was loosely pulled back into a pony tail.

"Rose said she heard something. My bad, I should have told you to go around back like everyone else. Come in."

Standing in the entry, Gerusha looked her over from head to toe.

"My God, are you still wearing panty hose? I'll show you to your room so you can peel out of them and get comfortable. Look through the drawers, there are sweat pants and Glen's rock band t-shirts. Try to pick one without a demon or dragon. Good luck with that."

"Room?" Lori-Ellen said.

"I won't take *no* for an answer. You're drinking far too much Chardonnay to drive home tonight. We rarely get them, but we're all set for guests. If you don't see what you need in your bathroom, just holler."

Up the curved stairway and down a hall, the guest room was bigger than her apartment.

"Take a few minutes to freshen up, then join us downstairs," Gerusha said.

In the center was a canopy bed with 11 pillows. She counted twice to be sure. The dresser was stuffed with clothes—

she found tiger-striped yoga pants and a voluminous 2XL Deep Purple t-shirt.

Come Taste the Band.

She was vaguely familiar with the band, but did not know anything about tasting any band. The silkscreen had wine glasses and no dragons, devils or demons.

She felt a desperate need to follow instructions to the letter.

In the bathroom, she washed her face and stared at her image in the mirror. The whoever looking back at her was a stranger.

Grabbing a washcloth, she sat on the edge of her bed and cried her eyes out.

She was a fraud.

I am not a princess, I am a scullery maid. I am a rat living in the walls. I am a cockroach. I don't belong here.

It took everything to fight off the urge to flee.

Instead, she got up and splashed more water on her face, then patted her skin dry with a fluffy towel. There was never a softer towel—it was as soft as cashmere. She loved the towel. It was beautiful.

I'm sleeping with this towel.

She arranged it on the bed.

"Wait for me," she said. "I'll be back soon."

While standing at the door with her hand on the knob, she changed her mind. After striding across the room like she owned it, she arranged the towel around her neck like a downy scarf.

"You're coming with me."

After descending the stairs, she was lost. She listened, then followed faint voices.

The kitchen was brightly lit. It wasn't just her and Gerusha, there were also two massive people, a man and woman. They were truly and extraordinarily large.

Gerusha grabbed her shoulders.

"You bad girl, you shoplifted my elegant fur. Do you know how many innocent Russian minks had to die to create that designer piece? But, damn it all, I have to say, it looks great on you. Makes your cheekbones pop. Okay, fine, I forgive you for breaking into the vault and stealing my exotic fur."

"It's a towel and tonight, my best friend."

"No. Tonight, it's a fabulous, million-dollar wrap made from endangered sables. Virgin sables who ate only diamonds and gold dust. Let me introduce the household. Rose and Marcus. Marcus is the big one."

It was true, Marcus was slightly larger than Rose, but they were both monstrous.

Rose waddled over like a buffalo and took Lori-Ellen's hand.

"You need to learn."

Tugging Lori-Ellen to the counter by one of the sinks, she poured Tang crystals into a measuring cup.

"Exactly half a cup of powder per quart of spring water."

She mixed the concentrate with water in a pitcher.

"Stir and keep stirring until the crystals are completely dissolved. Don't be lazy and stop too soon. No crystals left. Stir longer to be sure. Then, the important part."

She dipped an eye dropper in a bottle of red dye, then carefully put one drop on a tablespoon.

"One drop is too much. Wick off half with a paper towel. Then mix thoroughly."

After stirring in the dye, she held the pitcher up to the light.

"This is the exact, proper shade. You'll have to practice, but you'll get it."

Lori-Ellen looked over her shoulder at Gerusha who was tossing a salad with tongs. She shrugged.

"She's a painter. Color is important to her. Just roll with it."

She nodded at a chilled bottle of white wine.

"I lied, no Chardonnay. Château Pape Clement Blanc. I hope that works for you, because that's what we have."

Lori-Ellen poured an inch and sipped.

"If you like it, don't be shy. Help yourself."

Lori-Ellen seated herself across the kitchen island so she

could watch Gerusha chop radishes and red onions for the salad. She nodded at Rose and Marcus who were cuddling and whispering to each other.

"How do you know them?

"They came with the house."

Rose spoke up. "The house is mine, they just bought it."

"If you understand that," Gerusha said, "you're leagues ahead of me."

Rising, Rose framed Lori-Ellen's face with her beefy hands.

"I am so going to paint your beautiful face."

"That means she likes you," Gerusha whispered. To Rose, she said, "You can have her for ten minutes, then the lobster rolls will be ready."

Rose took Lori-Ellen's hand and led her down a hallway.

"This is my studio. Sit on the chair while I arrange the lights."

Lori-Ellen was instantly captivated by the lurid images on the canvases.

"I've seen your work before."

Rose nodded at Lori-Ellen's t-shirt.

"I did a cover for them. They wanted a fire-breathing dragon, but they got what they got and were happy to get it."

Lori-Ellen stood in front of a six-foot square painting showing a photo-realistic farmer feeding slop to pigs. In the background, surreal mechanical monsters were on the march.

"I call that one *Pig Farmer.* It's not for sale. In fact, don't get any ideas. None of these paintings are for sale. Now, sit. I have to get you fast. Lady G will filet me if we let the lobster rolls get cold. Sit!"

Rose moved the lights millimeters until she was satisfied, then arranged the towel so it draped around Lori-Ellen's neck the way she wanted.

"Hold very still, I need to work quickly."

She stood before a canvas and made a few strokes with a charcoal pencil.

It took a mere minute.

"Okay, go now. I got you. I got the essence of you. You are mine now."

"Can I have a peek?"

Rose looked at her as if she was mad.

"No fucking way." she said.

In the kitchen, Gerusha was serving. There was another stunning blonde sipping wine. Though she did not come to the company often, Lori-Ellen recognized her.

Angela.

Walter's woman.

"What's with the towel?"

For an embarrassed instant, Lori-Ellen wanted to run.

Instead, she said, "It's my best friend."

"Okay," Angela said. "Let's eat, I'm starving."

There was a formal dining room and a breakfast nook with plenty of chairs, but, cozy and informal, they stayed in the kitchen sitting on bar stools around the kitchen island. Gerusha lit candles. Dinner was cheese squares, crackers, lobster rolls and salad. It was a fabulous meal, far better than anything Lori-Ellen could get at Outback Steakhouse or Applebee's.

There was a warmth in her belly and it took a minute to figure out. Like magic, no matter how much she drank, the level in her wine glass was always an inch, just like her first pour. Gerusha was smooth in serving, but empty bottles by the sink told the tale.

With flushed cheeks, Rose stood and tugged at Marcus' hand.

"Brace yourself, here it comes," Gerusha whispered.

"Though we are not formally married in the eyes of the Catholic Church or Washington State, I don't believe Master Marcus should enter the lifetime state of holy matrimony without sampling the fruits of my sexuality. We will have not have any fraudulent misleading. So, we bid you goodnight with fair warning. There will be sounds of carnal lust coming from the far bedroom. Despite inevitable, insatiable curiosity, do not be alarmed or give in to the temptation to peek."

She led Marcus out of the kitchen.

Turning, Lori-Ellen caught Gerusha pouring a half-inch into her glass.

"What was that?" she said.

Gerusha shrugged. "They've been fucking like rabbits for six months. Always with a speech containing way more details than we need, but you get used to it."

She raised her glass.

"To us, the winners."

Lori-Ellen drained her glass. Immediately, Gerusha poured in a fresh inch, then the empty bottle joined three others by the sink. Gerusha popped the cork on a new one.

"I don't feel like a winner," Angela said. "I heard the news. You two are rich while I can barely scrape together a million in the bank from scraps I get from Walter. Bastard. He thinks, if he just pays my credit card bills, that's enough."

"You were offered a job," Gerusha said. "But, you declined. Besides, I've seen your credit card bills. You're doing fine."

"People like me aren't suited for day jobs," Angela said. "I am an actor. I need my days free for auditions and rehearsals. Besides, you don't know what I go through. Walter *experiments* on me."

"Shush," Gerusha said. "He experiments on everyone. He only does the risky stuff to the homeless."

"What are you going to do?" Angela said. "I don't want to go to Alaska. It didn't work out so well last time."

"Alaska?" Lori-Ellen said. "What's going on with Alaska?"

Gerusha poured a quarter-inch into Lori-Ellen's glass.

"You get top-secret clearance when this bottle is done—then I'll tell you what I know—which, granted, isn't much."

"Speaking of the devil," Angela said. "Where is Glen?"

"I think he's coming home. I hope so. Tonight, it's just us

girls."

Unsteadily, Angela stood up.

"I've had enough, so it's just you two. I'm going home."

Concern washed over Lori-Ellen's face. Gerusha laughed.

"She's not driving, they have a place one street over. Walking distance. Don't worry, Parker will see her home."

"Who is Parker?" Lori-Ellen said.

"Security, week nights."

The three walked to the back door.

"I can't believe you two are rich and I got nothin'."

"When opportunity knocks, you gotta answer the door."

Angela fingered the towel around Lori-Ellen's neck.

"I do love your wrap. Who is your furrier? Cotton Craft?"

Lori-Ellen buried her nose in the towel. It smelled good—as if it was freshly laundered with Febrez. Maybe it was.

"Fuck off," Lori-Ellen said.

Gerusha and Angela tilted their heads back and laughed.

"We're all going to get along just fine," Gerusha said.

After Angela left, they settled back in the kitchen. Gerusha carefully measured out wine until Lori-Ellen's glass was filled to one inch. From down the hallway, someone was squealing. They couldn't tell if it was Rose or Marcus. Slowly, Gerusha pushed the heavy door shut to muffle the sound.

"They'll be at it a while," Gerusha said. "Ask me something."

"I'm fuzzy on what happened at the company. Help me understand?"

Gerusha sighed. "I'll try, but I learned a long time ago it's best to go with the flow and not try to follow the gory details. Here goes. We were selling a process that rejuvenated wealthy clients. We transferred personalities and memories into a new host body. Unfortunately, it looks like the process created psychopaths—truly dangerous people, as you well know. As soon as Glen figured this out, he pulled the plug. Now you tell me something."

Lori-Ellen buried her face in the towel.

"I'm a fraud and I don't belong here."

"Good, imposter syndrome, we're in the same boat. I don't belong here either. For fuck's sake, I was a barista at Starbucks when Walter met me. And yet, here I am. Despite my good fortune, in an instant, I could have an aneurism and fall over dead—or worse, be paralyzed and useless." Dramatically, she flopped her head sideways and stuck out her tongue. "But, for as long as I am alive, I'm riding the wave. If not you, then who? We're all just passengers on this bus. Your turn."

"What's with you and Glen? He's old and a bit of a clown."

"That's a great question I ask myself all the time. But, for as long as he'll have me, I made a commitment and I am his. Yes, he's a clown, a braggart, a bullshit artist, greedy and selfish—and those are his better qualities. Good luck to you if you think there is a perfect man out there, somewhere. It's like a black box process. If good things come out, then it doesn't matter what's in the box. Glen, like God, works in mysterious ways."

"The guest room is heavenly. I will not want to leave."

"Then don't. We have a long day tomorrow, then we're free for a while. Stay here. What are you leaving behind at your apartment? By my calculation, you have three outfits. I'm not being critical, you accessorize and creatively change the mix, I give you that. Write it all off, don't even go back."

"You could have just given me a raise."

Gerusha laughed. "We aren't in the save-the-world business. How many times have I heard Glen say that? He says, 'I tried saving the world and it didn't work.' Hardship created you."

"You were going to tell me about Alaska..."

"Ah, okay. Did you know that Glen was duly elected to congress? The deep state machine chewed him up and spit him out. The whole thing was buried in a memory hole. If you think about it, it's amazing what they can do when there is a harmonic alignment of interests—Silicon Valley tech companies and swamp rat state bureaucrats enabled by a compliant, lapdog mass media. They work miracles. So, there's unfinished business in

Alaska."

Gerusha took a sip of wine, then continued.

"Though huge in area, the population of Alaska is only a shade over seven hundred thousand. To make the numbers easy, let's say there are five hundred thousand voters. Something like twenty percent—a hundred thousand—lean left. Glen says we don't have to get rid of all of them—he wants to focus on the 8,000 school teachers. He says, beyond government employees, they are the core group to attack."

"He's going to conquer Alaska?"

"No, he's going to free it."

These words echoed in Lori-Ellen's ears.

"How the hell can he do that?"

"I don't know exactly. Somehow, the Russians are involved, he thinks they will invest. The goal is to create a philosophically homogenous society like Sweden or Japan. I don't know exactly what that means, it's something I heard Glen say."

"That sounds smart—not like Glen at all."

Gerusha laughed. "He has his moments. None of that is important right now. Here's what you should be thinking about. Are you going to sit on your money like a mother hen—or, are you going to accept a job offer from Glen and move to Alaska for a few years?"

"Will Glen offer me a job? Something interesting?"

"He'll let you do whatever you want. And, if he doesn't, I will. Take the time you need and think things through. But, right now, we have more important decisions."

She walked to the freezer and slid open the drawer.

"Ice cream. If you make me eat it alone, I'll ask Parker to shoot you in the head. We have salted caramel, strawberry or Dutch chocolate. And Vanilla, of course. One scoop is enough for me, but you take what you like."

One scoop was enough for Lori-Ellen too. With tiny spoons, they savored and made it last. When they were done, Gerusha hugged Lori-Ellen.

"One more day and we're done with Immortality."

"It sounds funny when you say it that way."

"Ha, so it does." She yawned. "Sleepy. Leave your key out and Parker will move your car. If you're up in the morning, we can carpool to the office. If you're not, then I'll see you later. Sleep as long as you like."

"Before you go, look into my future. What do you see?"

Gerusha laughed. "Anything I predict will probably be wrong." She took a breath and thought about it. "Okay, I'll give you one. Now that you're rich..."

"Nearly."

"Close enough. Relatives you haven't talked to in decades will reach out to make sure you're okay and let you know about little Sally who needs a heart transplant or poor old Johnny who desperately needs a small loan until payday. All of your old boyfriends will reach out—they'll want to rekindle the flame or will have a sure-fire investment for you to look at. Be kind. Let them down gently. It will take you about five minutes to realize being rich does not solve all of your problems and that being famous really sucks sometimes."

"You make the lifestyle seem so appealing."

"Hey, don't ask the question if you don't want the answer," Gerusha said, laughing.

In the guest room, after using the toilet and the miracle of a bidet, she brushed her teeth, found a nightie in a drawer and slipped it over her naked curves. Testing and then finding the pillow she wanted, she moved the other ten onto a futon. She wrapped the towel around the chosen pillow and rested her head on it. She knew it was stupid, but the towel symbolized peace and a warm welcome into a different world.

Her head was filled with images and information, but woozy, it didn't take long to find sleep.

In the morning, moving slowly and nursing an aching head, she dressed in yesterday's clothes and wandered downstairs. Gerusha did not say anything, she just pointed.

Coffee.

Aspirin.

"Yes, please," Lori-Ellen said.

At the Immortality headquarters, the acquiring team was in place inventorying equipment and paying careful attention to anything said by the outgoing team. It's a stereotypical cliché, but the Germans were humorless and efficient. There were four already waiting in Gerusha's cramped office. The supervisor was Günter. The first thing they did was present a contract.

Lori-Ellen's offer was for around double her current salary with unrestricted stock options and a $100,000 bonus for staying six months.

"Are many employees accepting their offer?"

His English was clipped and precise, though heavy with accent. "Not as many as we expected," he said.

"I will take it home and consider it."

"I will take that as a *no*," Günter said. "We'll take what you offer—whether it be an additional day, week, month or year—at your terms."

She glanced at Gerusha who, very slightly, shook her head.

"Sorry," Lori-Ellen said.

"Very well, let's get as much done as possible before the closing bell."

With only a couple of bathroom breaks, they worked until 5:00 when literally, the closing bell rang out through the building. Gerusha and Lori-Ellen both stood and removed their hands from the keyboards and stretched their stiff backs.

The German team looked unhappy, but resigned to what they had to work with. It would take a long time for them to sort through the passwords, keys and keycodes, sketches, schematics, flowcharts, source code archive locations and network maps.

People mingled in the hallways. It took a half hour of hugs, tears and insincere promises to keep in touch before Lori-Ellen made it to the building's front entry. There she spotted her friend, Paul Butler; she weaved her way to him through the crowd.

"How did you make out?" Lori-Ellen said.

"They re-instated all the orders. I'm happy. I hear you're one of the one-percenters. Millions? How much?"

Lori-Ellen was embarrassed to say.

"I'm not sure."

"Right," Paul said. "There has to be a party. Can you get me in?"

"Damn it, Paul. Exclusive. You ask too much."

"I'm in sales. You don't ask, you don't get."

"Take care. I wish you well, Paul."

He grinned, but it was a sad, resigned grin.

"I'm in sales. I'm also used to being disappointed. Look, I don't suppose we could meet for dinner and get to know each other better?"

She glanced at her watch. 5:40.

That was fast.

"Aren't you married?"

"Maybe it's time I upgraded."

She spotted Gerusha waving by the front entry, then leaned over and kissed him on the cheek.

"Save your sales pitch for the new company."

She turned and was gone.

Doctor Zalooq's Little Show

On the top floor overlooking the entry, Walter stood and looked over the crowd. He waited until everyone noticed him and quieted.

"I'm not going to bore you with a long speech thanking you for your good work. You know what you did and what it means. Now it's time to move on to the next adventure—whatever that might be. With that, I will hand over the vault's key to the new owners and we'll be done, both literally and symbolically."

He reached under his shirt and pulled out a chain. On the chain was a small, golden key. With a flourish, he pulled the chain from around his neck and with thumb and index fingers holding the tiny key and the golden chain dangling, held it out to Rutger Pheyer, the President and COO of Pheyer, International.

The key grew larger until it broke the chain—which fell three stories to the floor. The key got larger and heavier. Walter adjusted his grip to hold it up until he staggered under its weight.

"Take it quickly before it kills me," he said.

The crowd laughed as he handed it over to Rutger. It was too heavy for the old man. He quickly handed it to his bodyguard.

"How did you do that?" Rutger said.

"Do what?" Walter replied.

He turned and walked away—headed toward the back stairway. Outside, at the bottom of the stairs, his limousine waited with the driver attending the back door.

After slipping inside, he kissed Angela and cupped her breast.

"How did it go?" she said.

"As always," he said. "Perfectly executed."

Glen Wilson—Secundo

IT HAD BEEN hot and humid in Miami, but after the long flight, the port city of Mazatlan stepped things up to full sauna mode. Once the stairs had rolled up to the plane, Glen was the first one off the aircraft. Though stiff from sitting so long, he was rested and ready to go.

The dossier was up to date as of a few weeks prior—and it said Murphy was taking a break and would be at the Pueblo Bonito resort Penthouse Suite 1 for an indefinite period.

Was she still there?

Glen's gut told him she was. If she could talk Elke into it, they'd stay there forever.

It seemed everyone at the Aeropuerto Internacional de Mazatlan had something to sell. Glen waved away business cards, brochures, flyers and coupons. He prepaid for a taxi voucher at the kiosk and was soon rolling through the sad decay of modern Mexico in his *Transporte Terrestre.*

On the way, he thought about asking the driver to help him find a weapon—at least a machete. A pistol was too much to ask. In Mexico, only Federales and cartel hitmen had handguns. He could probably find one, but he didn't need the attention.

Murphy and Elke were out-of-shape, middle-aged women. He didn't need much to take care of them and was sure he could kill them with his bare hands if he could get to them one-on-one, but that seemed unlikely. Per the dossier and his fragmented memories, he knew Murphy rarely left Elke's side. So, no gun and no hand-to-hand combat. Of all the options he considered, a one-pound rock in a sock seemed like the most appropriate weapon.

At the Pueblo Bonito lobby, he booked a room for a week though he only expected to stay a day or two. The clerk told him the only restaurant open at this hour was at the pool. On a map, she showed him how to get there.

After looking over the menu, he wasn't inclined to be adventurous. Burger, fries, tortilla chips, salsa and a Pacifico beer seemed safe enough. Activities around the pool included a Spanish lesson and young women painting pottery. There was an informal volleyball game going in the pool.

Did his eyes deceive him?

There they were.

Murphy and Elke in one-piece bathing suits casually swatting a ball back and forth across a net.

He tried not to stare, but it was hard. He'd flown 1,700 miles on a noisy airbus A320 to find these women and there they were, splashing around in the pool like adolescent idiots.

Would they waste time like this if they knew they were enjoying their last precious hours on Earth?

Squatter and more muscular, Murphy looked dangerous. She'd definitely be first. Taller, but flabbier, he could take his time with Elke if he could find a private place to do the job.

He briefly wondered why he hated them so much.

It was Glen who deserved to die for what had been done, so why bother with anyone else?

Because Glen deserved to know he caused all his friends to die before he died himself. It simply had to be.

Needing a sport bag to hold a couple of clothing changes, he took a Pulmonia to the Galerias Mazatlan shopping center. At the Adidas store, he bought sweat socks. Elsewhere he found underwear and a hooded raincoat—in case it started raining blood.

It just might.

Back at the hotel, after dropping off his purchases, he

walked to the open-air, back restaurant, Cilantros, and there they were again.

Did they ever leave the hotel grounds? Could he possibly be so lucky?

As he walked in, Murphy eyed him suspiciously.

Did he remind her of someone?

After seating himself at the bar where he could watch them, he ordered a Cadillac Margarita and wondered where he could find a rock, something round or oval between one and two pounds. Get a good-enough swing and a skull, as tough as it is, had no chance. The beach was sandy, but he wasn't worried, there had to be rocks somewhere.

Light's out.

He could feel it, the satisfying crunch. In fact, he could see the whole scene. In his imagination, there was enough room in their suite for a roundhouse windup. He would cave in the back of Murphy's skull and she'd be dead, instantly collapsing like a bag of rocks. Then, Elke. Maybe stun her with a lighter blow, then work her over from toe to head—smashing all of her bones and leave her quivering like a bowl of Jell-O.

Leave her alive so she can suffer a long time before dying?

It thrilled him to consider her fate—alive and damaged for the rest of her life.

Yes, that's the way to do it.

In the bar mirror, he studied himself. His beard had grown out an eighth inch. He was dressed very casually in a polo shirt, *Venados* baseball cap, khaki trousers and bare feet in sandals. With mixed memories, he knew of himself as an old man and he remembered himself as a young man. He also saw himself as a completely different young person. The three images blended and confused him.

What had the surgeons done to him? His jawline was different, it was as if they shaved off bone. Where his face had been oval, they had sculpted angles and edges. His gappy teeth and ears were different.

Those doctors were devils. It filled him with fury and he wished he could blow them up all over again.

While sipping and studying himself, he caught the eye of a young man sitting behind him at a table with another young man. Glen could be imagining it, but it seemed like these two were getting extra special attention from the waitresses. They were dressed very sharp with shiny boots, creased trousers and open-collar dress shirts. Gold. Lots of gold in their bracelets, watches, rings and necklaces with ornate tattoo sleeves extending an inch beyond their shirt cuffs.

He knew the type. Arrogant. Fearless. Cold eyes like snakes.

Cartel.

Was this random? Maybe the Sinaloa cartel watched out for the tourists. Hotel and restaurant businesses were key money-laundering systems. Were they watching Murphy and Elke? Or, were they watching him? The presence of these men tickled his spider-sense.

All possibilities needed to be considered.

He ordered another margarita.

He'd watch.

If they left before Murphy and Elke, he could conclude that his instinctual tickle was a false alarm.

Or, they might follow Murphy and Elke when they left. This would mean their business—whatever that was—was with them.

But, if they follow me when I leave...

That would not be good.

While sipping his fourth margarita, he watched Murphy sign their check, then the two women strolled, hand-in-hand, back to the hotel.

Two minutes later, *one* of the men followed.

The remaining one flicked his eyes onto the back of Glen's head every minute while nibbling tortilla chips.

I'll wait him out.

An hour later, Glen couldn't linger any longer. He needed a

piss. He scribbled his room number on the bar tab, added a miserly tip, signed and walked toward the public restroom on the path to the lobby. This one was too isolated...there was another toilet near the lobby where there were more people around. He walked to that one. When he came out, he peeked back at the restaurant—the remaining man was gone. Suspicious, he slowly scanned the area.

There, across the pool under a palm tree, the man watched.

This is not good.

Not good at all.

Glen Wilson—Primeiro

While sitting at the DFW airport, Glen decided to stop screwing around. It took several calls before he tracked down Iván Archivaldo's assistant.

"Change the protection order to a hit," Glen said.

The man's English was heavily accented, but easy enough to understand.

"Thirty-thousand, U.S. Forty-thousand if you want it to look like an accident or for the body to disappear."

"We'll wire thirty-thousand right away," Glen said.

Glen Wilson—Secundo

While he watched, the other man rejoined him. The first shook out a cigarette, then one for his partner. After lighting up, both pairs of eyes bored into Glen through the smoke. Though it was a no-smoking area, an unobtrusive pool attendant ducked in and placed an ashtray on the edge of the wall before them.

After a few minutes, the new guy glanced at his screen, then answered his phone. The conversation was very brief. A decision had been made. Now there was a different look in the men's eyes, one Glen knew well.

Murder. In the blink of an eye, the hunter becomes the hunted.

Fight or flight?

He wasn't going to beat two armed thugs on their home turf.

Shit.

Casually, while trying to look sleepy and inebriated, he yawned and looked at his watch, then walked through the lobby and down the hallway to his room. By the time his reached his corridor, he was running. There was no dawdling, he grabbed his valise and sport bag and ran to the furthest exit.

After pounding down the stairs, he was in the covered parking area. He slipped around the grand entry, then jumped in a Pulmonia.

"*Zona Dorada*," he said. "*Vamos.*"

In Mazatlan's Golden Zone, he jumped in another Pulmonia.

"Valentino's," he said.

Valentino's Night Club was the disco-bar on the nearest edge of Mazatlan's Malecón, or sea wall. It was a reliable place to hail a taxi and get a ride to the airport. With any luck, there would still be a flight to anywhere he could catch.

There was one and only one.

To Mexico City.

It was fine.

Anywhere but here.

In the first class cabin sipping another margarita, his nerves settled. He didn't feel ashamed for running.

Glen Wilson does not run from a fight. He simply postpones the confrontation until the right time comes—the time when he has the overwhelming advantage. It does no good for Glen Wilson to be killed before the mission is complete. Erring on the side of caution is simply a smart maneuver.

Despite his internal pep talk, he felt like a coward.

A worthless, miserable piece of chicken shit.

However, he knew the feeling would pass.

By the time he reached Mexico City, it was early in the morning. There were lots of flights to choose from. He decided to skip to the end game.

Seattle.

Glen.

Without their leader, he could take his time and pick off the rest of the team at his leisure.

Glen Wilson—Primeiro

IT WAS HARD for him to believe, but they planned a party without him. Seattle had long summer days, so at 8:30 PM when the Gulfstream landed at Paine Field, it was still light. Though it was a reverse commute, traffic was tangled and ugly. Arriving at the Canal Terrace in Fremont at 10:00, the party was in full swing mode.

Taking care of the important things first, Glen found a glass of rye whiskey and a cigar. Many of the people milling around were family and guests. Glen felt he didn't know anyone beyond an occasional face here and there. Instantly, Glen's good mood evaporated as black waves of depression attacked.

I travel halfway around the globe to save the world and this is the welcome I get?

Gerusha waved away smoke as she sat down next to him. She took a swig of his whiskey before speaking.

"I heard you were lurking around here somewhere."

Lori-Ellen took the seat on the other side of Glen. They both leaned in and kissed him on his cheeks at the same time.

Instantly, he felt better.

"You two have been getting to know each other? What else is new while I was gone?"

Lori-Ellen spoke first. "We're rich."

Glen shrugged.

"Did anything interesting happen?"

"I told you," Gerusha said to Lori-Ellen. "He doesn't care

half a shit about money."

She was tipsy. Glen grinned. That was the way he liked her best.

"I'm high on life," Glen said.

"I just decided," Lori-Ellen said.

"Decided what?" Glen said.

"I want to go to Alaska with you."

"Ah. What do you intend to do in Alaska?"

"Something important in an office. No scut work, something interesting."

"Fine."

"That's it?"

"What do you want? A contract? I'll put you in charge of contracts, so you can draft a contract with yourself, then run it by yourself for review before you sign it. What about my bronze bust from the lobby? Did some one pack it up?"

Gerusha shrugged. "The Germans own it now."

"Too bad," Glen said. "We'll have to commission another. When we get to Alaska, Lori-Ellen, that will be one of your first tasks."

"Great," Lori-Ellen said wryly.

"I told you to be careful what you wish for," Gerusha said.

"Let everyone know there is a meeting at the house at 10:00 tomorrow," Glen said. He looked Gerusha over from crossed legs to the top of her head. "Better make that 11:00."

"Tell me about your trip."

Glen settled back in his chair, took a sip of whiskey and stared off into the distance.

"Here we go," Gerusha said.

"It was my usual grand victory. I flushed the fake Glen out of the bushes and made him flee in terror of his life. He knew, if I caught him, it would be his ugly end, so he stayed far away from me."

Gerusha leaned across Glen and put her hand on Lori-Ellen's arm. "I will translate. He spent his time reading newspapers, drinking and chatting up waitresses."

"That's not fair. Anyway, while I was there, I bought a river boat as an investment."

"A river boat?"

"Yeah, pretty cool, huh?"

To Lori-Ellen, Gerusha said, "I almost asked him what we're going to do with a river boat, but we really don't want to hear it. Glen, we need to mingle. Give us an hour and we'll be ready to go."

"Us?"

"Yes, Lori-Ellen is staying with us for a while. And no, we're not all sleeping together."

Glen looked Lori-Ellen over.

"That was the farthest thing from my mind," he said. "If you have the guest room, then you are a few doors down from us. You'll have to live with heated sounds of carnal passion and the walls shaking."

"Glen," Gerusha said, "she's been with us a few days. We've been in the kitchen when Marcus and Rose retire for the night. She's heard the elephants mating."

"Oh," Glen said, disappointed. "We can't compete with that."

Roxy and Murphy

Murphy turned her cell phone on once a day. She had missed a call from Steve, but he didn't leave a message. She pressed the "call back" button.

It was a woman who answered.

"Is this Roxy?" Murphy said. "Steve told me that if a woman answered, I should hang up without saying anything."

"What? Oh, Steve's sense of humor. I get it. Yes, this is Roxy. I'm calling people in Steve's phone contacts. If you haven't heard, I'm afraid I have tough news to share. Steve died—murdered."

"That's horrible. What happened?"

"Bennie said it was one of the Immortality psychopaths—whatever that is. The Miami Beach Cannibal's sister. You know about that one?"

"Yes, I talk to Steve every week, give or take."

"This isn't easy to say, but Steve didn't have much time left anyway. Cancer. Pancreatic. He died protecting me."

Murphy thought back over the years. To her, Steve would always be her husky, gruff, gravelly-voiced mentor and colleague.

"It will take time to get used to the idea that he's gone. He was one of my dearest friends. Decades."

"Maybe this isn't the right time, but I'm going crazy here. Bennie says the team is moving to Anchorage. What do I have to do to get *in*?"

Murphy laughed.

"I'll text you an address in Seattle. Just show up and refuse to leave and you'll be in. Steve was a good man. I'll miss him."

"Me, too. Thanks, Murphy. These psychopaths are dangerous. Watch your back."

"Thanks, Roxy. You were a comfort in Steve's last days."

"I'm clinging to that and taking things day-by-day."

They disconnected their call.

"Steve?" Elke said.

Murphy nodded.

"He was a fine man."

"Yes, he was," Murphy said.

Saying nothing more, they sat and watched the sun set over the Sea of Cortes.

Glen Wilson—Secundo

IT WAS VERY strange...he'd never physically been in Seattle before, but he knew it intimately. The oppressive, solid-gray cloud cover. The clean, heavy-with-humidity air. The relentless emerald green foliage. The ubiquitous progressive wokesters with weird haircuts. The merciless traffic.

Home.

To be irritating, he rented a monstrous, lemon-yellow Hummer H2 from Hertz and drove it to a place he knew in the SoDo's industrial district. On a side street next to a roll-up door covered with graffiti, there was an unmarked metal door. After parking and getting out, Glen waved at the security camera.

"I don't know you," a disembodied voice said through a scratchy speaker. "Fuck off."

"I'm getting wet, Tommy. Let me in."

It took a few minutes while Tommy thought it over.

When the lock buzzed, Glen pulled the door open. At the back of the bare room was a large, felt-covered bench. The place smelled like machine oil and cordite. Tommy, looking skeptical, stood behind it with his hands buried in the pockets of a voluminous trench coat.

"Relax, Tommy, you're not going to shoot a good customer like me with that hand cannon in your pocket. RPG-7 and let's say two PG-7VMs and a half-dozen TBG-7V incendiaries. AK and a half-dozen magazines of seven-dot-sixty-twos. And a Colt 1911 dot-forty-five with five clips filled with cop-killers. I think that will do it."

"Starting a war?"

"No. Finishing one. Don't worry, you won't get any on you."

"Tomorrow, noon. You know the drop location and the protocol?"

Glen nodded. "Sure do," he said.

On a pad, Tommy added up the numbers with a pencil stub. He dropped it front of Glen, who shrugged.

Tommy didn't negotiate. With him, it was always a take-it-or-leave-it deal. It would take almost all of Glen's money, but he didn't care. There was always other money around for the taking.

"Plus sales tax, of course," Tommy said.

Glen laughed.

"Sales tax, my chapped ass." He pointed at the slip of paper. "I'll be at the drop tomorrow with that much in cash plus another two-grand for body armor. Nothing special, just whatever you have laying around."

Back in the truck, Glen thought things over. He had an evening free.

Fuck tonight, fight tomorrow.

There was a 24-hour place back by the airport where he could easily find a girl. He had a couple of thousand dollars in cash. Though barely, that was enough for dinner, drinks, a room at the Doubletree with an escort.

He grinned.

It was nice to be home.

In the morning, he had breakfast in the Doubletree's Coffee Garden coffee shop. While eating, he decided the Hummer was too garish. After eating, he took it back to Hertz and got a gray Hyundai Santa Fe instead. It would have been better to get a Subaru Outback—which was so common in Seattle they were practically invisible—but the Sante Fe SUV was almost as transparent.

As he knew they would, the Santander Bank complained about the cash he wanted and he spent over an hour dealing with them.

No, a transfer, bank draft, money order or certified check will not work. Cash. Now.

The withdrawal nearly wiped out his balance, but it was okay. Everything was okay.

The weapon sale was consummated on a stub of street off of Jackson not far from King Street Station. The driver of the battered white cargo van brought out a battery-operated cash counter and ran the bills through twice to be sure. He didn't mark all the bills and check the holographs, but he was careful and examined at least a hundred of the Ben Franklins—all while the escort stared at Glen as if daring him to try something.

Everything was in a wooden crate and it was heavy. By folding down the back seats of the Hyundai, the crate would fit, though only just.

After pulling open the van's back doors, the driver pointed to indicate that Glen should lift.

"The price includes free delivery."

"Fuck me," the driver said.

Grumbling, the passenger got out and helped to haul out the crate. If Glen was going to hijack them, this was the time, but there was a third man in back of the van cradling a MAC-10 machine pistol with suppressor. They were ready to rock and roll.

Glen laughed. He didn't care about the money.

Now the Hyundai was back-heavy and didn't have as much pep, but it rolled, so it was all good. He decided to take a tour through the neighborhood. He knew the address. He knew the gate code.

Along the way, he was stuck behind an Amazon delivery van. On a whim, he circled back. After waving at the doorbell camera, he grabbed the box.

This could come in handy.

As he drove by the house, he was disappointed to see the gate wide open.

What good is it to know the top secret gate code if the damned gate is open?

There were many cars in the driveway.

Some sort of gathering.

After passing by, he pulled off and watched the street in his rearview mirror. A taxi stopped and a tall black woman with a short-cropped afro hairstyle got out.

I know her.

He concentrated; he'd seen her recently, but where?

He figured it out.

She's Steve's friend...the one who threatened to cut me to pieces with a fencing foil.

Perfect, she can die along with all the other guests.

There were private places hidden in Discovery Park where he could prepare his weapons, but first he needed to visit the Ace Hardware and get some tools to open the crate—at least a pry bar and a screwdriver.

A Secret Meeting at the Wilson House

The library was big enough to hold everyone, though only just. Glen was half-dressed in boxer shorts and a ratty cotton bathrobe, his favorite. Walter wore an Italian three-piece suit and black shoes polished with a mirror finish. His white hair was swept back on his broad forehead like a rogue wave. He looked like a diplomat or English royalty. Disheveled Glen looked like Dude Lebowski. Walter pulled Glen's favorite chair to a spot along the wall and settled in.

Glen frowned.

That's my chair, but it would take a ton of TNT to move him now.

He counted heads. Walter, Angela, Gerusha, Murphy, Elke

and Lori-Ellen. Bennie would join via conference call. It didn't seem like a full team.

Glen felt a pang in his gut.

Steve should be here.

But, he was not going to join them and never would again.

Shit.

The intercom buzzed. Glen pressed the button to answer.

"Parker? What's up?"

"Boss, Collier has gate duty and says there is a woman who wants to come in and talk to you."

"Who is it?"

There was a muffled conversation.

"Her name is Roxy."

"I don't know any Roxy. We're busy. Take her Watchtower and tell her to fuck off."

Murphy pushed Glen aside and gave him a dirty look.

"Parker, this is Murphy. Tell Roxy to come around back—I'll let her in."

Murphy stabbed a finger in Glen's chest.

"Idiot. Roxy is Steve's friend. He died protecting her. You be nice or I'll slug you in the kidney and you'll piss blood for a week."

"This is a private, serious meeting," Glen said. "Invitation only."

As she left the room, Murphy flipped Glen her middle finger.

Glen addressed the room.

"Where was I? The replica-Glen knows everything I know and is therefore extremely dangerous. The hazard cannot be understated. He will be crafty and relentless. I urge you to take all security precautions until I kill this fucker. If you see him coming, hide."

Leading Roxy, Murphy returned to the room. She was bundled up with a knit hat and a down-filled long coat. After scanning the room, she walked up to Walter.

"Mr. Wilson, I've heard so much about you."

Walter tipped his head back and laughed.

"I'm Wilson," Glen said.

She turned and looked him over.

"Oh," she said, then looked for a place to sit.

There was a leather ottoman. She perched on it.

Glen grunted.

"Shall I take your coat?" Murphy said.

Roxy hunched her shoulders and tugged the collar closed around her neck. She looked like she wanted to be ready to leave at any instant.

"No, I'm fine."

Glen addressed the room.

"As I was saying, the fake Glen will be volatile and dangerous."

"Hold on," Roxy said. "I'm new. Give me some background, okay?"

"Because Glen and Walter are greedy and have zero common sense, they made fake versions of wealthy clients," Murphy said. "Younger versions. Unfortunately, they created murderous psychopaths, each and every one of them."

"It's more complicated than that," Glen said.

Roxy looked more carefully at Glen.

"There's a younger version of you?" she said.

"Yes," Glen said. "He won't be as distinguished or as handsome as me..."

"I've seen him," Roxy interrupted. "Mean-looking guy, hatchet-face. He was following behind the bitch that killed Steve. He looked a little like you, Glen, but younger as you said—with a stubble beard and a more intelligent, calculating look to his eyes."

"Do you know what he was doing?" Murphy said.

Roxy shrugged. "He had a knife and a gun. He was up to no good, I'd say. That reminds me, I don't know if this means anything, but as I was paying the taxi driver, there was a car parked down the street. Korean SUV. Gray."

Pushing Glen aside, Murphy marched to the intercom.

"Parker? Is the front gate closed?"

"Yes, ma'am," Parker said.

"Thank you. Tell Collier to keep a sharp eye out."

"Will do," Parker said.

Glen Wilson—Secundo

Finally ready, Glen drove by the house again. This time the gate was shut. He drove past, then backed up to the gate.

The guard walked around and stood by his window. His nametag said Collier. He was burly with close-cropped hair and a no-nonsense expression on his face.

"Private property. Move it along, pal."

Glen pressed the button to lower the window.

"Amazon delivery."

"Let me see it," Collier said. He examined the label. "This isn't even the right street. You need to take this a few blocks to the southeast."

As he leaned over to hand the package back, Glen jabbed his screwdriver into his eye. It sank to the hilt. Collier collapsed.

After getting out, Glen looked up and down the street.

No one.

The guard was heavy, but Glen was able to drag him through the side gate and hide his body behind the hedge. He punched in the security code and the vehicle gate slid open. He backed the car in and parked. The sensor would not let the gate close, so he was ready for a quick getaway.

Looking over the broad lawn, he saw figures moving behind shades on the first floor of the house.

Perfect.

He raised the Hyundai's back hatch and laid out the projectiles in the order he planned to use them, then loaded the RPG. Fire first, then explosives. The scene was vivid in his imagination. It would only take a few minutes. He'd blast incendiary grenades through all of the front windows. In half a minute, the house would be a fiery furnace.

Then he'd fire the explosive grenades and tear shell-shocked people to shreds. The bodies of the disoriented people staggering out would be framed by the flames and he'd pick them off one-by-one with his AK and handgun. Working quickly, he'd be long gone by the time the cops and the fire trucks arrived.

The bullet-proof vest was a beat-up, black Safe Life tactical carrier.

Cheap bastards. Fifty bucks at an Army-Navy discount store.

After considering, he decided to play it safe. He pulled the body Velcro clasps tight, then hefted the RPG.

He was aiming and ready to fire the first round when he heard a moan from the guard. Glen set the weapon back in the Hyundai and walked over to see Collier frantically clicking the button on his shoulder microphone.

Glen frowned.

"You have a screwdriver in your brain. How are you still alive?"

He put his shoe on the screwdriver and pressed down. The screwdriver resisted, then went an inch further in and Collier stilled.

"Okay? Any more interruptions? Anything more from you? No?"

Glen walked back to the SUV.

Some assholes don't know when it's time to die.

He lifted the RPG, flipped off the safety and aimed with his finger on the trigger.

It was time to rock.

Battle

PARKER'S VOICE CAME through the intercom.

"Something is happening at the front gate. Collier is nonresponsive. Stay away from the windows and move everyone to the back of the house. Now!"

Murphy did not hesitate. She pressed the group toward the door.

"Everyone out—back of the house, now. Go!"

Herding like a Border collie, she tugged Roxy to her feet and pointed.

"That way. Hustle up."

Moving quickly, Murphy fast-walked to the guardroom. It had a door to the outside—which was open. Outside, a straining Parker drew back on a compound bow. He let an arrow fly and watched its trajectory.

As he notched another arrow, he spoke.

"Crap, the fucker is wearing a vest."

Glen Wilson—Secundo

Aiming at the nearest front window, he increased the pressure on the RPG's trigger until he was knocked backwards by heavy blow to his chest. For an instant he thought he had fired, but the coffee-can incendiary projectile was still poking out the barrel of the launcher.

He couldn't breath.

A quivering arrow protruded from his chest. He dropped the RPG and stared at the arrow when a second arrow flew by and embedded in the SUV's back tire—which exploded.

Fucking hell.

He ripped at the Velcro of his Kevlar vest, tossed it aside and stared at the embedded arrow, then looked up.

Sixty yards away, a man standing in the driveway was drawing back. Glen took a second to think about jumping in the SUV, but it was not going far with the flat tire, so he bolted.

It was a good thing he moved, because the next arrow hit him in the calf instead of the gut. He stared at it poking through his leg. It didn't hurt, but it would.

The best he could, he ran.

Battle II

Parker stared at Murphy.

"The shithead moved," he said.

"You tagged him. Let's go get him. Handgun?"

Parker unsnapped the flap of his holster and handed her his Glock. Appearing from the house, Roxy stripped off her bulky coat and dropped it. Under, she wore runner's leggings and a loose-knit sweater. She stripped off the sweater to expose a sport bra. In an instant she took off running. By the time Parker and Murphy reacted, she was at the roadway, sprinting.

"Wow," Parker said. "She's fast."

Murphy shrugged.

"Let's go," she said.

Glen Wilson—Primeiro

Taking his time, Glen walked to the end of the driveway. He kicked the RPG into the grass and then turned to examine the arrow stabbed in the back tire of the SUV.

This thing isn't going far.

The keys were in the ignition. It complained, but rolled in

reverse and broke the arrow. He was able to get it off the driveway and out of the way.

He ran back and jumped in the groundskeeper's old Nissan pickup. It started immediately. At the end of the driveway, he turned right and followed the trail.

Glen Wilson—Secundo

Cruising on adrenaline and endorphins, the arrow did not slow him much...in half a minute he turned a corner and it was like he was a world away from the mayhem. The sound-deadening evergreen trees, Leyland hedges and rhododendrons in this upscale neighborhood were thick. It was as if he was all alone in virgin forest.

Furiously, his mind raced.

The immediate future was vivid in his mind. It was as if his escape already happened.

First, he needed a car.

With his pistol aimed at her head, he'd pull a blue-haired matron out her SUV. It would be worth investing a few seconds to kick her in the head so her call to the police might be delayed.

If he could kick her hard enough with his good leg, he could save a bullet and still, her call might be delayed forever.

That would be a good start.

Then, get out of the city. North? South? East? It would be best to head east. Once over the Cascade Mountains, Washington State was a different country. Rural and independent with fewer police. He could find a clinic where they would believe his elaborate story about accidentally shooting himself in the leg. If they patched him well, maybe he'd leave them alive.

The idea of being kind to people who helped filled him with warmth.

No. Better to leave no witnesses.

Glen's team might scatter.

Good.

Then he could pick them off one-by-one. First, the archer.

Flashing back, he could see the primitive look on the man's face. He had the cold eyes of a hunter.

How many innocent deer were murdered by this creep?

Maybe he'd enjoy an arrow in the gut.

Yes. That's the way.

Glen would have to get some gear, study and practice to get proficient with the bow and arrow.

Morons can notch, aim and hit a target. How hard would it be for a clever man like me?

He could be ready in a couple of days. He wouldn't have to heal completely first—he could practice with his leg bandaged.

The wound got serious about hurting. The dull ache changed to something raw and hungry.

He stopped to look. The arrowhead was barbed. Nasty. Evil. Mean. There was no way to pull it back, it would have to be pulled all the way through or cut off. What were the chances the stolen car would have bolt cutters? Not zero. If he cut the arrowhead off, he could pull out the shaft, wrap the holes with something and control the bleeding.

The blood was oozing, not spurting, so that was good. Still, the pain was building steadily and he needed to get off it quickly.

It was nothing a handful of Oxycontin couldn't handle.

Moving as fast as he could, he raised his head to the sky and asked for help.

Car. Bolt cutters. Oxy.

He tried to think of other things to ask for, but those three things were the most urgent.

They will do for now.

Looking ahead, he saw a cautious Subaru Forrester poke its nose out of a driveway and slowly turn toward a stop sign a dozen yards farther away. There it sat, emitting steam around its blood-red brake lights—beckoning while the preppy driver played with the Bluetooth connection on her iPhone.

His first thought was frustration. A bigger, more luxurious vehicle would be more comfortable—something like a Lincoln

Navigator or Cadillac Escalade.

He pressed away the ungrateful feeling. A Subaru is reliable transportation. That's the main thing right now.

Thank you, dear God, for answering my prayer.

Roxy and Glen Wilson—Secundo

The assailant had turned onto a side street, but there was a spotty blood trail to follow. Roxy ran past the turn, then slowed and slewed around the corner. There he was, ahead, limping like a wounded animal and marching toward a boxy car idling at a stop sign.

It took ten seconds, but she caught up and pushed him forward. Spinning, he flopped on his back and raised his pistol. She kicked it out of his hand—it skittered across the pavement. While the Subaru and unconscious driver turned the corner and cruised away, she raised his leg, got a careful grip on the slippery arrow shaft and pulled it through.

Gasping for air like a beached fish, Glen spoke.

"Thank you for helping me."

"I'm not helping you," she said. "I'm killing you."

Placing the arrow under his chin, she pressed it in as far as she could, then reared back and put her foot on the nick. Putting her weight into it, the arrow head lurched forward into his brain and the fake Glen Wilson was no more.

Panting, Parker and Murphy ran up to the scene and looked down on Glen's body.

"Damn, you're fast," Murphy said.

Roxy shrugged.

"As a girl, I wanted to qualify for an Olympic medal in hundred-meter sprinting, but I wasn't fast enough."

At that instant, Glen pulled up in the pickup. After exiting the truck, he joined them in staring down at the fake Glen.

"Let's load this piece of shit and get him out of here before the neighbors get excited," he said.

As if loading a heavy trash bag, he and Parker threw the

body in the bed of the pickup.

While watching Glen and Parker drive off, Roxy said, "I guess he'll thank me later?"

Murphy threw her arms around Roxy and hugged her tight.

"Good luck with that," she said.

Glen and Parker

"What will we do with him? "Parker said.

Glen considered the options.

"Let's take him out back and compost him," he said.

And Now, the One and Only Glen Wilson

While his team quietly sat in the library collecting their wits and nursing drinks, Glen was on the phone bringing Bennie up to date.

"When the fucker got a look at me, he ran like the hounds of Hades were on his heels. When I caught up with him, he begged for his life, but there's no mercy when you cross Glen Wilson. I sent his murderous soul straight to hell and that was that."

Murphy caught Roxy's eye.

"Do you see how this shit goes for us?" Murphy said.

"Yeah, I guess," Roxy said.

Murphy grabbed the phone out of Glen's hand.

"Hey," he said. "I'm talking."

She pointed her index finger at him and spoke sternly.

"Don't even start with me."

She turned away to talk to Bennie.

"Be ready, Bennie," she said. "As quickly as we can get to a plane to Anchorage, we're coming."

Author's Rambling Afterword

IF YOU'VE READ this far into Glen Wilson's deranged adventures, then you're one of my closest friends, even if we have never met. Thank you for joining me on this journey.

Thinking back over the years is poignant for an old man.

Let's go back.

Way back.

From my teenage years, there was a dead certainty in my gut that I would be a novelist. Not only that, but a well-known and successful one. I thought, once I applied my wonderful self to the task, I would automatically excel and the world would drop to its figurative knees and worship before the metaphorical altar of my overheated ego.

Ah, the sad death of a grand dream of youth.

By the time I was forty, I had written a few odd pieces (some are captured in *Mesh*) and started a couple of lame novels that quickly fizzled...and that was it. Like a hammer, it struck me that time was running out and if my dream of becoming a novelist was ever going to happen, my writing life had better get started.

Soon.

Or else.

The genesis of my worship of the written word is not hard to fathom. As a kid, I grew up in rural poverty in Southern Oregon and my only portal to the sparkling wonder of the outside world was books. I loved them. Still do. In addition to a steady diet of science fiction from the Eagle Point Public Library, I read everything I could get my hands on, including Mom's lame-brained women's magazines and the fine print on cereal boxes.

Mom was a reader, but Dad was most assuredly not. One of the key motivations of my life was to NOT be like my damaged, inept alcoholic father. In fact, much of the driving force of my life has been to prove to him that I'm not a loser. This is really pathetic considering that he died of cirrhosis of the liver at age 56 way back in early 1988. Decades later, I still carry around the burning desire to prove myself to him.

If you've ever sat down to write a novel, maybe it was easy for you, but it was hard for me. I couldn't think of an idea strong enough to support a long-term, sustained effort. I was lucky to meet my writing partner Mark Bothum—who is a far superior natural writer than me. Working with him on the first book (confusingly, the second book in the Continuing Adventures of Glen Wilson), *Alligator Alley*, was a real pleasure and it was like having training wheels on a bicycle.

Once I got going and found my voice, it was relatively easy to keep going.

When we wrote *Alligator Alley*, there was no thought of doing more and creating a series. But, I liked Glen and his odd associates and I knew there was more to his story.

As it turns out, there was much more.

Growing up as I did, I am completely hopeless with anything mechanical. It's not like we had a lawn mower to practice on. Most of my life was spent in the strange inner space between my ears. I could complain about my dismal and hopeless formative years, but I developed a very vivid imagination. Desperation and sensory deprivation will do that to a person.

By the time I wrote *Hartz String Theory*, I was feeling really good. I truly believed that novel would pave my way to fame and fortune. Innocently, I entered it in the First Chapters writing contest hosted by a defunct social media platform called Gather. To my despair, *HST* promptly died. Of the 2,600 entries in this contest, maybe mine came in last place.

As it turned out, the contest was a fraud and there was incredible anonymous sock puppet vote manipulation and something common to us now, but new back then: relentless, vicious trolling—including by me. The contest judges had no confidence the writing community would produce a publishable book, so the $5,000 prize and publishing contract was awarded to a wired-in hack, a pre-selected shill: Terry Shaw. However, other than Terry's dreck, the top entries were quite good, so they also awarded a first-place prize to Geoff Edwards.

When I feel depressed, I enjoy reading the bad reviews of authors I dislike.

> *When USA Today said of* [Terry Shaw's] *book: "The novel is driven more by plot than its writing or characters" apparently they mean that it's written in an amateur style whose characters are flat, unlikable and have an obsession with anal sex."*[1]

If you care to look up these books and test my literary taste, Terry Shaw's is *The Way Life Should Be* and Geoff's fine historical drama is *Fire Bell in the Night.*

A good thing came from the creepy disaster of Gather's first chapters contest: a community of authors formed a loose-knit writing group called *The Writin' Wombats.* At its peak, there were 350 scribblers in this group with varying skill, but a general seriousness about writing. We shared critiques, tips and encouragement—mixed with inevitable hostility and boorish nonsense.

While it lasted, it was fun and I learned a lot. The most

[1] From a one-star review of Terry Shaw's *The Way Life Should Be* at Amazon.com.

important lesson was how my writing skill stacked up against people who genuinely knew what they are doing.

And, I had a lot of work to do.

It was a humbling and harrowing experience—like a literary boot camp—but the end result was very good for me.

After Stephen King (in the 1970s), Dan Simmons is the best commercial writer I know of, but I vehemently disagree with him about something. As a former teacher, he thinks the only way to improve writing craft is to immerse oneself exclusively in well-written, successful books. As part of the Gather First Chapters contest, I saw a lot of really crappy writing. It was informative to see weakness in a novice writers' work and realize I was doing exactly the same thing and should stop.

One flaw I see in beginning writers—they think a story is a bunch of exciting events all pasted together.

That's nonsense.

A good story is a bunch of things that happen to characters you care about. I believe the author must love the characters. If he or she doesn't, how can the reader be expected to care about them? And, who can love a book filled with characters who do not move us? It won't happen.

After years of writing and publishing, what else have I learned? The main thing is to write and keep writing.

> *My advice to the young writer is likely to be unpalatable in an age of instant successes and meteoric falls. I tell the neophyte: write a million words–the absolute best you can write, then throw it all away and bravely turn your back on what you have written. At that point, you're ready to begin.*[2]

[2] David Eddings

I've written my million formative words, but I'm unwilling to flush them. My characters are alive and real to me—often more real than people I encounter in the outside world. That mentality is probably a very serious psychological condition. Perhaps a pharmaceutical cure will someday be discovered.

I sincerely hope to do Glen's mad menagerie justice.

When the writing is going well, I am not in control. The characters do what they are going to do and I'm often surprised by their antics. This feeling thrills me and I hope it thrills the reader too.

In the Glen Wilson series, eight books are planned, so there are two left. Whew. With everything else I'm doing, they will be hard to finish, but I promise to try.

Many have asked me if I am Glen Wilson.

No.

No way.

But, as I got older, I found that the more I acted like Glen, the better my life got. Try it, dear reader, and let me know.

For now, farewell, my friends. I'll see you in the next book.

www.ingramcontent.com/pod-product-compliance
Lightning Source LLC
LaVergne TN
LVHW091117080826
845145LV00008B/1950
* 9 7 8 1 9 4 9 2 6 7 6 0 0 *